The Intrepid Women Series

"do not tell me No"

KATHRYN JANE

do not tell me No

~ is dedicated to my own hero Al, to my sisters Barb and Judy, to my friends, and to the Lethal Ladies – all of whom contributed to the birth of this book by keeping me fed, clothed, exercised, encouraged, edited and somewhat sane. *I love you all.*

The Intrepid Women series

~ is named for my courageous, amazing, one of a kind friend, Anne. *I miss you still.*

Table of Contents

Chapter 1

Ten floors above the Vegas Strip, the bathroom door opened and my life went down the toilet.

This being a first for me, I hadn't given much thought to the morning after a one night stand. I suppose I'd expected him to leave. Huh. One more item for the "wrong again" column.

Waking up to a flushing sound was my first clue. Then the door opened and there he was.

Tall, dark, handsome and sexy as hell, wearing nothing but a pair of faded-in-all-the-right-places, thigh-hugging jeans. Fly still fastened. Top button? Not. A line of silky dark hair aimed like a laser pointer. A living cliché. Yup, all the rest was there too, the required six pack, pecs, biceps, and shoulders, all tucked into smooth golden skin. City girls would tag him "buff." Country girl like me? Speechless, barely able to breathe.

Closing my eyes won't make him less enticing because his gut clenching male scent was lodged in my nostrils. Keeping my eyes open doesn't seem to be a better option. He's right there. Six feet of body-humming, smiling male. My face flamed at the sudden slide-show of memories.

Instinct was urging me to jump out of this playground-sized bed and run screaming from the room but I'm buck-naked and it's a classy hotel. Still, I'd be hard to catch that way. Or I could drag a six-hundred thread-count sheet from the bed and—

"Don't even think about it." While commanding, his voice was low and sexy - as it had been all night.

Do I detect a hint of laughter? Is he reading my mind?

"Maddy?"

Not my real name, but I like the way he says it—part of what got me into this embarrassing mess. My first, morning-after-a-one-night-stand. What the hell had I been thinking? Well, actually, it was curiosity about monkey sex. Note to self, cut back on steamy novels. But they'd started me wondering, pondering, wishing? Oh yeah, I know—be careful what you wish for.

"Maddy."

I gave in, opened my eyes and there he was, standing beside the bed, watching me.

Holy jumpin' Jehoshaphat. He was beyond beautiful. His mouth, surrounded by the requisite sexy stubble was perfect, sinful. He smiled and my heart made for the exit like an angry calf on the end of a rope.

Even his strong white teeth were perfect.

His eyes, a deep sensuous blue, outlined by even darker navy, were filled with humor. He was laughing at me. No doubt my hair was a tangled mess from hours of delicious romping and I likely had raccoon eyes by now.

"What?" Lord did my voice actually squeak?

"You're freakin' out, aren't you?"

Okay, nail on the head, but did he need to know for sure? Could I bluff my way through this? I'd been known to win the odd hand of poker — but never when I was naked.

He planted one knee on the bed and leaned dangerously close, bracing himself with a hand on either side of my shoulders, his face mere inches away. I could smell toothpaste. And man. Oh man. My body went on full alert. My mind switched to hibernate. He lowered his mouth, inch by painstaking inch. I was beyond help. I wanted this, him. To heck with the consequences.

But in the last hundredth of a second, somewhere in my mind, a voice screamed, "Morning Breath!" I zipped down the bed, beyond his grasp, and bolted for the bathroom as fast as my feet would carry me. I refused to think about what my bare ass looked like in retreat.

I leaned on the marble counter, stared at my image in the mirror, and groaned. What sane man would be willing to kiss that? Way beyond bed-head, it looked like an entire litter of kittens had spent the night wrestling in my hair. Evening Black, mascara had migrated to a place more fitting for a quarterback and I had a pillow crease across my cheek. And I was worried about tasting like the bottom of an irrigation ditch?

Half an hour later, showered, brushed, coiffed, made up and wrapped in a sumptuous hotel robe, I emerged to find myself alone. No gorgeous fellow waiting to lock lips and reacquaint himself with my tonsils. No visible evidence of a man having been here at all.

I stared at the bed. It was pulled together as though a maid had been in. Pewter-colored pillows were plumped and Egyptian-cotton sheets smooth under the navy-blue spread. No sign of late night bedroom antics. My clothes lay folded in a tidy pile on a burgundy leather chair. What the heck? Had I been dreaming?

I stuck my head out into the hallway. Not even a lousy room service tray to be seen.

I closed the door, walked into the bathroom and studied myself in the mirror. Was I losing my mind? Had I been off the ranch for two days too many? Had I made the whole thing up? Huh, like I had that kind of imagination. But what the heck? One minute he's willing to kiss the bride of Frankenstein and the next he vanishes without a trace.

Well okay, so I'd taken a little more than a minute. But why the mysterious departure? Why put the room back in order as though to hide that he'd even been there?

Oh hell, maybe he was married. Holy Hanna, I can't believe I slept with a married man. Well, not that we did much sleeping but that's even worse. I have never, would never, consider poaching. It's just not in my nature. But then, neither is sex with a total stranger, so what the devil does that mean?

It means that I took a little vacation from reality. No more than a side trip. A wander past the property line. Well maybe a bit worse than that but you get the drift. Just a few hours of mindless sex, no harm, no foul. Huh.

I about jumped out of my skin when the hotel phone rang. "Hello?"

"You're going to be late." The deep, rough voice made my skin—in numerous and varied locations—tingle. My body temperature jumped about ten degrees and my brain cells drained into an unnamed file.

"Who is this?" Cripes, like I don't recognize his voice… and I'm squeaking again.

Click.

He hung up? What the heck?

Late? The synapses began to fire. Oh, shit, nine o'clock. I have a meeting with the NFR, Head of Security. In fifteen minutes.

It had been a long ten days at the National Rodeo Finals, studying the faces of cowboys, looking for something familiar, hoping I'd find the brother I hadn't seen since I was five years old—he'd been ten. I remembered so little of his face now, but I was sure I'd know him if I ever saw him again.

Unsuccessful in my search, depressed and sad, I guess I'd hoped one wild night with a gorgeous cowboy could be about pure mindless pleasure, no strings, no guilt. Right, like I'd ever been able to avoid guilt… thank you mother.

Dirk Swanson agreed to an interview the day after the Finals, and I was hoping to wheedle a mailing list or two out of him. To see if my brother's name was there or maybe a name close to his that I'd recognize as an alias.

I know of course that mailing lists aren't Swansen's department, which is exactly why I'm targeting him. Through years of searching for people—both my own family and clients of my internet business—I'd learned to never make a request for information to the place or person who could and would, say no. Approach from a different angle.

I'd planned to walk to the venue but there'd be no time for that now. I punched in the number for the hotel's concierge, requested a cab, threw on underwear, a skirt, a blouse, grabbed my purse and laptop, then flew out the door to the elevator, still buttoning up.

But the interview was a bust. I was informed that the Head of Security wasn't available. My meeting had been rescheduled, postponed until tomorrow morning. The buzz, the adrenaline, the anticipation of answers? All suspended. Uneasy in a holding pattern.

I hiked back down the Strip to my hotel, shut out the noise, the people, the chaos, and tried to put the setback into perspective. It was like any day at home on the ranch, where cattle or weather or a particular fifteen-hand buckskin stallion with a Napoleon complex, could screw up the day's plans in the proverbial blink of an eye.

By the time I'd waded through the colorful crowds on the casino floor, wound a path through clanging banks of slot machines, and ridden a silent elevator to my room, my disappointment over the postponed NFR appointment had all but evaporated. I'd switched gears. Begun planning. For my late afternoon meeting with The PBR Publicity rep. He too had been too busy to talk to me until the Rodeo Finals were over. I got that.

Heading straight to the bathroom I scooped handfuls of cold water onto my face before I remembered the makeup I don't normally wear. Oops. So I scrubbed my face clean, unwound the cleverly sophisticated knot I'd made with my hair and shook it free. I stared at myself, contemplated, then decided to go with real.

I peeled off the skirt and the lace-trimmed blouse. Had my hands behind my head, weaving my hair into its usual comfortable and convenient braid as I went to retrieve my jeans and shirt from the suitcase I'd never unpacked.

A scream lodged in my throat. I froze in my tracks.

There he was, standing by the floor to ceiling window, in the shadow of the dark heavy curtains as if he'd just materialized out of thin air.

What did I do? Did I run back to the bathroom? Cover-up? Nope. Nothing so predictable. Instead I stood gaping at him, armpits exposed, holding the half-finished braid like a frozen wannabe lingerie model.

Huh. No self-respecting model would be caught dead wearing mismatched underwear. Granted, the peach-colored barely-there lace bra was just as sexy as the red satin thong—but together? Not a pretty sight. Well, at least they weren't the granny cottons I wore when I knew I'd be spending a day in the saddle.

He stepped out of the shadow and his grin was delicious. "Nice."

I groaned, finally had the wherewithal to drop my arms, and spun to retrieve my clothes while muttering, "I was in a hurry this morning." Nope, I didn't mention that it was his fault, either. Nor did I ask the obvious question about how he got back into my room when the door was locked.

I grabbed my favorite oversized flannel shirt from the chair where I'd tossed it yesterday and pulled it on, hoping to cover up the obvious signs that I was cold from the air-conditioning—or far from immune to his presence

Once covered to mid-thigh, I turned to confront him. Had plenty to say, but the words died in my throat. He was right there. Real close. In my personal space. If he'd been a horse I'd've shoved against his chest and told him he was hoggin' my oxygen. This was no horse.

Still, I placed a palm on his chest and pushed. I think. Mostly I just stood mesmerized. By his eyes, his mouth, the heartbeat under my hand. The whole package was way too stimulating to ignore, so instead, when he leaned in, I met him halfway.

Lord have mercy. Bronze those lips. That tongue, those hands. Shit, was that my leg way up there? And was that his... oh yeah, come to momma... what happens in Vegas...

*

Sometime later, as the humming in my body slowed and I became reacquainted with several of my own brain cells, I glanced at the clock and said, "Um, I have a meeting in an hour."

The skin around his eyes crinkled, his mouth quirked up in the corners and my heart did a curious little bump. "Wanna be late?"

I shifted, slid out my own side of the bed and made for the bathroom. "Hold that thought just a minute. I'll be right back."

I'm sure I was less than five minutes. I'd taken a little time to brush my hair—the braid was long gone—and apply a tiny bit of makeup. But when I came back out, he was gone.

He'd done that tidy up, fold the clothes, make the bed thing again. Odd. But nice, sort of.

I shrugged, then the phone rang and I reached for it with a laugh. The guy was definitely into games.

But it wasn't him.

The strain in my ranch manager's voice was acute. Another murder. There was a ticket waiting for me at the airport—a flight out in thirty minutes.

I called the concierge for a cab while I pulled on jeans and the flannel shirt. Grabbed my purse and laptop. Stuffed my feet in sneakers and made for the lobby—it would be weeks before I'd realize that my suitcases, the rest of my belongings, had been left behind.

A relentless loop of four words played in my head— dead in the corral... dead in the corral... —as I followed procedures by rote. Ticket. Boarding Pass. Security check. Gate number. Seat number, buckle up.

Somewhere along the way, possibly over Colorado, for just a moment or two, my thoughts slipped to the mystery man I'd left behind, and the brother I still hadn't found. I gave myself a mental shake. Fantasy time was over.

I'd just been sucker-punched by my real life.

*

Ignoring the yellow crime scene tape, I braced a sneakered foot on the bottom rung of the corral fence and leaned forward, careful not to touch the oil treated rails. Discarded purple latex gloves, and strips of yellow crime scene tape lay garish among hundreds of footprints highlighted by the watery light of dawn. I spotted tire tracks. Probably from the ambulance. A man - someone I didn't even know—died here.

No sign of the buckskin stallion. I'd been down this

road before and it had ended badly. No, "badly" could be overcome. The last time this horse had been on the loose, it was my father who'd died and I was the one who'd found him.

Now less than eight months later I was reliving that day in Technicolor. I closed myself off from the memory, the gruesome picture of human death and decomposition - the gut wrenching moment I'd realized I was staring at my father. The knowledge that my search was over and he would never tell me he loved me or explain why he'd left. Why he'd taken my brother with him but left me and Syd behind.

It was easier for me to think about the horse instead. He'd been on the other end of the rope wrapped around my father's arm, and tied at his waist. A suicide move if you're a horseman—which my father apparently had been. To the core.

I didn't believe that he'd wanted to die that day or that the horse had killed him. The buckskin's hide had been covered in dried sweat-lather and bloodied welts that spoke of extreme cruelty and although my father had made himself a stranger by walking out of my life when I was only five, I couldn't believe that he was a cruel man.

I had crystal clear memories of the day he left. The day my family split down the center. He'd taken me into the bedroom I shared with Sydney, sat me down on one frilly pink bedspread and he'd sat on the other, facing me. He'd told me that he had to go away for a while and Dean was going with him. I asked to go too. Said I liked fishing. He'd laughed sort of and told me he wasn't going fishing this time and I needed to stay with my mother and sister.

He'd said it was best. I hadn't liked how his face looked. Or how my stomach had felt sick. In the way of children and intuition I'd known that something was terribly wrong. When I'd cried, he'd pulled me onto his lap and hugged me. Hard. Told me I had to be a big girl and help my mom to look after my little sister.

Thirteen years later, I'd begun my search, and in the twelve years it took me to find him, I'd never had so much as an inkling that he'd been anything but kind. And an extraordinary horseman.

"Cass?" My foreman Jared's voice penetrated the memories, forcing me to turn. His lined face was drawn and pale beneath the leathery tan. He ran a gnarled hand over his stubbled chin, seemed at a loss for words.

Connie, his wife, came out on the porch behind him and called to me. "Come inside Cass."

For ten days I'd been living under the alias of "Madeline." Now my own name sounded strange to me. I shook off the odd feeling and dealt with reality. When I'd called Jared from the local airport, he'd filled me in about the dead man—a drifter they'd just hired to work on machinery—answered all my questions about the man's family and what needed to be done next. He'd told me the Medical Examiner had to notify Border Services and Homeland Security because the dead man had more than his own ID card in his pocket and the ranch was less than twenty-five miles from the Canadian border. The Sherriff wasn't happy about the Federal interference.

"Where's Buck?" I was hoping my foreman would tell me the horse had been found, was locked up in a safe place. My gut said it was a stupid hope. And that pissed me off.

"Gone." He draped an arm around my shoulders and tried to walk me away from the empty paddock. "But we'll find him, everything will be fine. We'll work it all out just--"

I wrenched away. "Stop it! Quit looking after me. A man is dead and the horse is gone. Okay, I got that. It looks like Buck has killed again. Got that, too. Now, what I don't got, is what the fuck went wrong?"

Jared's jaw was clenched. Connie stepped past him to lay a hand on my arm and speak softly. "He's lookin' out for you Cass because that's what your father would have wanted." She held a hand up as I was about to growl again. "Honey, you're not gonna like any of this, so maybe we should all grab a coffee and sit down inside."

I hate backing down. But I respected both Jared and Connie. They were solid folk, had been ranchers for eons. My father bought this ranch from them about five years ago, and instead of taking over and changing things, he'd left them where they were. Built his own house a little ways from theirs and paid them a decent salary to continue running the operation.

When I showed up out of the blue eight long months ago looking for a man I believed to be my father, they'd welcomed me as though they knew me—in spite of name changes and conflicting stories. When I'd discovered my father's body just days later, they'd been there for me, encouraged me to stay, helped me move into the big house. They'd come to feel like family to me. That made them family.

I took a deep breath and marched into their house, not stopping until I'd filled a mug with coffee and dropped into a chair at the kitchen table.

"Okay, I'm listening now so somebody'd better start talking." Connie's dark eyebrows lifted and I nearly squirmed in my chair like a scolded child while muttering, "Sorry."

"I understand you've had a shock. But so have we." Her snappy tone was something I'd never heard before.

Whoa. Okay, I was being bitchy and insensitive, great time for my mother's personality to emerge. I pressed my fingertips into my temples. "I love you guys and I'm sorry I wasn't here when all this happened."

"It's okay honey, we know how important it is for you to find your brother. It's not like you went to Vegas to party. Did you have any luck at all?"

With humongous effort I flicked the mental picture of my mystery cowboy from my mind, swallowed a guilty groan and struggled to keep the grimace off of my face. Did I mention before about my guilt issues? My mother had raised us to believe that seeking personal pleasure with no ulterior motive was an illustration of a weak nature -- therefore, my one night indiscretion was inexcusable.

Thanks to the gods of reason, Connie was nothing like my mother. I shrugged. "No. Nothing regarding Dean. And my client, the one who insisted upon a face to face meeting? Never showed up."

The years I'd spent searching for my own family had morphed into an online business where I helped other people find missing loved-ones. It started with a simple website, sharing some of the techniques I'd discovered along the way. Then, with an email from a single mother of five who didn't have the time to track down her kids' deadbeat-dad, my pastime, became a business. I'd found the woman's husband—a John Doe in an Alaskan morgue—and his life insurance helped her support their children. That was ten years ago.

Jared interrupted my thoughts. "I'll give you the bare bones of this mess for now." I nodded and cradled my coffee mug.

"Couple days after you left for Vegas we hired a drifter named Pete to overhaul the engine on the blue tractor. Seemed to know his stuff. Said it would take him a week or so. Gave him room and board with a promise of three hundred cash when he got the machine running. Let him stay in the cabin out back, took his meals in here with the rest." He shrugged. "Yesterday morning, the men were coming up from the bunkhouse for breakfast, they spotted Pete lying in the stud paddock. Buck was standing over him."

Connie added, "In all the scramble getting to Pete—thinking he was hurt and not realizing he'd been dead for hours and there was nothing anyone could do for him—the gate was left open and Buck slipped out when nobody was looking."

I closed my eyes, dropped my head into my hands. "Do we know the cause of death yet?"

"Way too soon, honey."

"Speculate for me."

Jared's voice was low and I heard both sadness and resignation in it. "There were marks on him. Head and chest. Like hoof-print shaped bruises."

I fought back the swell of emotion, swallowed hard. A man was dead. Apparently killed by a horse I'd previously defended like a mother bear. If I was wrong, this one was on me.

"Cass?"

I lifted my head and gave her a poor excuse for a smile. "I can't change what happened to the man, but I'd bet this ranch that Buck isn't responsible. I'm going after him. Could you drum up provisions for a couple of days?" I looked over at Jared. "I want three of his pregnant mares. Daisy, Winsome and Elvira were the last three he bred. Saddle Daisy, put the overnight pack on Winsome. Elvira will be my spare. I'll ride out in an hour." I shook my head at my own lack of manners. "Thank you both, for everything."

"I'm going with you." Jared's voice held an edge of steel.

"No. You're not. Even if I'm lucky, I'll only have one chance to catch the crafty bugger and if I'm wrong, if he is what they say he is, and smells a man, I'll be forced to put a bullet in him."

"You'll have to do that anyway, missy." Another voice chimed in from the doorway.

We all swung to stare at the big man standing outside the screen door. That's when it dawned on me that the dogs had been barking and I hadn't even paid attention. The four blue heelers didn't like Sherriff Porter. Neither did I. He was a whole lot of sexist attitude filling the doorway at over six feet tall and probably weighing in at about two-sixty. He had cold brown eyes and a soft spooky voice that sent chills down my spine.

"Come in Sherriff," said Connie, always polite.

The hinges squeaked in protest. "I'm sorry Cass," he

said as the door banged closed behind him. "The horse has killed too many men for me to let it go again."

Sorry, my ass. "You don't know that. No one has ever seen him kill. You know he didn't kill my father. The horse was framed."

He gave me one of those patronizing smiles that made me want to slap his arrogant face. "Now missy, I know you love horses--"

"How about the lack of rope burns on my father's arms? Where the hell were the rope burns, Porter? And what about the welts? The ones you say my father put on the horse? Where was the whip that made those? I told you then and I'll say it again now, my father was murdered. And it wasn't by a horse that is so terrified of most men that he'd run a hundred miles to get away from one unless he was defending his mares."

"Come on Cass. How many times have I stood at that fence out there and had him run at me, threaten me with snapping teeth?"

"Because he was defending me." You idiot. "He's a stallion, protective of what he perceives as his."

"Oh." He gave me one of those arrogant, open-mouthed, nodding smirks. "He told you this did he?"

Just as I was about to explain a little about understanding animals, he went on.

"And how do you explain away the death of the other man that menace killed? Tony Brown's death was unprovoked." He narrowed his eyes at me but I didn't back down.

"Bull. Shit."

Jared placed a hand on my shoulder and said quietly,

"Cass, not now."

I shrugged away the hand, stepped into Porter's personal space and asked, "You willing to state under oath that Brown had no history of abusing animals? You willing to look a judge in the eye and say you can think of no reason why the horse attacked that man when he was simply walking across the paddock? How about the scars on Buck? You got any idea what kind of force it takes to break skin with a whip?" I tapped his badge with my index finger. "You want that horse dead sheriff? You'll have to go through me. See you in court."

He grabbed my pointing finger and squeezed until furious tears started to well. "Missy, you touch me again and you'll be in court alright. Defending yourself." His voice dropped even lower. "A woman livin' way out here should respect the law for the protection we provide."

I jerked my finger away and ground my teeth at the poorly disguised threat. "Oh, I respect the law. I respect it so much that my lawyer has all the evidence I've collected, plus a letter written by me and notarized. All up front and legal, with documentation of my suspicions. You know, the kind of thing that says," I lifted my hands right up into his face and did finger quotes, "In the event of my untimely death." I smiled grimly. "A woman living way out here can't be too careful, can she?"

I backed up a step. "That stallion has become my greatest source of comfort. Knowing I'd be safe from any man just by stepping into that pen gives me an amazing feeling of security. And of course my dogs." I smiled at the heeler lying on the mat outside the screen door, eyes glued to the lawman. "Did you hear? Just last month Blue took on

17

a nasty cinnamon bear. Yup, ran it off my porch and down the driveway like an unwanted suitor. Dog's got jam. Course, he's the runt of the litter, Connie and Jared's three are much bigger. Stronger too."

"Cassie." Connie's cool voice made me rein myself in. Nobody else got away with calling me Cassie. "That's enough."

I clamped my jaw shut but stayed firmly in place. Porter backed away, grabbed his holstered gun, gave it a lift and squeeze as though rearranging his nuts. "Once I get a court order to have that stallion shot, I'll be back to do the job personally."

My tone was neutral, calm, "You are on private property Sherriff. I suggest you remember that I not only own three thousand acres but have the rights to all the surrounding land. Be very careful not to step inside my boundaries without an invitation. My cowboys are modern fellows, all packin' video equipped satellite phones in their other holster. They're always on the lookout for rustlers and poachers."

An icy stare his only response, he marched out the door. The screen slammed behind him.

I plunked back down at the table and reached for the coffee mug with a shaky hand. I looked around the room and muttered, "What the hell did I just do?"

Connie shook her head at me. "Honey, seems to me, you declared war."

"Shit."

Chapter 2

What the hell was I doing putting my hands on her?

Figures, when he needed to pace, he was confined to a small luxury jet. Gage Meyer, drew on years of Special Ops training to ensure that his expression didn't give away the fact he was fuming. Pissed at himself and not a damned thing he could do about it until they landed. Didn't help that his brother and sister—also members of the family's Secret Security Company - sat across from him wearing expressions a hell of a lot closer to amusement than concern.

Gage scowled. "You'll both back off if you know what's good for you,."

Angie's instant grin said she wasn't afraid to tug on the lion's tail. At five foot nothing and dressed in her usual manly looking flight suit, it was always her bright red hair slicked back into a tight knot that gave the first indication of what she'd be like to deal with. "First time we've seen you twisted up like a pretzel over a woman.

Quinn stretched long legs out in front of him, and dropped one booted foot over the other. The bland expression on his face didn't match the intensity of his blue eyes. "Good to see you're human after all bro."

Gage turned to stare out the tiny window of the private jet. Nothing to see but clouds. "Cassandra is sweet, kind and defenseless." *Not to mention wildly responsive.* "She hasn't got a fucking clue she's in danger. She thinks the biggest problem she has is a stranger's death on her property. She believes that her parent's marriage broke the family up, has no idea that her dad and brother went into witness protection. She suspects that her father's death wasn't an accident." He rubbed the back of his neck. "And I'm pretty sure the only Minnows she knows about have fins, not guns, so what part of that do you two think is so fucking funny?"

Angie rolled her eyes. "Oh for crying out loud, Gage. We don't think this mess is the least bit amusing. But the fact she's got your knickers in a twist, well, it's only fair we get to tease you."

"I had an assignment. Fucked it up. Now I have to fix it."

Quinn's was always the voice of reason. "Your assignment was to get her out of Vegas before the Minnows got hold of her. Seems to me, that part's handled."

His sister sat back, enunciated her words carefully. "You couldn't know she'd get called back to the ranch and bolt without a word."

Gage rubbed his hands over his face. "Instead of securing her, doing a simple extraction, I tried to win her over."

"Well, yeah," his sister agreed. "That was stupid. But you're a man so it's expected."

He tossed a glance at Quinn hoping for backup but saw no help coming from that quarter. "I thought it would be easier on her if I could make her understand what kind of trouble she was getting into. Convince her she needed protection." He could tell Angie was about to add something so he cut her off with, "Yes it's my fault that she's in more danger now. My fault that we're currently somewhere over Colorado or Oregon, but –" He ground his back molars and sucked in a shallow breath before he started making more excuses for his own stupidity. "Fuck."

"Hey, bro," Quinn's voice became serious. "We'll get her out of there. We're a team, it's what we do. She'll be okay."

Gage wasn't ready to be placated. "How? She had a four hour head-start. We may be good - hell we've pulled off rescues that would even impress my old running mates - but how do we stop a group of organized criminals from getting their hands on her when we're twenty thousand feet in the fucking air?" He checked his watch.

There was a warning in Quinn's low tone. "You need to focus on the facts. First off, Jared and Connie have her back. Second, the Minnows have been content to watch her up until now. Stands to reason they're going to wait and see if her brother makes some kind of contact when she gets home."

"But she didn't find Dean. Had no luck whatsoever."

"And they know this how?" He shook his head. "We're talking Minnows not rocket scientists."

Angie added, "Just a few smart guys leading a bunch of muscle-bound morons around by their dicks. They likely thought you were Dean when you first made contact with

Cass."

"Great. Then I put her in danger from the get-go." He turned to stare out the tiny window; maybe ignoring them would shut them up. He let his mind wander back to the first meeting with Cass. He'd sat there pushing the buttons at the slot machine beside hers, waiting for an opportunity. When his machine lit up and bells began to clang she'd looked right at him and grinned. Just like that, she'd spoken to him, opened the door to his mission. But instead of simply maneuvering her into an area, a position, where an extraction could be executed, he'd become a man instead of a soldier. The sound of her laugh slid through him, the look on her face hours later as he'd touched her...

He shook off the memories, brought his mind back to the reality of her slipping through his grasp and into danger. The Minnows would use her as bait - at the very least.

Quinn nudged his sister with his elbow and tilted his head toward Gage. "Is he having what you girls call a pity-party?"

Angie half-snorted. "Could be." Then she scowled and gave Quinn a solid punch in the shoulder. "And don't say girls like I'm twelve. I've got four years on you."

He grinned. "I'll be sure to point that out when you hit forty. And fifty, and sixty..." When she thumped the same spot on his shoulder, reminding him she was pretty darned tough for her size, he added, "Geez, shouldn't you be in the cockpit?"

Angie nodded. "Feels like punishment sitting back here." She gave Gage a steady look. "You know, we could change tactics. One word from me and the guys up front will drop this baby right into the airport at Oroville. The strip's long enough, just. Then we'll beg, borrow or steal a vehicle, go in guns blazing. Your call."

Tension plus the studied effort to hide it had created a screaming ache between his shoulder blades which stormed up and over into his eyes "Tips our hand. Too risky." Her point of course. "The time it takes to get to the Steed, we get back double, so your favorite, rocket fast, almost invisible helo still makes the most sense." He fought back the urge to heave a huge exasperated sigh. "Yes. You're right. You're both right and I'm wrong again. Happy now?"

Angie unbuckled her seat belt, went to the compact bar built into the bulkhead behind the cockpit and poured a generous glug of scotch whiskey into a glass. She held it out to Gage. "Drink."

"I don't need my senses messed up any more than they are."

"True, but you could use a smack up-side the head and I think the whiskey would be a better choice than one of your sibs decking you. Course then you could ride the rest of the way strapped onto a bunk." She tipped her head to indicate the space behind him.

Gage didn't need to look. He knew there were two skinny bunks back there that folded down from the interior walls. He didn't like the chances that his siblings could actually overpower him, but all three of them had gone through the kind of elite training reserved for Special Forces and Navy SEALs so the battle would be messy.

He took the glass, stared at it until Quinn added, "Drink up, bro, the effects will be long gone by the time this crate is on the ground."

Gage threw the fire down his throat and handed the

empty back to Angie with a grimace to cover any hint of a gasp. He hated the taste, relished the burn. Pain was good. Felt right.

He laid his head back against the seat and sighed. "See, all better now."

Quinn laughed. "Yeah, right."

Chapter 3

I climbed the three steps onto my porch wishing I was wearing boots. There was something both affirming and comforting about hard sole riding boots clomping on wooden planks. Even without the jingle of spurs.

I pushed the door open and Harris, my dirt-brown-tabby, popped his head up, staring at me from his bed of towels on top of the dryer.

"*Pprrrlt.*"

"Hey pal."

I scooped him up and headed for my bedroom. Buried my face in his thick fur, absorbed the vibration of rusty purring. He stretched his neck out while I scratched under his chin.

"Miss me?" I set him on the bed and began pulling open dresser drawers.

It was imperative I dress and pack in the most efficient way possible. December wasn't the best time to go for a ride in the mountains. Frigid air would bite at exposed skin, seep in through every seam. I stripped down, tossing my clothes on the bed where Harris quickly made them his newest favorite spot. With his butt planted in the middle of my flannel shirt, he began to knead, wearing a goofy happy cat expression on his face.

"Sure," I said, "You don't even care that I'm leaving again, so long as you have my clothes."

When I peeled off a pretty matched set of turquoise lace panties and bra, I caught my naked reflection in the mirror and a memory of my mystery man flashed. His eyes had met mine in the hotel's smoky mirror. His arms slid around me from behind, and fingertips skimmed my flesh, caressing me, teasing me. I could feel the length of him pressed close, heat, the rasp of his jaw on the sensitive skin behind my ear. I heard the hum of pleasure from his throat, smelled the heady maleness that surrounded, enveloped and owned me.

I shook myself out of the sensual fog and replaced sexy with careful, practical layers. Cotton panties, sports bra, silk long johns, sweat pants, turtleneck sweater and a pair of woolly socks. I grabbed two more pairs of socks, another turtleneck and a spare set of long johns to stuff in my saddle bags. Harris got one last scratch under the chin before I left him with a promise I wouldn't be gone for more than a couple of days and Connie would look after him as usual.

Back in the laundry room, I yanked a set of saddle bags off a hook by the door and crammed in my extra clothes, gloves, a scarf and three bottles of water. I stuffed myself into heavy-duty overalls and shrugged on the matching jacket. Checked pockets to make sure I had all the necessary survival tools, the little things like a compass, tin foil and butane lighter that no one with a brain rode into the mountains without. I slipped the chain over my head that held a girl-sized, pink, razor sharp pocket knife. While I hefted a huge plastic jar of scotch mints off a shelf and filled a baggie with Buck's favorite treats, I had a momentary flashback of the minty toothpaste smell when my mystery lover leaned over me, his warm breath awakening... hard to believe that was only yesterday. I gave my head a shake, reached for my satellite phone and glanced at the clock.

Just enough time to call my sister, Sydney, let her know what was going on. I used the land line, rather than waste my satellite battery. Who knew how long I'd be in the mountains.

Because Syd was one of those people who could never resist a ringing phone, I was stunned when I heard her canned voice telling me to leave a message. Momentarily at a loss what to say, I bumbled out, "Syd? Where the heck are you? Call me. Not life or death but we've got a situation here. A hell of a mess really. Don't talk to anyone but me or Connie or Jared. Do not talk to Porter. He's part of the mess. I'm packing my sat-phone, kiddo. Call me, please?" I reeled off the number.

Syd and I had been apart for a few months, since she'd fallen head over heels for a rodeo cowboy and got burnt. He'd moved on, leaving her behind like arena dust.

Less than an hour after arriving home, I rode out of the yard and into the hills with two mares in tow. The collective steam of our breaths created a dancing mist in the crisp morning air. Brilliant sunshine pretended to heat but I felt no more than faint warmth on my face.

Over the heavy and wonderful smell of the pine trees, I caught a faint whiff of manure and glanced back to see

Blue step carefully around a fresh deposit. The dog trotted in typical Heeler fashion behind the last horse. The steady creaking of saddle leather, thumping of a dozen hooves on frozen ground and the occasional snort were a mixture of familiar sounds that used to make me feel comfortable in this wilderness. But not today.

I had way too many jumbled thoughts rocketing around in my head, like pin-ball gone wild with six or seven little silver balls instead of one.

Ping. A dead man in the paddock. Ping. A murderer on the loose. Ping. Where the blazes is my sister? Where's the damned stallion, and my brother for that matter, where the heck is he? Will I ever see my mystery man again? Feel that amazing mouth, taste ... *Arrggh. Stop it. Focus on one thing at a time.*

"Calm, I will be calm. Study this mess from all angles." Daisy's ears swiveled at the sound of my voice. I twisted in the saddle to check on the other two and smiled. "It's okay ladies, I'm just trying to sort things out in my mind and it's easier to say it all out loud."

Their heads all nodded. I grinned. Of course they did. Watch any horse walking uphill and their heads nod up and down with their stride. I settled back around to watch where we were going. Not that there was much chance Daisy would go off the trail.

"Let's start with Sydney. She's not picking up, even though she always answers her cell. I'm worried about her because she's been so sad since that Wesley-jerk dumped her. I did try to warn her that falling for a rough-stock cowboy and taking him home to her city life, would be like transplanting wildflowers. But would she listen? Of course not. She was so stupid in love she ignored all the warnings. Hell, she even brought him here once between rodeos. I suppose she figured that having a ranch in the family would be a handy card to play."

I sighed, feeling bad for Syd. "I just wish I could have reached her this morning to tell her about what was going on out here."

A squirrel raced across our path and up a tree, chattering and scolding.

"Hey, shouldn't you be hibernating?" No, wait, they gather their nuts for the winter, stock up with food for when the snow comes, bury everything, but don't hibernate. Right. I smiled, thinking about how much I'd learned since arriving here less than a year ago. I'd always had horses in my life but this kind of wilderness? Nope. And yet, it already felt like home—as though living in furnished apartments in cities all over the country while I searched for my father and brother had been a penance and these mountains my reward.

Tucked away in the remote north eastern section of Washington State, we were a two hour drive on dirt roads from a town in any direction. Oroville being the biggest.

We should be belly deep in snow by now, being December, but the weather had been unseasonably warm and dry for months. Warm being relative of course. If things didn't change soon, all the ranchers would begin worrying about next year's grazing without the melting of winter snowpack to feed the grasslands in the spring.

I stopped on a wide ridge, to give the horses a breather and found my own breath stolen by the panoramic view. The hundreds of miles of mountaintops made me insignificant. Like a speck that was a single sparrow in the sky. My place in the world so much less than I'd thought. I loved this feeling yet it made my heart hurt.

I absently ran my hand down Daisy's neck, my thoughts turning suddenly to my mystery man.

"Wonder what he'd think of this place, ladies? He wore those jeans and belt buckle like he owned them, but who knows? Could be he was just a city boy, playing cowboy for a few days in a place where he could get away with it."

I grimaced at surfacing memories of photo shoots where I'd pretended to be anything but what I was. I'd worn corsets and garters before my fifteenth birthday thanks to my mother the manager. I'd had a lucrative career as a model that began when I was only five. A strict diet and exercise program ensured steady work from the time we arrived in New York, shortly after my father left us, until I'd made a run for it at the age of eighteen. Illusions. I still used them didn't I?

I bet my mystery-man would have a good belly laugh if he could see me now. Hell, he'd have to get right in my face to even guess that there was a woman under all the layers of clothing.

As a tall, gangly teenager trying to hide my body when I wasn't in front of the camera, I'd started shopping in the men's department. Turned out to be a lucky move as I'd learned the secret to finding clothing with longer sleeves and inseams.

Now, living on the ranch, I wore men's gloves, jeans and boots for their fit and durability. The only working clothes I ever bought in the ladies department were long-johns. Men's have that damned double flap in front with the extra room I have no use for. Of course, when I'd had no choice but to buy men's, I'd cut out one flap and then wear them backwards. Never hurts to have extra room in the butt as long as that reinforced edge isn't there to leave a painful groove in a cheek.

Today, I was wearing my favorite two piece Carhartts. Heavy canvas overalls and jacket with fabulous insulation and big brass snaps I can operate with my gloves on. I used to love my one piece - coveralls and jacket attached - but having to pee outdoors now and again? Not a good thing. In order to drop your drawers, you have to peel from the neck down, then while your naked hind end is exposed to sub-zero temperatures, you have to struggle to keep everything gathered up so you don't pee in the hood.

One of the mares chose that moment to stretch herself out, lift her tail and water a large patch of ground behind her and I grinned. "Fine for you, show-off."

Steam rose as the other two also took a private moment. Once they were all back standing square, I prodded Daisy with my heels and gave a light tug on the lead line. "Rest stop's over ladies, let's get a move on. Time we found that rotten old boyfriend of yours."

We followed signs of the missing horse, hoof-prints in the powdery dust covered frozen ground. Not stupid, he was following a trail he'd traveled many times before. It was the route Jared had first taken me on, a loop trail that stretched up through the ranch property and then wound back down through the pastures surrounding the area where the houses, barns and pens were located. The entire journey was considered a three day ride, but I didn't expect Buck would stay on the trail that long. If he was intent on running away from humans, he'd branch off eventually, go into unknown territory. Perhaps follow the scent of the wild horses rumored to roam the wilderness to the north. Thinking about ghostly sightings of mythical horses sent an extra chill through me.

I rode in silence past the place where I'd spotted what had turned out to be my father's remains nearly a year ago. I'd spent the months afterward trying to prove that he'd been murdered by a man, not trampled by Buck. But in the end, I accepted defeat because really, what difference would it make in the long run? He was still dead.

Weeks after the gruesome discovery, a clue arrived in the form of a letter addressed to him. An invitation to a bullfighter's reunion at the Calgary Stampede. Turned out, my father had spent years hiding in plain sight, in the make-up and costume of a bullfighter volunteering at local rodeos. Dressed up like a clown he risked his own life to keep bulls from goring or trampling cowboys that were bucked off.

I'd hoped that if my father was able to hide in plain sight for so long, maybe I could tug this thread and find some connection to my missing brother. But the reunion netted me little. Only one old guy recognized the outdated picture I had of Dad and Dean. He said that the kid, my brother, had looked solid back in the day. Always finished in the top three at the Little Britches Rodeos and figured to go on to Pro, riding rough stock.

That's why I'd gambled. Hoped that even though he wasn't listed as a competitor, the National Rodeo Finals might draw my brother out as a spectator or maybe I'd find someone who recognized him from the age-enhanced photograph I'd taken with me.

The NFR/Vegas plan also involved getting my hands on old membership and mailing lists—using the pretext of writing a historical article with a 'where are they now' segment. I hoped to use past rosters to check out cowboys who only showed up for one or two seasons. Maybe I'd luck into a pattern of aliases. Grasping at straws for sure, but what else could I do?

And did I ever wonder why my brother was so hard to find? Did it never occur to me that maybe he was dead or just not interested in his sisters? Of course it did. But I couldn't help myself. The only concrete memory I had of Dean was his whispered promise that he'd come back and find us when it was safe. And for some stupid reason I clung to that. He'd been ten, I was five, and I thought he hung the moon.

A sudden tenseness, bunching of muscles under the saddle, brought me back to the present with a jolt. All the horses were uneasy, ear's flickering, nostrils flaring in search of identifiable scent.

I glanced around, saw nothing but scenery. Skeletons of bushes whose leaves had long since died and blown away, bristled among the prickly pines and elegant fir. Tall grasses, baked golden by last summer's sun stood upright and proud. No cattle had grazed this area. The smaller plants had been browsed by deer and elk.

I urged the horses forward until we rounded a bend in the trail and the line shack, my destination for the night, came into view.

"Holy Hanna," I muttered and swung down. Winced

as my boots met the frozen ground for the first time in hours. Shooting pain reverberated from the soles of my feet to halfway up my shinbones. I'd forgotten to wiggle my toes and flex my feet in preparation for landing because my mind had been otherwise occupied. I'd been staring at the tiny cabin, wondering what the hell had happened to make it crumple that way. Looked kind of like a giant Sasquatch had stomped right in the middle of it.

The skin at the back of my neck tingled.

Blue was standing statue still, his ruff up, on full alert. All three horses were fidgeting, nostrils flaring, ears flicking back and forth. I tied all three to a tree at the edge of the clearing, and approached the cabin, watchful, ready for anything. The dog kept pace at my side.

When I got a good, close up look, I realized that something very human and focused, caused the shack's demise. A chain saw had been used to dismember it. All four walls and supports cut through before it had been shoved over. No, probably pulled with something strong. Horses or maybe a machine of some kind.

I backed away. Even though the destruction was likely weeks old, this was still a crime scene. I nearly snorted out loud. Who was I kidding? Sheriff Porter would call it garden variety vandalism. Not even a big deal. Or worse still, he'd think it was drug smugglers using the cabin on their way across the Canadian border and he'd have the National Guard or some such entity out here en masse. I grimaced at the thought of Porter having free reign, a legitimate reason to be on my land.

Nope, not reporting this to anyone right now. I was on a completely unrelated mission. I had a horse to find.

I retreated, swung back up on Daisy. "Sorry ladies, I know you're tired but I just don't feel comfortable making camp here."

We pressed on. I knew of some caves about an hour's ride away. We'd make it by dark if we didn't dawdle. Winding our way through the ponderosa pines, following a wide elk trail, I struggled to make sense of the reality I'd seen. Someone had totally destroyed a line shack. Why? To what purpose? It was probably only used half a dozen times a year, but a damned handy place to take shelter when you were a day's ride from home.

Not much to it. Four walls, a roof, a wooden bed-shelf along the side, a table built into one corner and a potbellied woodstove in the other. Cupboards under the bed held first aid supplies, and a couple of those weird foil blankets in a big metal rodent-proof box, and a sparse selection of canned goods as well as hiker-style dehydrated meal pouches. A descent selection of ropes and an old, make that ancient, rain slicker hung on the back of the single door.

Nothing worth destroying. It just didn't make any sense. I doubted kids would come all the way up here to vandalize a line shack that was decades old and in disrepair.

I shuddered and looked around, using the scenery as a distraction, trying to absorb the tranquility of the mountainside. Pine needles thick on the ground, muted the horse's hoof beats. Sunset was bathing everything with rich golden light - my second favorite time of day. But nothing compared to dawn, when sunlight leaned gently across the land and the earth glowed in anticipation.

Pushed by the fast approaching nightfall, we reached a small clearing near a tiny creek that would serve as a holding pen for my horses in about forty minutes. I untacked the mares while they drank from the creek, dug into Winsome's pack for the long rope and wound it around several trees to create a pen to contain the ladies. They had dried grass to nibble on and could drink from the creek. Knowing that there was a stallion running free, I'd've preferred hobbling all three horses, but there could be cougars in the area. Instead, I retrieved a ten pound bag of oats from the pack and sprinkled it on the ground in a big circle just inside the rope to keep them from wanting to wander.

Once the horses were settled I shouldered my pack of food and bedding, whistled to Blue and headed up a narrow trail. I stopped at the first cave and set a little booby trap of balanced sticks, stones and a tin plate to trigger a warning if anyone came that way. The second cave was a little bit smaller than the first but it would do. I tucked my pack against the wall, dug out a sandwich, a bottle of water I'd filled at the creek and a baggie of kibble for Blue.

We ate in companionable silence. Blue was like that. He rarely had much to say and preferred I didn't carry on solo conversations—he always looked confused, as though uncertain how to respond. Most of our communication was silent. He understood body language and even the slightest eye signals. He just didn't speak human and considering I don't speak dog, I suppose that's fair.

When I settled into my sleeping bag, Blue curled up against me, a warm comfort and dependable guardian. Darkness was complete with not even a shadow of demarcation.

Sleep was elusive. As I lay there, thoughts of my last

twenty-four hours in Vegas entertained me. How could such a short time feel like it meant so damned much?

I smiled in the darkness. *Butch Cassidy and the Sundance Kid* was an old movie I'd watched many times. I'd called my mystery man Sundance because he was smooth but not slick, funny without being comedic. And his voice was—my tummy muscles tightened—well it was something I'd never forget.

When he'd insisted we walk the strip and take in the sights I'd had no idea I could be seduced so easily. We'd stood at the rock and wrought iron wall, watching the dancing fountains. The lights, the music, the sound and motion of the water had just begun to wash over me when he leaned down, his lips barely brushing my ear and his voice had gone straight to the middle of me. The words he'd said never even registered. I'd simply arched my neck and my insides hummed when his mouth slid down and around to rest in that spot where I'm sure my pulse must have been visible.

Lord but I'm afraid I made some kind of sound like a groan or a whimper because he chuckled and pulled me back to lean against his chest. His hands looped casually around my waist while he was careful to keep space between our lower halves.

After the dancing-waters show was over, he'd taken my hand and we'd wandered along the sidewalk in the neon glow. Stopping under the replica Eiffel Tower to stare up at the structure, we'd talked about travel in Europe. Neither of us had been overseas.

It was different when we came to the miniature Statue of Liberty. Seems both of us had done time in New York.

I'd felt like a prisoner, under my mother's control, but I didn't share that story with my cowboy. And he'd known I was holding out on him.

"Miss Maddy" he'd said—because I'd told him my name was Madeline, "I sense a deep dark secret. Is it bitterness or fear I detect?"

I smiled. "A little of each I'm afraid. But this is supposed to be my fantasy night. I'm not revisiting my past. I'm having a present. A here and now with a nice man I've met in one of the most exciting places on earth."

He lifted my hand to his mouth and kissed each knuckle while never taking his gaze from mine. My heart did a little back flip and amazingly remained in my chest. I let my other hand touch his cheek, my thumb brushing across the hint of bristle on his chin. And then, just as though it was something I did every day, I leaned in and kissed him. Right there, on the wide warm sidewalk, with people swarming past us as though we were a boulder in a stream.

When I finally stepped back, putting space between us, I heard myself ask, "Who are you?"

And he'd just smiled.

We'd made our way back to my hotel and found a nightclub. He wanted to dance with me. I wanted to get naked with him. Turns out we both had the same goal, he just had a slower, more civilized approach.

I was starving. It had been a remarkable six years since I'd had sex and I was pretty certain the drought was nearly over. Dragging out foreplay wasn't in my plans for this cowboy. At least not the first time. And the little mini orgasms that were happening on the dance floor were about killing me. So I'd been bold. Again. Second time in an hour. Hah. Second time in my life—like who's counting. But I was getting the hang of it.

I pressed against him and found more than his belt buckle hard and exciting. "Sundance, I'm not very good at this tippy toeing around stuff. So I'll just come out and ask. Would you like to go up to my room with me?"

There in the darkness of a mountain cave I found myself grinning at the memory of how I'd just grabbed the bull by the horns, so to speak.

His smile had been slow and sexy but he hadn't answered with words. He simply dropped a lip-lock on me that curled my toes and made my heart pound. When we came up for air, he led me out the door and straight to the elevators. Our next kiss had lasted seventeen floors, until somehow, remarkably, we were inside my room and I was naked.

The man had then proceeded to light my entire body on fire with his hands and his mouth, demonstrating the meaning of implosion. Then it got better. By the time he finally came inside me, I didn't know my own name—let alone my alias.

But now, in the cold evening air, tucked into a cave with only a lumpy pack to lean on, and a herd dog to keep me warm, I wondered about my alter ego. Was that wild and sexy woman someone I could tap into outside of Vegas? Did she exist under the manly clothes and efficient rancher persona? What would happen if my mystery man saw me like this? Would he be turned on by the real me? Or would he look through me, over and around me just like all the other men? Too bad I'd never know one way or the other. A one-night stand didn't warrant a man chasing a woman half way across the country. And even if he'd wanted to find me, he didn't know who I was, or where I lived.

I sighed, and wriggled against the pack, trying to find a softness that just wasn't there.

*

Steel horseshoes clanked, scraped, thumped the hard packed dirt and rocks while we climbed the narrow mountain trail. A long and restless night of hot sexy dreams had had me awake and ready to roll by first light. My lower back muscles and quads burned from keeping my ass out of the saddle and my center of gravity forward so I wouldn't impede the action of the mare under me. With a steep rock wall on one side and nothing but air on the other, there was nowhere to dismount, nor could I allow the horses to stop moving.

One misstep and I'd be a first time base jumper… sans parachute. A shiver ran up my backbone. I concentrated on the end of the torture, just ahead, where the trail would take us over a ridge, and onto a grassy plateau surrounding a natural spring. A perfect place for a recalcitrant stallion to hang out.

"Food, water, and rest up ahead ladies," I promised as we trudged on.

Coming over the rise I smiled. What had been lush green grass surrounding the tiny pond last summer was standing pale gold and crisp, moving like a gentle wave in the cool wind.

Icy-cold spring water bubbled up through the ground.

Blue was already lapping at it when his head jerked up.

Following the dog's frozen stare I spotted the buckskin stallion when he flicked his ears to listen behind him. Cocky bugger was neatly camouflaged in the shadows of trees. I tipped my chin in his direction and huffed out a breath in greeting. His nose raised and I'm sure he huffed back.

I laughed. "So what's the plan big boy? You ready to come home?" I slid slowly off my horse and stood still, waiting to see if he'd approach. He stood his ground.

I slipped a hand in my pocket for the baggie full of peppermints, plucked out a candy and offered it to Daisy. She lipped it from my palm and crunched happily while I watched Buck take one step forward. I handed another to Daisy but Buck didn't advance any further.

I dropped my rein to ground tie the mare, and strolled slowly away to lean on a tree at the edge of the clearing, keeping my gaze fixed on the bag of peppermints in my hand. Buck edged my way but I ignored him, instead crouching and poking around in the pine needles.

When the stallion's hot breath tickled the back of my neck, I smiled and murmured, "you can't stand to be ignored, can you big guy." I moved just enough to blow a soft breath on his nose. He answered in kind, then pushed at me with his muzzle.

"You lookin' for candy Buckster?" I fisted half a dozen peppermints and offered just one between my thumb and forefinger. He lipped it with care, stepped back to crunch and enjoy.

I went back to my saddle horse, adjusted the tack, checked the straps on the pack horse, reached down to pet

Blue and felt that hot breath on the back of my neck again. I straightened and smiled at him. "More candy Buck?"

Within minutes, I'd slipped a halter onto his head and tied him to a tree with a standard slip knot in the cotton rope, then turned the three mares loose to nibble bits of grass from the rocky ground while Buck and I had a one sided discussion. Like Blue he wasn't big on human communication. But we understood each other pretty well anyway.

"You know, if I thought I could trust you to stay on my land, I'd be sorely tempted to leave you out here. But smarmy Sheriff Porter is still itching to put a bullet in that handsome head of yours. So for now, you're better off in your paddock near the house, where I can watch out for you." I ran my hand down his golden brown neck, patted the big muscular shoulder, and bent to check his legs for cuts or injuries. I lifted his hooves. The steel shoes were still snugly in place and there were no rocks or bits of stick imbedded. "Somehow, someday, I'm gonna prove that you didn't kill my Dad. Then big boy, I'm gonna turn your ass loose and let you live out your life." I sighed. "But for now, we have to take you home."

It was time to gather the mares and get a move on. I checked the cinch for tightness, before climbing aboard Daisy. I rode her to where Buck was tied to the tree, leaned out of my tack, and reached to release the slipknot. I smiled as the mare under me snickered to the stallion. She sidled coyly away from him forcing me to put almost all my weight in one stirrup to reach out a little further for the rope. *What a flirt.*

Boom!

Chapter 4

The sharp crack of a rifle, the explosion of bark peppering my face, and Daisy jumping sideways—leaving me suspended in midair for a heartbeat before my left hip bore the brunt of my graceless landing—all happened at once.

I'll never know if it was reflex, accident or instinct. But keeping my grip on the stallion's lead rope, becoming the anchor that kept him from bolting with the turncoat mares who'd skedaddled in Daisy's wake, may be what saved my life. I scrambled to get behind the tree, never conscious of deciding from what direction the shot had come but knowing for certain which way to go.

Another shot. Single action. Had to reload.

I made for the rocks beyond the tree to follow the trail the mares had taken. A frightened rumble came from Buck's throat as he strained against my hold. Grabbing a handful of mane, I swung myself onto his back. He needed no urging, just a better sense of direction. He spun on his haunches, took off at a flat run—the wrong way. The mares were headed home with Blue at their heels. We weren't.

I laid low, my stomach on his withers, my chest

43

pressing into his mane as he picked up speed. With nothing more than a halter on his head and a fat cotton rope in my hand there would be no slowing him down for a while. My arms wrapped around his neck, and gripping my own hands for extra security, I prayed he wouldn't stumble while we rocketed over what felt like miles of mountain trails.

Minutes that seemed like hours later, Buck's frantic gallop slowed to a tired lope. I sat up, pulled back on the rope and quietly talked him into stopping. He gave in, obliged me, and wound down. Canter to trot, to walk, to standing with his front feet planted wide, his sides heaving. I stayed motionless, listening for sounds of pursuit.

Buck's ears swiveled back, sideways, forward. He lifted his head. Nostrils flared while he searched for scent. For a moment I thought he was reacting as I was to the fear that someone out there was shooting at us. I was struggling to hear the slightest noise, see any miniscule movement in the trees. Unlike the recalcitrant stallion.

Astounded, I recognized his look. The panic was gone. Replaced by a desire to find his mares. Too bad he hadn't thought of them before fleeing to higher ground, like a wild animal. Now we were lost in the mountains—after almost having a hole blown through us—and his only concern was a piece of tail. Great. Testosterone and linear thinking. Sounds like he could use a night in Vegas. Hmmm.

Jeez Louise. What was with my mind?

Okay, blame it on adrenaline or wishing some big strong man was riding to my rescue. Right, like I'd ever needed a man at a moment like this. Of course, I'd never had a moment quite like this but I'd gotten myself out of plenty of jams before, so this would likely be no different.

I glanced around, trying to figure out where we were. Crap, nothing looked familiar. Well not specifically anyways. Just familiar like all the pine trees and rocky hills did, for miles and miles around. So I kept Buck pointed uphill and we continued to climb. He wasn't pleased but I needed a decent vantage point to figure out where exactly home was.

It only took about twenty minutes to break out above the trees and discover that we were way beyond my comfort zone. We'd galloped clear off the ranch, and deep into government land.

I chose a clearing with a view in the direction I thought we'd come from and pulled out my compass, silently thanking Jarred for one of the many in-depth lessons he'd given me. Although I'd learned to ride when I was really young—for a commercial I worked on—I had little more than city-girl knowledge of anything ranch. Last summer, I'd become Jared's shadow and the intense training he put me through probably helped both of us get over my father's murder.

By September, I could ride for days on end without saddle sores, throw a rope, find my way around with a compass, control a grass fire, ride anything that moved and operate all the equipment. Besides that, I understood wildlife, domestic animals and everything in between. I could survive in the woods for weeks on end; deal with almost any medical emergency of human or animal—including snake bite. Shudder. Enough cheery thoughts.

"Okay Buck, westward ho." I turned his head and nudged him with my lower leg. He grunted and refused to move. I gave him a pretty good poke with my heels—wishing I had my spurs—but again, he didn't budge. "Oh for crying out loud." I got off, headed the direction I wanted to go and pulled the reluctant beast along behind me. "Okay, for now this'll work but if anybody starts shooting at us again we go back to doin' it my way. Got that?"

He didn't answer.

After about two miles downhill on a rocky trail, I'd had enough. I snapped the lead rope to the left side ring of his halter and tied the tail end to the right. Grabbed a handful of mane and swung up onto his back. Reaching out to pat his neck, I spoke firmly, nudged him with my heels and he stepped forward without protest.

I smiled, sighed and settled back a little on my rump as we were still headed downhill. When the ground leveled out in a nice wide meadow, I prodded Buck into an easy lope, glad to be finally covering some ground. Home was still probably a two day ride away unless we lucked into picking the right trails and avoiding ravines or cliffs that could force us to double back.

It was starting to get dark. But I hadn't found a decent spot to hole up for the night so I rode on, hoping. In less than two hours, full night would settle on the mountains. Then, seeing my own feet let alone where we were going would be impossible. The ridge we'd been travelling on was wide but risky in the dark.

Buck was nervous all of a sudden. Hesitating every few steps rather than plodding forward. There was lots of ripped up deadfall around, solid evidence of bears feeding. I suppose hibernation could be late this year—with the weather being weird. Bears could be taking advantage of the long fall and stocking up on extra food before tucking in for the winter. Buck was terrified of bears.

Sure enough, he came to an abrupt halt and I felt his muscles bunch under me.

Oh. Crap.

A smallish black bear stepped onto the trail in front of us.

Buck spun on his haunches and sold out. Didn't we do this already? Thank heavens riding bareback wasn't a problem or I would've been supper on a platter *just right* for Baby Bear. I clung with my legs and wrapped my arms around Buck's neck, again. "You know, this panic and run thing is getting old," I yelled. "It was a freakin' *little* bear."

He ignored me of course, head down, ears flat, legs pumping.

After a while, I grew annoyed with his foolish fleeing. I'd allowed him his moment of panic but it was time to get a grip. I sat up and see-sawed on the rope, putting pressure on the halter where it crossed the bridge of his nose but he seemed oblivious to my efforts, ran on like an idiot. He didn't seem to realize that we'd already put about five miles between us and the bear. Stupid horse would probably run 'til he dropped.

Intervention time.

I reached forward, wrapped my hand around his left ear, slowly tightened my grip, then twisted and bent. Hah. Great. No effect whatsoever. Fine, maybe if I could slide my hand down to his mouth and grab the corner, kind of like a bit pulling on him. I leaned further across his wither, good thing he's pretty short-necked. I used my right hand to pull the rope from the left side so maybe he'd cock his head a little as my left hand reached for his mouth. I concentrated, edged my fingers closer and then his front end dropped.

Shit! I sailed over his head. Slammed into mother earth. Pain shot from limbs to throat and when the back of my head exploded… my world went black.

*

Gage circled the clearing as fast as he dared, studying the footprints, hoof prints, and the tree with a chunk of bark missing about twelve feet up the trunk. The bullet was too deeply imbedded in the pine for him to dig it out quickly. He'd send his team back for it later. Right now, he needed to find Cass before the Minnows did.

He'd already followed the ATV tracks, and pocketed two 7mm shell casings. Not your average hunting rifle. But a professional shooter wouldn't have left that kind of evidence behind. Could be either a good or bad sign.

Evidence so far, pointed to the bad guys wanting her alive. Most likely, the shots were supposed to spook the horses away so that Cass would be on foot. Vulnerable. They'd capture her. Use her to lure her brother out of hiding

But Gage found enough evidence in the thin skiff of dust covering the frozen ground, to know that Cass had left the clearing on horseback, presumably on the stallion. The question was, where were they now.

He stuffed his arms back into the straps of his big back pack and settled it into place as he strode off following the imprints of the horse's steel shod hooves. They were deep in the toe and widely spaced, indicating he was in full flight. No tellin' how far away they were by now.

He checked his watch. Two hours since he'd heard the gunfire and barely escaped being trampled by three terrified horses barreling down the trail. Lucky for him he hadn't been on the nasty narrow path carved into the side of the mountain. Ten minutes later and he'd have been run down or knocked clear over the edge.

With tracks so easy to follow, Gage maintained a swift pace. Swift considering that he was climbing steadily up a mountain. The Steed, with all its heat seeking electronic gadgets, would have been faster and more efficient. But detection of the high-tech helo could alert the enemy that they weren't the only ones looking for Cass.

So far, the Minnows' pursuit of her had been more opportunistic than aggressive. Gage wanted to keep it that way.

He also suspected that the gangster group was using Sheriff Porter as a pawn in their game. He'd likely been the one to whack the guy that was found in the stallion's paddock. Chances were good it had been a means to prove his worth to the big boys.

Gage shook his head and picked up the pace, breaking into a jog for a while, still mentally flogging himself for screwing up so badly in Vegas. In all his years in both Special Forces and then the family's security agency, this was the first time he'd totally blown a case. Hell, it was the first time a woman had ever come between him and duty and it wasn't sitting well, at all.

How many times had he slapped at his brothers for making decisions with their dick. Man did he have payback coming or what.

Even worse, it wasn't like all he could think of was getting her naked and watching her, hearing her when he was... nope, it was more than that. Dammit he liked her. Liked her tenacity, her sense of humor, hell he even liked when she talked in bed. That was a first.

Not that he didn't like women for more than sex. He had sisters and a mother that he liked. And they always had lots of their friends around and he'd never—he shuddered—never been turned on by one of their sexy looking friends, even in bathing suits around the pool in the summer.

He was a big brother. To everyone.

As for sex, he chose to play with women who weren't looking for anything but a physical relationship. Nice, clean, hot women. He smiled to himself, he'd been on both ends of a booty call now and again. But Cass was different.

He gave himself a mental head slap. Yes. She was different. She was sexy and funny and fun to be with and she made him feel like doing the chest thumping Tarzan thing. But all of that would mean squat if he didn't get her off this mountain—alive.

*

I woke up to warm, moist breath in my ear. In Vegas that had been a delicious turn-on. Here, in the mountains with nothing but a chunk of granite pressing into my hipbone, the only thing turned on was my panic switch.

Please oh please let that be horse breath and not one of Yogi's cousins sniffing at me. How long could I play dead?

And was that the smart move? Oh crap. Like I had a choice right now. I tried to keep my breathing slow and even, from the gut, no chest movement, shoulders motionless.

Oh man enough already. It was touching me, sniffing at me like it wasn't sure if I should be supper or not. I hope to hell I smell bad. Jeez if I was a guy I could conjure up one of those killer farts. NO. Do not laugh. Calm, stay calm. Think, dark, thoughts.

Finally. Finally it happened. A loud snort. A horse snort. And my eyes popped open in time to see Buck saunter away.

Wait.

"Buck. Whoa." Well jeez, that whisper didn't even sound convincing to me. I cleared my throat and sat up so I could muster a good commanding yell. But pain flashed through my head and I fell back with a groan. Oh man just let me die.

I managed a couple of those ankle deep steadying breaths I'd learned as a model when some idiot had decided that snakes would make the shoot more dramatic. Even with this walloping storm in my head I knew that if I didn't catch the damned horse it was going to be a really long walk home.

Satellite phone. Why was it that I'd never think to ask for help? I gave myself a mental head slap and reached for that handy bit of technology. Then remembered. The darn thing had annoyed me, an unnecessary weight in my jacket. I'd moved it to the saddle bags.

Shifting, slow and sure, knowing I had no choice, I sat up, then turned so I was on my knees with my hands braced in front of me and forced myself to stand. Once upright I discovered that the pain in my head wasn't so bad—compared to the screeching agony where my knee used to be. Walking out of here had just reached the category of nearly impossible—at least before spring thaw. I needed the damned horse.

I couldn't count on the mares making it home and a search party finding me before the guy with the gun did. Guy with a gun. Shooting at me on purpose? What the hell was up with that?

I did a mental channel change. Checked my pockets and was pleased to find I did still have the two things I needed most to handle the problem. Compass, and the bag of peppermints.

I glanced over at Buck. His ears had pricked at the sound of the rustling plastic. I plucked out a candy and popped it in my mouth.

"Wanna share with me?" I held the bag toward him, gave it a little shake and sucker that he was, he came right to me. While he lipped at my left hand where I'd fisted the sweet treat, I snagged him by the halter with my right. *Yes!* I still had a ride home.

Time now to get a little *MacGyver* creative. No way was I riding this bugger again without brakes, and maybe a steering wheel.

Using the tiny pink pocket knife, I pulled the drawstring from my sweats and cut a four inch wide circle of fabric from the bottom of my left pant leg. I rolled the canvas material and wrapped it with the string to create a loop style bit I slid into Buck's mouth and fastened to the halter rings. Next I used another strip of pant-leg to wrap around his nose and hooked it to the noseband of the halter in a way that left it low enough to be a pressure point above his nostrils just in case I needed extra control. I attached the lead rope as reins then stood for a moment to admire my handiwork.

It took another ten minutes to hop and hobble to a spot where I could crawl up on a boulder and slide onto his back.

Now, where was I?

Compass in hand, I prodded the horse forward and pointed him east toward the power-lines where I knew there was a service road to follow out to the highway. True, it was the long way around, but better footing and a route that would make us easier to find. Unfortunately it would also make us sitting ducks for someone with a gun, but the pain in my head was beginning to make me feel weird and I was just a little bit scared now.

Buck behaved himself and we plodded along, finding the road I'd aimed for just before the blackness and silence of night wrapped itself around me and made me feel very, very small and insignificant. Only the body heat of the horse between my legs kept my thoughts from turning gloomy and eventually, concentrating on that warmth, my thoughts drifted to my mystery man.

I wondered where in this vast world he may be. What was he doing? Had I even crossed his mind? Did he wonder why I disappeared? Oh how I wished I'd been thinking clearly enough to at least try to leave him a message when I checked out. I mean, just in case he ever wanted to maybe give me a call or something.

I sighed. Guys like that didn't call. They knew how to enjoy the moment and move on. Here for a good time, not a long time.

Oh what I'd do right now to have him keeping me warm instead of this silly horse.

The rhythm of movement, the steady thump of hooves on the dirt road traveling straight down the mountainside, the bothersome hum of the high power wires overhead lulled me into a state of near sleep. I couldn't see where we were going so there was little point keeping my eyes open. My center of gravity had drifted and lowered, settling somewhere around my tailbone as I swayed with the movement of the horse's back. My legs hung slack down his sides. I gave in and leaned forward, crossed my arms over his neck and allowed my weight to settle just in front of his withers.

In my head a new tape wore on, over and over. I will not fall asleep, I will not fall off, I will not fall asleep, I will not fall off... And I prayed for daylight.

I could have stopped, lay down and rested, tied Buck to a tree or one of those big steel towers that supported the power lines. But I was cold. And scared. Afraid to fall asleep. So I thought about my mystery cowboy, relived that night in Vegas, detail by fabulous detail, every touch of his hands, of his mouth. His breath against my skin.

Chapter 5

Gage's breath caught and his forward motion ceased. The horse, bathed in pre-dawn light stood head low and hip cocked, less than fifty feet away with Cassandra sprawled over its back. Keeping his attention on the stallion and his movements smooth, he keyed the electronic locater to send his signal to the team, and pulled Jared's scented gloves from a pocket. He understood the purpose of the aromas, and could get on board with the smell of leather and peppermint, but the added perfume of lavender was sickly sweet.

Jared also instructed him to hum, but now, the only tune Gage could come up with, was a ditty his sisters used to sing to drive their brothers out of the room. Shaking off the ridiculous memory he managed happy birthday, while fear clawed at his throat. Cassandra was limp, appeared lifeless.

The horse's nostrils flared and his head came up. With all four feet planted, muscles tense, and ears pricked forward, the beast was poised for flight.

Gage started forward but not directly toward the animal, angled instead to pass him and was careful not to look him in the eye as he rubbed the palms of the gloves together in an attempt to release more scent. If he could just get to Maddy before the damned horse moved and dislodged her. Rushing wouldn't work. Instead he edged sideways, offered a gloved hand, palm up for the horse to sniff.

Once a thorough examination of the glove and Gage's sleeve was complete, the stallion lowered his head and made chewing motions—horse speak for acceptance.

Gage tugged off the gloves, stuffed them in his belt, slid a hand to Cassandra's throat and relief poured through him. Her pulse was strong. Years of training took over as he gently probed her scalp to find the source of the dried blood matting her hair. The cut was small but surrounded by swelling.

Forcing himself to remain silent, he crouched to check her face the best he could considering her right cheek was pressed against the horse's neck. Dirt was imbedded in the deep scrapes and muted the bruising on her cheekbone but didn't hide the dried blood beneath each nostril. He needed to get her off the damned horse, now.

With his mouth beside her ear he poured urgency into his whisper. "Cassandra."

No response. Was she unconscious, or deeply asleep due to pain, fatigue or exposure? He slid a hand between her and the horse, dug his knuckle into her breast bone and rubbed back and forth a couple of times while he kept after her verbally. "Maddy you need to wake up baby. Come on Maddy. Cassandra. Wake up."

"Ow." It was faint, barely a mutter but Gage's body went slack with relief.

She opened her eyes just enough that he could see her pupils looked somewhat even. She lifted her head for just a second, muttered something like, holy crap, then went instantly still.

"What hurts?"

"Head, everything."

"I need you to go freeze-frame for me. Do not move so much as an eye-lash," he said while reaching behind him, grabbing a black plastic c-collar from a pocket on the side of his backpack. He slipped the collar around her neck. Tightened the straps then probed down her spine with practiced hands. "Does anything I'm doing hurt?"

"My head."

"What else?"

"Not sure. Arms and legs are asleep."

Fuck. "Can you feel them?"

"Heavy, like when I sleep on my arm."

Determined not to think the worst, and not to rush what had to be done properly, he fell back on clinical routine. Walked through the steps. Pinched her forearm, she pulled reflexively pulled away. Ran a nail across her palm, and her fingers closed. He checked the other arm and then her legs, careful to place reassuring hands on the horse as he walked around him.

As confident as he could be that she had no paralysis, he held his breath and eased her off the buckskin to lay her on the flattest part of the dirt roadway. He checked the readout on his locater, estimated pickup wouldn't be for at least twenty minutes.

Trusting the horse not to wander off, he concentrated first on Cassandra's circulation. "Think from the core out.

First your shoulders, flex and rotate them a little, then your elbows and on down to your finger tips."

The frown on her face only added to the level of gruesome painted there by dirt and blood and bruises. "Pins and needles." She wiggled her fingers.

"That's good, means they're waking up. Now start down your legs. First clench your butt muscles a couple of times."

"Ha, ha," she muttered.

He tried to smile, but failed. "Just like the arms, work on down a little at a time until you're moving your toes." He dug in his pack for the foil blanket, showed it to her and tipped his head toward the horse. "Will it spook him if I unfold this?"

"Nope."

Not taking his attention off the stallion, he kept the blanket low, and unfolded it to cover her legs. He tugged off his jacket, tucked it in around her shoulders and studied her face.

"You're staring," she said.

"You have blue lips."

"New trend, matches my bruises." She clamped her teeth together but he'd caught the subtle shiver. He unclipped the locater from his belt. Checked the read-out, slid a tiny keyboard from inside and sent a brief text. She muttered something about satellites and power line interference.

He shook his head. "This thing gets a signal anywhere, anytime, so long as I don't go off the planet."

"What did that cost?"

"Everything." He gave a glance over his shoulder.

"I'll take the horse to the edge of the trees." He pointed up into the sky. "Your ride's almost here." He led the buckskin the short distance and tied him to a stout tree. "Ever been in a helicopter?"

"Jared can bring the truck up the service road."

"You need x-rays and a CAT-Scan, not a bumpy trip in a pickup. I'll take the horse back to the ranch."

He watched her face as the helicopter approached soundlessly. Her eyes widened with surprise and for the first time since she'd left him in Vegas, he found himself smiling.

"Steel wool," she muttered and he cocked his head. "Takes away the shine. Won't get spotted in the woods."

He caught himself before he told her that was exactly the point of the finish on the stealth copter his family affectionately called the Steed, to make it as difficult as possible to be seen or heard by the enemy.

He leaned over to shield her from debris stirred up by the rotors.

As soon as the blades stopped, Gage glanced up, and used his hands to signal what was needed. Quinn hopped out the rear door, dragging a backboard with him. Then pulled tack for the horse from inside as well, dropping it on the ground before making his way over to them.

"Hey pretty lady, I'm Quinn, your personal flight attendant and cheerleader." He grinned as he set the board on one side of her and dropped to his knees on the other. Gage stayed silent. Moved to position himself above her head. "We're going to roll you onto your side, then back down onto this board. Okay? On the count of three."

Kneeling above her, Gage placed his hands alongside

her head to stabilize her neck, and nodded. Quinn counted, rolled her up, slid the board into place then lowered her back down and secured her in place. A routine of movements they'd practiced and used dozens of times. The entire procedure took less than two minutes but it ramped Gage's tension up even more, added a new layer of real to his concern.

Loading her into the aircraft, Quinn kept up an annoying banter. "Family sends a thank you for bringing Gage to his knees, sweet lady. Never been done before you, so my hat's off." Gage's teeth clenched. "You're probably a real heartbreaker under all that dirt, but still, not is usual type. Way to tall. He usually goes for curvy little blondes."

"Hey." The word escaped and only made his smart ass brother's grin widen. Not much a guy could do with his hands full now. Besides, he was a believer in, don't get mad, get even.

Quinn set the head end of the board on the edge of the deck, jumped in. Gage waited for the signal, then pushed her into place on the floor, watched his brother fasten the motion clips, pull on his helmet then lift a finger with a swirling motion. Gage slid the door closed.

He scooted to get past the reach of the rotors but didn't stop, didn't give in to the urge to watch until they were out of site. Instead, he did what had to be done next.

*

My stomach lurched as we shot into the air. No wings, no feathers. Just a metal pod and people I didn't know.

I should've done something, refused to go, or at least

said something. Instead I'd given away my control, forfeited decision making, allowed them to pick me up, ship me off, and that was just wrong. At the age of eighteen, I'd taken my life in my own hands and promised myself that I'd never be anyone's puppet again.

Yet here I lay on the floor of a helicopter, heaven knows how many hundreds of feet above the ground, helpless, strapped down so well that only my eyes could move. My destination was unknown and I was truly at the mercy of others. I tried to take a calming breath but my chest couldn't expand. I concentrated, fought the scream. Kept my wits. Tried to shout, "Help me."

The collar hampered mouth movement. The sandbags they'd put beside my head blocked the sound of my voice. Panic ramped up. Swiveling my eyes to search for help sent fresh pain through my head while all I could see was the back of the pilot's helmet left, and Quinn's knees above me on the right. If I could just reach out with a finger tip, touch his pant leg, or turn my head the tiniest fraction. But they'd tied me tight, I could barely see anything, couldn't hear, couldn't move, couldn't anything, strapped into a weird craft with total strangers and someone had shot at me and ... a greasy wave of nausea slithered up my throat. If I puked, I'd choke to death, aspirate, terror bloomed and a volley of silent screams ripped through me.

A cold hand touched my cheek, sliced through the panic, drew my focus to the man leaning over me. The frantic pounding of my heart registered as his blue eyes stared from inside a black helmet. His mouth moved but I couldn't hear him.

"Help Me." My yell was just as soundless. He shifted,

knelt close, held up a mike attached to a set of earphones, then tapped the side of his helmet. He lowered the mike to my mouth and I squeezed words through teeth forced closed by the combination of collar sandbags, and straps. "Can't move. Help me. My hands."

His glance raked the length of my body. I flexed and wiggled my fingers to get his attention and without hesitation, he loosened the straps to released my arms. Pain shot through my shoulder while the panic began to recede. Facts, observations registered with increasing pace.

The man watching me looked an awful lot like his brother, my mystery cowboy from Vegas. I couldn't help but wonder what the hell the two of them were doing in Washington State. Had he followed me, and if so why? Had he showed up at the ranch and been recruited for a search party when the mares showed up without me? I glanced as far sideways as I could to try and get a good look now that Quinn had sat back in his seat.

All I could see was a pair of pant legs of a material that made me think about Gage again. Gage, I liked the name that went along with the man. Liked it better than the phony one we'd used in Vegas, I'd been Madeline and he'd been Sundance. Geez could it be more corny?

I focused again on the fabric and carefully slipped a hand out to feel the same velvety softness over a canvass strength I'd noticed when I'd grabbed Gage's sleeve—a camouflage print of black, brown and grey. Quinn wore black, but it was definitely the same stuff. A texture I'd never felt before today. And in my thirteen years as a model, I'd encountered pretty much everything invented.

I was startled to realize that Quinn had leaned forward

and was staring down at where my hand gripped his pant leg. I let it go, would have shrugged if I could. I watched him smile and he met my gaze with an odd expression. I lifted the mike from where he'd left it resting on my stomach. "What?"

His mouth twitched as though he was trying not to smile.

I tried again. "What?"

He shook his head, said something and the smile grew as he glanced toward the front of he craft. I followed his gaze. Watched the pilot turn slightly toward us and was surprised to see the face of a woman. Her mouth moved, obviously in conversation with Quinn through mikes and headphones in their helmets. Then she turned fully and looked down at me. My heart did a funny bump as an eerily familiar smile spread across her face for just a moment before she returned her attention to the front of the helicopter.

Was I seeing things? Making things up? Was I superimposing Gage's face on everyone? I started to wonder, at this point, if I had indeed fallen down a rabbit hole. Or more likely, sustained a major head injury.

Head injury, right, funny how pain gets worse when you think about it. Maybe if I didn't think, didn't try to move, the pain would ease up. I could lie here, frozen in time, suspended hundreds of feet from the ground in a little tin machine with two total strangers who looked ridiculously familiar, while we put miles between me and everything I know, everyone I trust. *Ohmygod.*

I didn't like the look on Quinn's face as he leaned over me, with an oxygen mask. I really didn't need it but he must think I did as he held it very firmly in place.

First I noticed the odd odor, then the funny feeling at the back of my throat. Something was off. My toes began to wiggle and flex. I tried to draw a deep breath, but I still couldn't even though the straps didn't feel tight anymore and the nasty plastic collar had stopped biting into my skin. That was good.

I knew my head hadn't stopped aching, but it didn't seem to matter. Weird. I closed my eyes and absorbed the idea of my mind being not quite up to par. There was an understatement.

*

Surfacing from the heaviness of drugged sleep took effort. The brightness was like shards of glass in my eyes as I focused on a plain white ceiling. The breath I held, eased out as I turned my head with care, to take in my surroundings. I blinked at huge golden cat eyes, surrounded by short white fur.

I tried twice to speak before my raspy throat parted with the single word. "Hello." I swallowed, wincing from the effort. "Who are you?"

In response, the cat's mouth opened in a wide, leisurely feline yawn. Ears flattened back, he stretched out first one front leg, then the other, spreading his toes and flexing his claws. When he stepped forward to bump his forehead against mine, I found myself smiling in spite of the pain shooting from the roots of my hair down through my neck and spreading out across my shoulders.

I swallowed a groan, sat up to look around and a new,

peculiar pain ricocheted through me. I clamped my jaw, squeezed my eyes shut and held my breath for as long as I could. Did it help? Of course not.

This was no time to fold up and be a wimp. I needed to find out where I was. Needed to contact Jared about Buck. Had to get ahold of Sidney.

I tried to distract myself and get a handle on my circumstances by cataloguing the room and its contents.

The blinking, blipping electronics I was hooked up to in one way or another were housed on shelves near the head of the bed. There was a standard IV pole and oxygen tank. One of those red, rolling cabinets filled with skinny little equipment drawers was parked against the wall, a box of purple surgical gloves resting on top.

The room itself was huge, like a fancy hotel room if you ignored the medical bed and equipment. Three walls were painted pale orange, like the inside of a ripe apricot. The fourth wall was glass blocks from floor to ceiling, and daylight filtered through. Nestled alongside the glass wall was a tidy arrangement of light brown leather chairs and a sofa with a low oval wooden table as a centerpiece.

Besides the feline being out of place, the place smacked of money from the electronics and luxurious bed linens to the high-end furniture. My conclusion at this point was a simple one. I was most certainly not in a hospital.

I looked at the cat. "Well pal, at least I didn't land in a dive." I reached out to touch him and he stepped forward, arched his back under my hand and began to purr.

The door opened and several people walked in.

A tiny redhead in a lab coat put her hands on my shoulders and eased me back against the pillows. "How are you feeling?"

"Pretty good aside from the pain. Who are you?" I winced at the sharpness of my own voice and she glanced toward the machines behind me. She reached for the tube that ran down from the IV bag and slid a needle into the little y-joint.

I opened my mouth to ask what she was giving me, but no words came out. My vision blurred and I descended into darkness with questions in my mind.

The next time I woke up, the pain in my head was borderline excruciating and definitely ranked a much higher score than all the other pains I was having. My knee for instance only hurt when I tried to move, my shoulder and wrist, likewise. If I thought about it for a minute, there were a gazillion little aches all vying for my attention but the head won, no contest.

On top of that, I felt green—like a comic-book illustration of sea-sickness. I closed my eyes, took long slow breaths and the tingling in my fingers eased although my stomach felt no better. I squinted one eye open and said to the cat nestled in on the foot of the bed, "Is this how you feel when you have a burning need to eat grass and puke?"

His response was a steady look that said, *better than a hairball.*

I groaned and used the edge of the sheet to wipe my damp face, then turned on my side and curled up like a shrimp in hot oil.

I heard the door open but didn't bother to lift my eyelids. A cool, soothing hand rested against my forehead.

"Cassandra? You awake?" It was a female voice, smooth, professional.

"No."

First I heard the chuckle, then real concern. "Are you in a lot of pain?"

"Just a headache," I lied, not knowing why.

"Considering your concussion, I'm not surprised."

"Don't have a concussion. Took a header when my horse tripped. No big deal."

"I have x-rays, an MRI and a CAT scan that say you've got no permanent damage. But you do have a concussion." Her voice was quiet but there was a 'no nonsense' tone about it. "You don't want me to shine my trusty light in your eyes do you?"

I cracked one eye-lid open and stared at a very tiny woman with a big attitude. She was pretty and had the kind of curves that made men stupid. I focused on her face, emerald green eyes surrounded by laugh lines and a mouth that twitched and made me pretty sure she was smirking at me. Something niggled in the back of my mind.

"You were in here before. You drugged me."

"I needed to change your pain meds, take you off the industrial strength stuff. Trust me, you didn't want to be awake for that."

"I have to get home. There are things to take care of." Without thinking, I made a move to emphasize how serious and determined I was, did something way high on the stupid scale. In one bold move, I sat up and swung my legs over the side of the bed.

Holy Hanna. I held on to that first sucked in breath while I waited for the double thump in my head to subside and my gag reflex to chill. I gave up before I turned blue in the face, and dissolved back down into the bedding. There was a vague realization that the woman eased my legs back up while I was swallowing hard and trying to get a grip.

"Dare I ask again if you're okay?" that cool hand was on my forehead again.

I eased over onto my back and whispered, "For my next trick..."

And she responded with a stern, "For your next trick you will lie quietly for an hour or I'll have to knock you out again."

Not sure if she was joking or not, I decided to be obliging. "Okay, I'll be good if you'll answer some of my questions."

When she smiled I had the feeling I knew her from somewhere. "First of all, my name's Eve, although I'm sometimes referred to as Doc, or Dr. Meyers. She smiled again. "You were injured and in danger so Gage had you picked up and brought here."

Still confused, I pushed past the pain but was careful to keep my head on the pillow. "I think you should explain why--" I did a one-handed air-quote thing, "Gage had me picked up." I finished with another set of finger folds. "You can start with who the hell Gage is. I mean besides a guy I met in Vegas and... Well, anyways, why would he be plucking me out of danger using what seemed like the kind of helicopter and people that I read about in fiction novels. And from there you can move right on to why I wasn't just returned to my own home, which would have taken about four minutes in that fancy machine, and I'd be in my own bed right now with my own people looking after me instead of strangers and I wouldn't have to ask all these stupid questions--"

You go girl.

I blinked. "-- and on top of everything else, I'd swear that cat just talked. Again. Oh lord I must have a head injury."

The good Doc wrapped her fingers around my wrist, perhaps to steady me because she could obviously see the digital readout of my pulse which had jumped from sixty-seven to a hundred and twenty-eight.

An odd warmth ran up my arm from where she touched me, spread like a comforting blanket. The tightness of panic eased in my chest. I'd felt no needle. Hmm.

The cat distracted me by stepping onto my stomach. He stared into my eyes with some sort of silent message before hunkering down, folding his toes into his chest, closing his eyes and beginning to purr.

Before I could return my attention to the odd feeling caused by the woman's touch, she'd removed her hand, turned away to fiddle with the machines. Her words were clipped. "With our intense, cutting edge therapy, you'll heal very quickly. And the facility is completely secure."

I frowned, wondering why that sounded like an odd thing for her to say, but she continued before I could ask a question.

"It will take a few days for the effects of the concussion to ease. In the meantime, we'll keep you comfortable with medication. All you have to do is lie back, and relax. As well, the people here are all quite friendly and would love to drop in and keep you company." She turned toward me with a smile. "But if I catch you having conversations with that cat, I'll toss you both in a padded room."

Comprehension dawned. "This isn't one of those weird, health retreats is it? Because I'll tell you right now, I'm not eating grass or tree bark. And anybody comes near me with a rubber hose, well, let's just say it they'll regret it."

She was grinning ear to ear. "Cleansing and purging not your style?"

"Ev--er," I said with a big gap between syllables to make sure she didn't miss my point. "But as for the cat conversations? You'll just have to live with it. I talk to animals. Always have, always will. Never had one answer back until now though."

"Far as I know it's a first for him too," she said with a straight face. "Before I go, is there anything I can get you?"

"How about an explanation or two? Like where exactly I am, and why I'm here. Why I was brought here. And why do you look so familiar when I'm almost certain we've never met?"

"Perhaps it's the family resemblance. My sister, Angie was your pilot in the helo--"

"I barely saw her face, didn't hear her voice."

"Gage and Quinn are our brothers."

Oh. Well. Isn't that interesting. She was watching me as though I was supposed to have some kind of reaction to that tidbit. So I scrambled for something.

"Quite the family. Doctor, pilot, medic, cowboy? Who are you people really and what is this place?" Why was everyone I'd met either a brother or a sister? All in the same age range? Weird thoughts about cults started to circle in my mushy brain.

Her brows tipped up. "You're safe here, and now that

the new pain treatment is starting to take effect, you need to rest." She touched my shoulder. "Relax. I'll be back to check on you a little later." She ran a hand down the cat's back. "And you behave yourself Merlin."

*

Who knows how much time had passed. I'd been drifting in and out of sleep for what felt like days, talking to the cat, puzzling over my situation and dreaming about my cowboy lover. Yummy, steamy dreams that distracted me from the odd situation I'd found myself in.

Now, completely awake, I wasn't sure I wanted to behave myself and stay here. The blinking, chirping medical machinery was gone. The only evidence of the previous hospital setting was the bed with folded down railings.

I swung my legs over the side and very, very slowly eased upright, waiting for my head to begin that nasty thumping thing I'd experienced before. Didn't happen. A thick achiness radiated down my neck and into my shoulders, but no drums. I turned from side to side, found nothing majorly uncomfortable. The cat watched me from the foot of the bed.

"Well Merlin, I think it's time I got a move on." Thank heavens I was dressed in sweats instead of a draughty, butt-flashing hospital nightgown. I slid down from the bed, settled my feet on the floor and my knee screamed foul. Right, I'd hurt my knee before the stupid horse stumbled and knocked me out cold. Or maybe it was at the same time? Geez, shouldn't I know one way or another? Do concussions mess with your memory?

Duh.

I swung around. "What did you say?"

He blinked, said nothing of course.

"Oh you're a slick one aren't you. Just wind the people up and watch them dance. That's your game isn't it?" I shook my head at him. "And here I thought you wanted to be my friend."

I turned away from the cocky white fur ball and limped to the door, stared at the knob, wondering. What if it was locked? I'd never know if I didn't try.

Don't do it.

Was that my own internal voice or the damned cat again? I glanced over to see he was still on the bed, as though settled in to watch a good show.

With my gaze fixed on the doorknob, I reached for it and as usual, my timing sucked. I suppose I'd been too distracted to notice the sound of approaching footsteps, or perhaps the door was soundproof. In any case, even the turn and click didn't register. Nope, I didn't have any warning before the door came at me and...

Chapter 6

Whack!

I didn't see stars when the door connected with my forehead, but the pain shot through me like a lightning bolt. And I'm sure whatever kind of sound I made, was drowned out by a deep voice cursing—loud and creative.

After I wilted onto the shiny wooden floor, the door was shoved fully open and strong arms slid behind my back and knees to swing me up and carry me back to the bed.

The first thing I saw when I managed to focus was the smug look on the cat's face. I gave him an evil glare. Or at least the best version of one I could muster at the moment, which I'm assuming was borderline pathetic.

I looked up at the face belonging to the strong arms to recognize Quinn, Gage's brother.

"Are you okay?"

"Glad I was looking down. You missed my nose. "

He smiled. I felt a little internal buzz and scolded myself. Yes, he had the same smile as Gage. No need to get stupid over it.

"I'm Quinn. We met on the Steed."

"I remember. And that makes the doctor and the pilot

73

your sisters." Right on cue, Eve walked in. "Feeling better?"

"Up until a minute ago." That put an instant frown on her face.

She stepped up close and tried to put her fingers on my wrist but I pulled away. "My pulse is fine. I had a bit of a surprise meeting with the door. I'll live." I winced when I moved my legs back over the side of the bed so I could get to my feet again.

Eve settled a hand on my sore knee and her fingertips rubbed gentle circles. "The door?" She studied me like a bug under glass.

Quinn explained, "I was talking to Lissa, shoved the door open while I was looking the other way and walloped poor Cassandra in the head."

I heard snickering and squinted at the cat. "Hey."

Quinn raised an eyebrow and Eve said, "Don't ask."

His mouth quirked. "Side effects?"

She shook her head. "Why were you behind the door?"

I shrugged. "Figured it was time to find out if I was locked in here."

"You are free to move around as you wish."

Quinn added, "It's not a bad place to be stranded. And with the rest of us stuck here for a few days, you've got great company." He flashed another one of those Gage-like smiles.

"Stranded? Why?"

Eve sighed. "No transportation available."

I nearly gaped in disbelief. Talk about lame. No transport. Huh. I'd check that out for myself, later. For now,

I'd play their game. I gave a little half shrug. "If you'll show me where the kitchen is maybe I could get a glass of juice or something."

Eve's smile was back, although something about the look in her eyes made me think she wasn't fooled. "Never mind juice, Lissa has supper ready. Quinn was sent to get you."

"Lissa? Another sister?"

"Cousin. By marriage." She gestured outward with her hands. "This is her house. We just drop in and keep her company now and again."

The light bulb lit and I finished the sentence for her. "When you need a safe-house." There were fragments of memories teasing me. Words like safe, secure and protected, flitted around in my head. "How long have I been here?"

"Four days."

I let that settle. Waited for more memories to surface but nothing happened aside from my stomach growling.

Quinn's lips twitched.

I slid off the bed and started for the door. "Supper sounds like a great idea." I stopped dead in my tracks after a few steps. My knee. There was no pain. I took another step, this time tentative. Nothing.

Quinn had come up beside me. There was a smile in his voice when he said, "Gage always did have a thing for brains."

I stared up at him and he smiled. "Not saying you don't have looks..."

"At this point, I'll just say thanks and perhaps we could move on?" Later. When I had some food in me and felt a bit stronger, I'd try to figure out how Eve made the pain go away just by touching my knee.

He offered his arm, elbow crooked toward me. "Dining room escort ma'am?"

I shook my head at him. "Charming men must run in the family." *But don't think for a minute that you've got me snowed.* I was willing to pretend to go along with them for a while, at least until I figured a few things out.

As we exited the bedroom, Merlin jogged past and left us to follow his tailless rump. "Hey, he's got no tail," I said like an idiot. Full points to me for observation. How the heck had I missed that obvious detail? No pun intended.

"Actually, he has one, it's just very, very short," said Eve.

The cat stopped and glared over his shoulder at Eve.

Quinn chuckled. "Not a nice thing to say about a guy."

Hmmpph

Merlin turned and continued to lead the way. Who knew if that was his comment or just what I expected it to be. There were far more important things for me to concentrate on.

I studied my surroundings as we walked a long hallway. Doors on both sides were cracked open just enough to see each room had a bed and a distinct color scheme. Mine had been pale orange. Passing these others I mentally ticked off the colors, yellow, pink, blue, green, purple, gray, and stark white.

At the end of the hall, we stepped into a magnificent great room, with a vaulted, glazed-beam ceiling. A massive field-stone fireplace and chimney stood in the center. One wall was all window and showcased a stunning view of mountains that gave me an overwhelming sense of relief.

I knew where I was. Only southern Alberta had this view of the Rockies.

I squelched a smile, turned my back on the window—as well as the gorgeous collection of leather furniture and Navaho blankets—to stare at a kitchen area worthy of any chef's knives. It was a work of art featuring stainless steel, copper, polished wood, granite, several ovens, and a stove with at least a dozen burners.

Eve went to the stove where a woman with short spiky blonde hair was standing with her back to me, stirring the contents of a steaming pot.

A long, rustic-looking table with about a dozen chairs, was set for six. Thick white plates rested on bright woven placemats along with heavy flatware and mason jar drinking glasses. All suspiciously homey. It made me itch.

A second hallway, piqued my curiosity so I decided to check it out.

Quinn was quick to catch up. "Where you headed?"

"Exploring." I didn't break stride. "Eve said I was free to wander, right?" By now I had reached the first closed door. I turned the knob and discovered an amazing pantry—shelves loaded with clear glass containers containing every imaginable ingredient from rice to dried fruit—and a wall of glass fronted freezers. I peered in and read some of the bold printed labels. There was every imaginable kind of meat, vegetable and fruit, plus plenty of prepared meals like lasagna and cabbage soup. Yuk, I thought, who invented cabbage soup?

The next door opened to a professional looking fitness

room. Half a dozen machines—stair-climbers to bikes—faced a side wall with a big screen on it. I shuddered at childhood memories. For years I'd been forced to spend hours in the gym to keep my body perfectly toned, while being half-starved to death.

I threw an evil look at the big weight apparatus in the corner of the room, glanced at a stack of free weights and grinned when I spotted the punching bags. "Now that would have been useful."

"What?" Quinn looked confused.

"Sorry, thinking out loud."

I perused the rest of the room, took in work-out mats and exercise balls in front of a glass block wall where sunlight filtered in. "Don't suppose there's a pool out there?" I asked Quinn.

He hesitated. "No. But sauna, steam-room, hot tub, and showers are that way." He angled his head toward a set of doors I hadn't noticed.

"Nice." I'd lost interest. To me, exercising indoors was like eating canned spaghetti. Okay in a pinch but nothing at all like the real thing. I'd much rather do a ten mile run in the rain than one mile on a treadmill.

While I moved on down the hall, opening all the doors as I went, a part of me felt rude and uncomfortable as though I was prying into other people's business, but the driving need to know about my surroundings, and to find an exit in case I wanted to leave, was far stronger.

Along the way, I discovered an office and a den as well as another bedroom. There were small rooms filled with medical equipment, and doors labeled MRI, CAT, X-ray and LAB.

The room I found most disturbing, was like a miniature clothing store with floor to ceiling racks of clothes in styles from urban chic to homeless. Cubby-shelves filled with everything from packaged underwear to shoes and watches lined one whole wall.

I shivered and backed out. Ideas were beginning to form and I wasn't sure I liked them.

When I came upon a locked door, Quinn placed a hand on my shoulder, quietly saying, "Off-limits."

"Why?" Stupid question, because if I wasn't allowed to look inside, he wasn't about to tell me what was in there. But I was wrong, one more time, and when he did tell me, he said the one word that would make me back off and never ever try the door again.

"Snakes."

I shuddered, jumped back and kept moving to get away as though something was going to slither out under the door. Another full body shiver ran from the top of my head to the soles of my feet while my voice came out little more than a horrified whisper. "Fuck."

"Cassandra, wait."

"Damn you," I muttered as I marched back to the great room, dropped into a chair near the window, pulled my feet up off the floor, wrapped both arms around my legs, rested my chin on my knees and rocked. Forced myself to breath deep, and clear the nasty images out of my mind. Snakes were my phobia. And because I had only one, well, it was a biggie.

I could endure anything, face any danger, deal with any problem but show me one little garden snake? I'm cooked. I mean, completely, utterly useless. The only cure, the only thing that ever helped even just a little bit? Blowing one away with a shotgun. As an animal lover that appalled me. But as a woman terrified of snakes? It helped me get through that day.

Now, as the shaking eased and my bones stopped rattling, I wondered why the hell would these people have snakes in this house? Not like they're great pets or anything. Hell they're nasty, slithery..."

"Cassandra." Eve was crouched in front of me. I blinked my way back to reality, focused on her face.

"What?" A final quivering chill was chased away by the heat that ran through me from where her hands lay over mine.

"Are you alright?"

"No. I have to leave here. Now. I can't stay. I can't breath."

"What happened?"

Quinn answered before I could. "It's my fault. Again. When she asked why that door was locked I said 'snakes' and she lost it."

Eve stood, and quite handily cuffed her brother. "Idiot." She settled on the arm of my chair and put an arm around my shoulders. Put herself between me and Quinn. "Cassandra, he was lying."

"Thought it was a good way to make you not want to go in there. Sorry."

"Damn your fucking hide." The words, once said, seemed to unlock me. Release me from the clutch of unreasonable fear.

"How was I supposed to know snakes would send you off all freaked out?"

"Stop saying that word." If I'd been standing I would have stomped my foot. "It should be in the girl-boy handbooks. Most females are afraid of them. And spiders. Just like boys are supposed to be afraid of going blind. Of course, there are exceptions to all the rules. I'm not afraid of spiders and most guys will risk blindness but--"

Eve laughed and was joined by the blonde woman, who had apparently been standing behind me. Always susceptible to that kind of influence, I felt a giggle burst in my own throat and just like that, we were all laughing together, even Quinn.

Once we'd wound down, Eve said, "There is nothing bad in that room. But it is private. Lissa," she tipped her head toward the woman with the spiky hair who was reaching over to shake my hand, "and her husband Kyle often share their house with strangers and only ask for privacy in their own room."

"I'll show you if you like," offered Lissa as she handed me a glass with water in it. I automatically took a swallow.

Now I felt foolish. "Not necessary." I turned to glare at Quinn. "No telling why men opt to lie when the truth is so much simpler."

Eve's look was thoughtful. "Funny, you don't strike me as a woman who would stereotype that way."

I sighed. "Sorry. Tender spot from a few of the species I've bumped into over the years." I glanced at Lissa. "You don't need to open the door. I respect your privacy, and appreciate your hospitality."

It was just the tiniest of movements I caught out of the corner of my eye but I could have sworn I saw a silent signal pass between Quinn and Eve.

"Well," Lissa said, "Supper's ready so why don't we get to it?"

Quinn held his hand out to help me up. "Friends?"

I placed mine in his and gave the appropriate, "Sure." But I didn't trust him. Or the two women for that matter. There was too much silent communication going on around me.

My head was beginning to pound again. I could hear a faint hum that nobody else seemed to notice. My vision blurred. Shit.

*

Mmmm . What a lovely way to wake up. A warm, hard, body. And that unmistakable scent of a –

My eye-lids flew up and I'm sure my eyes widened cartoon-style when I focused on the sexy as hell face of my Vegas lover. A voice screamed inside my head that this was creepy and wrong but my body disagreed. Stalemate.

Gage simply smiled.

"Oh." I'm a woman of many words. But at the moment, my brain was too busy registering the sight, smell and feel of him to produce enough words to form a sentence.

"Good morning," he said.

Well. The deep sexy voice tickled my eardrums as a delightful harmonized response built under my skin. All I needed now was a little taste and I'd probably have lift-off. Speak, I thought, and my lips moved but no sound came out. He smiled like he knew what was going on in my head, and brushed his mouth across mine.

Instinct is a remarkable thing. At least I'm assuming it was instinct that kept me from parting my lips for the sample I craved. I needed a toothbrush first—again. But this time there was no bolting to the bathroom. Not while pinned to the mattress by an arm and a leg. Secondly, some sense of preservation prevented me from fighting for my freedom with the kind of fast move that would aggravate the headache I'd had before.

"How's the head?"

Huh? Now he's reading my mind? I wanted to answer, say something, but that morning breath thing was an elephant in the room—not that he of the foraging lips, seemed to be noticing any pink pachyderm.

When I resorted to wriggling like an impatient toddler, he allowed me to slip away and I scooted to the bathroom, happy to find I was headache-free. With the bathroom door between us and a mouthful of Crest, I scrubbed back and forth, up and down, thinking about how stupidly I'd wanted that good morning kiss until I noticed the bright colored, tropical fish on the shower curtain. My shower curtain. The one at the ranch.

I spun around. Stared at my turquoise tub and matching toilet. My towels. How the hell did I get here?

I turned back to the mirror and eyeballed my image. Bed head, faded bruises, toothpaste foam dripping off my chin. I spit, rinsed, spit, wiped my face, stuck my toothbrush in the blue glass beside the sink. Ritual type moves to help settle the queasy uncertainty in my belly.

Opening the door, I was surprised to see Gage in the bed where I'd left him, propped up against the headboard, his expression relaxed.

I leaned against the door jamb and studied my bedroom. Took in the details I'd missed only minutes ago because they were so familiar. Pictures on the walls, the quilt I'd made, a hooked rug, tiny beads sewn along the edge of the window blind. Each detail was there. Yet I was afraid to lift those pretty blinds and look outside, for fear this was all some freaking bizarre hallucination.

"Maddy."

There was understanding in his voice along with concern and warmth. I fixed my gaze on his eyes, firmly ignoring the pull of that sexy mouth and the gorgeous body visible above the sheet.

"My name. Is Cassandra."

"I know. But sometimes I think of you as Maddy."

"Sometimes? Come on Gage, it's not like we've got a long history." I had to fight the pull. Even without looking at his mouth, I felt the heat of his smile.

"You were Maddy to me."

I shook off the argument, his attempt at distraction. "Last thing I remember was passing out. They must have put something in the glass of water. How did I get home?"

Each word was carefully enunciated. "You're recovering from a head injury."

My nostrils flared and my jaw clamped shut. Through grinding teeth I spit out, "You are playing games with my mind. This whole freaking thing has been orchestrated and I want to know why."

"Cassandra."

Something new in his voice reminded me that in spite of our physical intimacy, we were strangers. Fear slid in alongside my mad.

"Whoever the hell you are, you need to quit playing games right now. Do not placate me. This is not a dream and I don't hallucinate." I've been shot at, dumped twice by the same horse—which really pisses me off—been plucked off the open range by two people in some kind of a mysterious helicopter, woken up in a blinkin' safe house on the other side of the Rockies, then, somebody twitches their nose or hits a switch and poof, I'm home in my own bed with a man who--" I was running out of steam. "Just tell me why I'm being played."

His gaze stayed fixed on mine. "Come. Here."

I started forward automatically. Stopped. I desperately wanted to go to him and forget the confusion of time and place. But I had a brain. A backbone. Abhorred weakness. Hated to acknowledge what was no more than a basic human need for comfort, in the middle of chaos.

For my entire life, I'd longed for a soft place to land. For years I'd searched for my father, craved the warm strong arms that used to hold me tight while his rumbling voice promised everything would be okay. He was my fairy tale. I hadn't seen him since I was five—when fairy tales stopped being real.

I recognized my needs. Tried to rationalize. Blended emotions and blurred edges, were not going to help me here. My father was dead. I would never find the kind of solace I'd sought in my search for him.

The freedom and exhilaration I'd felt with Gage in Vegas had nothing to do with misplaced childhood feelings. Yet, what he was offering now seemed different.

He studied me in silence. His face expressionless, but

his eyes had the intensity of someone trying to catch the hands of a clock moving.

Having weighed the situation and prepared to sacrifice pride, I went to the side of the bed, allowed him to pull me down and wrap me up in his warmth. He tugged the cover over us and I refused to let my mind ruin the moment. Because it was just that. A single moment of weakness. It would pass, and then I'd move on.

His lips played with the edge of my ear. I felt his breath and before I had a chance to talk myself out of it, I turned to meet his open mouth with mine. Submerged myself in pleasure until it felt like my heart would crawl up my throat. I pushed away, trying to gather my scrambled wits.

"Okay," I said, "so I needed that." I cleared my throat and tried to get my voice to climb back up an octave. "But it doesn't change anything. I still need to know what the heck is going on. Why didn't you just have that helicopter bring me here when you found me, or to a local hospital first? And does anybody know who was shooting at us? Was it the sheriff after Buck?"

He did nothing but stare at me for what seemed like a minute or two, then shook his head. "You've had a concussion. Side effects can include memory loss, blurred vision, ringing in your ears, confusion, hallucinations and--"

"Stop right there. I happen to hold an advanced first aid ticket and I don't remember hallucinations being on that list."

His smile was accompanied by a narrowing of his eyes. "Memory loss perhaps?"

"I have no memory loss."

"Then why haven't you asked me about the horse you were all fired up determined to save from the sheriff?" The words were clipped and decidedly unfriendly.

I'm sure my jaw dropped open right about then. Buck hadn't crossed my mind. Well except for being aggravated that I'd come off of him and ended up with a concussion. "You rode him back to the ranch?" I couldn't interpret the look that flitted across his face before he answered.

"I brought him here for you."

I sat up. "He has to be protected. The sheriff wants to kill him."

"Don't worry about the horse. I've made sure he's safe."

"Where?"

He got out of my bed and stood there in nothing but navy blue boxers with his back straight and his jaw set. "I said he's safe. No." He shook his head when I started to speak. "I'm not going to tell you where he is and I'm not giving him back until you and I come to an understanding about another matter."

I threw myself out the opposite side of the bed and stood just as determined, with the bed between us like a line in the sand. He did one of those down and back up glances that reminded me I was only wearing a camisole and panties. I refused to acknowledge the evidence in his shorts that he was liking what he saw.

"I want my horse back so spit it out. What is this other matter you're talking about?" According to my internal antennae, this wasn't about sex, chemistry or flings in Vegas anymore.

"I want you to shut down your website."

"Huh?" I'm usually a little more articulate than that but his statement had come right out of left field and to say I was flummoxed, would be a major understatement.

He repeated himself, one word at a time.

I nearly said *huh?* all over again. I gave my head a shake, *ouch* . "What the hell does my website have to do with you?"

"Everything. My business is being directly impacted by your little hobby and I need you to stop."

"Little hobby? Do you have any idea how much sarcasm I heard in those two words?"

He scrubbed on his face with both hands, took a deep breath, then shook his head. "Could you put on a robe or something."

I dropped my gaze down the front of myself first, then him. Granted, my nipples were on full alert and the camisole accentuated their condition. But his naked chest and tented boxers were a much more blatant illustration if you ask me. I looked him in the eye. "Ditto."

He bent and grabbed his jeans off the floor. Good luck with that, I thought, while I skedaddled to the bathroom where I'd seen my robe hanging behind the door. Halfway there I changed my mind and went to my closet for jeans and a t-shirt. I opened the door and sucked in a startled breath. The closet didn't exist past a door on a wall. I spun around and jerked open a dresser drawer, then the next and the next. All empty.

With a nasty swirling sensations in my stomach, I went to the bathroom and grabbed the robe. I stared at myself in the mirror as I pulled the belt tight, took a long steadying breath and reminded myself I needed to deal with one thing at a time.

Chapter 7

The bed was pulled together all neat and tidy like before—there must be a proud mother out there somewhere—but at least this time Gage hadn't vanished. Instead he was standing by the window, hands in pockets.

"Okay, I'm ready to hear your explanation now." I crossed my arms over my traitorous breasts.

Silence.

Did he think I was going to accept that? "Look. Gage. The person you met in Vegas. Maddy? She's a figment of my imagination, everything I'm not. I'm Cassandra. I don't take orders from strangers." I held up my hand when he started to speak. I was on a roll. "Yes, we *are* strangers. Spending about eighteen hours together in Vegas didn't change that status. Naked or not.

"So, this is where you hit a mental switch, think of me as an ugly old business man you're dealing with and explain why my website is causing you a problem. It might be smart to start by introducing yourself. Then you can try to make me understand why you've been manipulating me..." I made a blatant visual sweep of the room. "because I'm pretty sure all this insanity began long before Vegas."

Silence. Hmmm. Was he trying to stare me down? Attempting to intimidate me? Or was he looking right through me while he contemplated his next move. Hard to tell. But whatever he was up to, I'd said my piece and was prepared to wait him out.

"Michael Gage Meyer." His tone was cold, impersonal. "Retired Special Forces, currently part of Meyer Security. Protection of the innocent is part of our business. Especially the innocents forced to start new lives or die. We've been monitoring your site since it's inception and until recently had no problem with what you were doing. However with one particular success story, *ICanFindAnyone.com* became newsworthy and the publicity upped your status to liability."

"What does that mean exactly?"

"Since your last big find hit the news and was linked to sites world wide, you've acquired six new clients. Four of them are searching for people who have disappeared on purpose."

"Witness protection?" I rolled my eyes. "I'm not stupid you know. I always research the requests to be sure that's not what I'm dealing with. I check court records for restraining orders and such, always aware that a client could be a stalker. I have ways to access data bases that cover everything from arrests, convictions, acquittals, even person's of interest."

"Well isn't that handy." His flat voice reeked of sarcasm. "You run an *online* business. You don't actually know who's sending you requests and emails. You have no way of knowing if they are legitimate. They could be using fictitious or stolen identities and you'd have no clue. You can't even be certain what *country* your requests come from."

"Oh, get *over* yourself," I snarled with a foot stomp for emphasis. "You're not the only person in the room with a brain. My contacts, the people who check out my requests, are highly respected officials in the US, Canada, Great Britain and Australia. I have connections within Interpol, the FBI and CSIS. I don't accept a client until they've been thoroughly vetted and the person they're searching for is cleared by all agencies."

He was pacing the room now, back and forth from door to window. That's when it occurred to me that this room, while dressed up to look like mine, was quite a bit bigger. Curiosity got the best of me. I went to the window and lifted the blind. Glass bricks. The whole wall was made up of glass bricks. Wall-board painted pale blue hid all but the hole where the window should be. I'd already known that this was nothing but a copy of my room, but for some reason, seeing the raw edge around the non-window, got me in the gut. I wheeled around.

"When did you get inside my bedroom to know what to do here? And where the hell is here?"

Realization clawed its way up my backbone. *I don't know where I am, who I'm with, why I'm here or if I'll ever be allowed to leave. I have no control. At all. Over anything.*

Panicking was not a normal response for me before I'd become mixed up in whatever this mess was, but— nothing about this situation was normal so I guess all bets were off as I was about to come unglued. An invisible weight pressed against my chest, squeezed my throat. Air. I couldn't get enough. I needed more air. My nostrils wouldn't open wide enough. I tried to gulp air through my mouth. Tingling started in my fingers and moved up my arms, sparkle filled the room as the light dimmed and my legs, my bones seemed to liquefy.

Gage's arms wrapped around me. Held on. Hard.

His voice slid past the roaring in my ears but I couldn't make out the words. With the weight of his hand on the back of my head, my face was pressed against his throat. Warm skin and familiar scent registered in my mind along with the light rubbing of his fingertips on my scalp.

The pressure in my chest began to ease. Tense muscles loosened as my breathing returned to normal.

"Better?" His mouth tickled my ear.

Feeling far too comfortable with the physical intimacy, I pushed away. Went back to the bed, sat cross-legged in the middle and tugged at the robe for descent cover.

Gage had his back to the window—make that faux window—his hands stuffed in his pockets, and the man didn't look happy. Well tough. I was a long freaking way from happy myself so I might as well just continue from where I'd left off.

"So you started watching me because of the website. Thought you saw something off about my new clients. You assumed gangsters were trying to use me to find people who were in witness protection or at least hiding for their own safety.

"Did anyone think to approach me? Ask?"

"That wasn't possible or appropriate."

"But kidnapping was?" An idea formed. "Am I under

suspicion? Do you think I'm playing along with the bad guys. Maybe you've even made a giant leap and suspect I'm being paid off or something." I held out my hands in exasperation. "See? This is why I need you to come clean. My wicked imagination is already getting away on me, and fear affects me one of two ways. I become either scary smart, or pretty little blond in a horror flick stupid. I need the truth. And I need it yesterday." I shot what I hoped was a steely gaze at him.

His shoulders lowered and he approached the bed. Sat on the edge with his back to me, leaned forward with his elbows on his knees and fiddled with a black stone he'd pulled from his pocket.

"Once we identified some of the players—your clients—we put a recon man into your operation."

"Who?"

"Wesley."

"You sent the bastard that broke my sister's heart?" He started to speak and she snarled, "Don't even think about using the phrase *collateral damage*." When he turned and raised an eyebrow at me, I muttered, "I read a lot, shoot me." I thought he was about to smile but he managed to squelch it.

"Your sister's involvement with Wesley is something I really don't want to get into right now."

"Fair enough." For the moment. First things first. "Okay, so while he was screwing with my sister's mind—to say the least—he was spying on my business, poking in my house. I get it. And what earth shattering conclusions did he come to?"

He gave me a sideways look I refused to interpret.

"He thought you were completely misguided, unsuspecting and-" he hesitated as though editing.

"Uh-huh. And what did you just leave out?"

I saw a definite smirk. "Absurdly innocent."

I was pissed. But I'd asked for straight and honest so how could I yell at him now? Damn. I gnawed on the inside of my cheek for a minute or two, gave myself a couple of mental head slaps and let it go. There were worse insults.

"Okay, so then what?"

"Then we had to figure out a way to get you to stop what you were doing."

"And of course that good old Y chromosome got all stirred up and you decided, hell, Wesley's doin' one, I'll do the other. After all, seduction has always been the best way to get a woman to forget she has a brain. Right?"

He was turned now, fully facing me, his lips a thin, tight line. The groove between his eyebrows deepened and his nostrils flared ever so slightly. Gorgeous blue eyes darkened like a stormy ocean, but my own mad wasn't about to back down.

"I've got a news flash for you cowboy, unlike a man, I don't shed brain cells when I have an orgasm. The big O doesn't stand for obliging. I don't get all squishy inside, long to cook your meals or iron your clothes. You want this girl to bend to your freaking will? You'd better have more than seduction in your bag of tricks."

Moving cobra fast, he was on his feet, dragging me up until we were face to face. With the fabric of my robe bunched in his fists, and eyes hard as flint locked onto mine, there was no doubt in my mind that I was on a precarious ledge.

Hearing the vibration of fury in his voice, I wondered at my lack of fear. "This is the first time in my life I've ever wanted to shake a woman until her teeth rattled. At the same fucking time I want nothing more than to strip you naked, tie you to the bed and torture you until you're screaming my name and begging for more. Because rant on all you like lady, you want me just as much as I want you." His eyes worked back and forth, studying mine until he growled, "I'm so fucking mad I want to hurt you."

My brain was yelling *payback's a bitch,* but my body was on fire. I *wanted* to scream his name and beg for more, dammit. What the hell was wrong with me. I dug my nails into his wrists. I needed to get away now. Right now. Before I embarrassed myself. Oh hell.

Too late. We locked lips and I'm sure sparks shot out my ears.

As if rising to the challenge, my brain catalogued all the input from my senses while my body turned traitor. His mouth was hard and his teeth just a little bit nasty. I retaliated, leaving an impression on his bottom lip. His taste was too right, too familiar. I wanted to cry out, *mine* while my heart started up my throat. The kiss was all wrapped up in anger, need, denial and desperation as we fought for control. Over ourselves. And each other.

I tore my mouth from his and turned my face away, breathing hard, staring blankly at the wall until I dredged up enough control to form words. "Let me go." The whispery pleading tone of my voice ruined the effect I was after but it was the best I could do.

When Gage released his hold on the robe, I sunk back onto my heels. Without a word or a backward glance, he marched to the door, jerked it open and left.

I slumped back against the pillows, tried to wrap my head around the idea that I could have such an undisciplined response to a man who was totally manipulating me. A man who lied to me without compunction.

The game had begun in Vegas where he'd softened me up, stirred my hormones and if I hadn't been called home, he'd have kidnapped me then. Or would have worked at getting me to close my online business, from a different angle. I glanced around the familiar looking room and thought, no, my incarceration here had been too well planned to sail as a last minute idea.

I notice a wooden tray with a coffee pot and mugs, on the dresser. It must have arrived while I was in the bathroom earlier. Suspicious of everything now, I lifted the lid and sighed at the rich aroma. There were two mugs, along with a tiny cream and sugar set.

Would it be drugged if Gage was supposed to drink it too? Did I dare? I poured just a bit into mug and took a tiny sip. It was wonderful. I waited, expecting some kind of drugged feeling, but nothing happened. Feeling confident I poured a full cup, but looked at the cream and sugar with suspicion. That's where the drugs would be because Gage drank his coffee black. Or he had in Vegas, so I'd be following his lead, for now.

With nowhere to sit but the bed, I plumped the pillows against the headboard and settled back with my coffee. Time to put my hormones on ice and figure a way out of this mess. After all, problem solving and puzzles had always been my forte.

I needed to find an exit. If I was correct in assuming I was still at the safe-house, and this was the room they hadn't let me see into, I was in southern Alberta, not far from the Rockies. I did a quick mental search of the towns and highways in the area. Luckily, being rural, once I escaped, I'd be able to catch a ride because ranchers and farmers rarely hesitated to pick up hitchhikers.

I yawned and gave my coffee cup a glance. Geez, maybe this was decaf. I downed the rest and snuggled into the pillows. My vision began to blur in a way I was becoming annoyingly accustomed to, and a little voice in my head cussed ugly.

*

My drug-befuddled mind scrambled to register information as I came to. This was becoming a new habit for me as I used to be someone always reluctant to wake up, to relinquish the last dregs of sleep.

I discovered that this time, I'd been placed on one of the leather sofa's in the great room of the safe house, confirming my earlier assumption that I hadn't left the building. I was dressed.

Surprised, I did a quick mental check and found absolutely no recall of putting on clothes. Great. I pulled out the neck of the pale blue cotton sweater and peeked, pleased to see the camisole I'd had on earlier. At least whoever had dressed me hadn't done it from the skin out. I was also wearing jeans I'd never met before. Well, no point dwelling on things I couldn't change.

With care, I sat up and swung my feet to the floor. My

head hurt just a little, probably from the drugs. I turned to survey the room. Lissa was standing near the long dining table, holding a stack of plates. Watching me. She didn't seem inclined to speak so I did.

"Look at this. I'm awake again. You'd best run off and report to someone so they can get my next knockout drink ready."

"Gage administered the antidote, you were only out for a few minutes." She smiled. "He left because he figured you'd wake up angry. Suggested I cover my ears for the first few minutes."

I sighed. "No point wasting my energy on an innocent bystander when he's the one pissing me off." I frowned for a moment. "You are innocent, aren't you?" I wanted to like this woman, but knew I shouldn't place blind trust in my instincts—ever again.

The corner of her mouth twitched. "I did help dress you."

"Help. Which means Gage participated?"

She took a few steps toward me. "Wrestling clothes onto an unconscious adult takes two people."

Hmph. Seeing little point in arguing, I let it go. "What's next on my agenda?"

"You and I get to hang out for a few hours. We could start with breakfast."

"Does that mean it's morning?" I'd lost track of days and times with all the knockout drugs."

"Eleven-thirty."

"You're not going to slip me more drugs are you? I'm growing real tired of other people hitting my on/off switch."

"No drugging, I promise. Are you hungry? What can I make for you?"

I narrowed my eyes at her. "You're trying too hard."

Good grief, the woman blushed, made me feel like a bitch. "Sorry. I'm not usually like this."

She smiled and for just the tiniest of moments I thought I saw satisfaction on her face—whatever the heck that looked like. She turned and spread the stack of dishes, one by one on eight plain red placemats. "I don't need this set until tonight but I always figure it's simpler to put them on the table than in the cupboard when I unload the dishwasher." Going to the fridge, she opened the door and surveyed the contents. "Would you like a Spanish omelet?"

Although she appeared to be talking to someone on the middle shelf, I answered, "Sure if you'll split it with me."

She passed me the eggs. "Still don't trust me?" She dug into the crisper for veggies.

"I can't trust anyone right now, besides, I can't eat a whole omelet." Or at least the four egg kind that Connie built for the ranch hands.

Lissa and I went about chopping and mixing and cooking like any two women in a kitchen. One led, one assisted. She pointed to the cupboard where more plates were stacked, I pulled out two, then searched a couple of drawers until I found cutlery. The routine helped me relax a bit.

I set two places at the polished granite breakfast bar and that's where we ate, perched on tall chairs. By the time we finished and started to clear up the dishes, Lissa began to ask important questions. She was subtle. She was good.

And I was suitably impressed, although not inclined to play the game by her rules. I waited until we'd settled into big comfy chairs in the living area. Then I got straight to the point.

"Is this your version of good-cop bad-cop? Gage gets me all riled up and pissed off and then you sooth the savage beast and become my best buddy? I suppose you work for him?"

She smiled and I saw the change. Her eyelids lowered from innocent to calculating, which was reflected in the turn of her lips. "Okay. I'll be honest if you will."

"Let's start with you." I tucked my feet up under me. "Who are you and how are you and-" I lifted my hands and twisted them in the air, "this place, connected to Gage's problem with my website?"

"Everything you were told before is true. I'm Gage's cousin, I live here with my husband Kyle and we provide a safe place for people... who need it."

"That would be those Gage is helping to establish new identities." She nodded. "And prisoners like me."

"No. You're a first. And I'd rather not call you a prisoner because you're here for protection."

"From what? Who?"

She sighed. "I thought Gage explained. People are trying to use you to find a relocated witness."

I'm sure my attempted smile fell short, but I wasn't feeling particularly cheery. "Most of what he said got lost in the translation after he called my business a little hobby." I stared out the window. "What I do is way more important than that. And I can't quit."

"Why not?"

I took a deep breath and looked at her. Did I trust her? Maybe. Did it really matter considering I'd already had one spy in my home who had stolen my sister's heart and another one in my bed?

"Okay I give. It's ultimately about family, so first you need a condensed version of my life. Sorry, none of this makes sense otherwise."

She settled back into her chair, crossed her booted feet in front of her and said, "Okay shoot. But if I start to snore, take a timeout."

I caught myself staring at her boots, I had an identical pair. Granted mine were much more well-worn, but identical is still weird.

I shook off the distraction and gave her a thumbnail version of my life, from when our family was split up, until I walked away from the tabloid circus of my modeling career by changing my name. Slipping under the radar, I'd dedicated my life to searching for my father and brother.

She raised a questioning eyebrow. "One giant contradiction. No wonder Gage is confused."

Choosing to ignore the Gage part, I tried to explain myself. "I know what it's like to not want to be found. I understand how important it can be to leave your old life behind." And how painful and lonely it can be when you get what you wish for.

"Why do you search for people if you understand the need to hide?"

"All I ever wanted was to find my family. The business was accidental."

"How?" She got up and went around the room plumping pillows and refolding the blankets draped over the backs of most of the furniture while I explained.

"It began with watching all the TV shows about missing people and unsolved cases—I was always looking for new ideas plus when you're hiding from the press, television's one of the tools that helps keep you from feeling so alone and isolated.

"Anyhow, I got thinking that while I was searching for my own family, why not use some of what I'd learned along the way. So, I picked a couple of the cases I'd seen and tried to find clues or threads that I could follow." I shrugged. "As they'd say on TV, I hit pay dirt."

Lissa cocked her head like a curious puppy—or a skeptical woman. "How were you successful when trained professionals weren't?"

"Turns out, being formally trained often leads to linear thinking because of rigid protocols. They have rules and expected paths to follow. I don't have any of that interference." I decided not to talk about my other tool, my gut instinct, due to its recent short-circuiting.

"So, using your own haphazard methods, you were able to locate people."

I frowned at her. "Unorthodox maybe but certainly not haphazard."

"Sorry, I must have misunderstood. How do you do it then?"

Positive now that she was orchestrating, and being no violinist, I stopped playing the game by her rules and took a time out. Standing, I stretched and strolled toward the big wall of windows, Stared out, watched a bird circling high above.

"Cass?"

"Let's just say I was discreet in the manner I worked. I shared information with the appropriate authorities and stayed anonymous for a very long time."

"What made you give up your anonymity, create your… website?"

It was more than a website. It was a place where I reunited the lost, consoled and cheered on people who needed me. A lump grew in my throat and tears starting to build as I stared blankly at the scenery and struggled for control. *Stop. Do not think. Look at the mountains, the way the sun is drilling down without mercy.* I swallowed hard, did the slow deep breathing that always gave me some measure of control. Studied the circling bird. Was it a golden eagle or a red-tailed hawk? Hard to tell at this distance. I concentrated on his size. Compared it to the surroundings, figured in the distance. I was staring hard, hard enough to see what was wrong.

The picture was an illusion.

Chapter 8

Feeling ill, I made my way back to the chair and plunked down. Leaned forward, rested my elbows on my knees and dropped my head into my hands.

"Cass?"

I shook my head, not yet ready to speak. Still attempting to sort the facts in my head. They came together like a slide show.

What looked like a window was some kind of elaborate technology running digital imaging on or through a glass-like surface. Put together with the space age helicopter—nearly invisible, and silent. Then add in the extraordinary knockoff of my bedroom, Gage's satellite phone gadget, rooms equipped with millions of dollars worth of high-tech medical machinery, the nifty drugs they kept hitting me with, and the room full of clothes for disguises.

I sighed out loud and asked the questions without looking up. "Who are you people? FBI? CIA? Private Mercenary? Wizards? Aliens?" I lifted my chin, pinned her with a look. "Who the fuck am I dealing with here and how the hell do I get back to my nice simple life? I don't have any pretty red shoes to click together."

"Your web-site--"

My fingers locked together, tight, as I swallowed back the lump of fear trying to rise up from my gut. "Done. Shutdown, yours, Gage's, whoever wants it. Done. Take my computers, my addresses, my contacts and go away. Just let this be over. I want no part of some underworld of--"

My heart skipped, then pounded against my ribs. Too fast, too hard as I recognized a flicker of sadness in her eyes. They wanted more than my business neutralized. The air around me thickened and sparkled. I shook my head. Not going to let it happen again. *Must. Not. Lose. Control.*

Without thought or plan, I spun in the chair so I was upside down, lying on the soft leather seat with my legs draped over the back and my head hung nearly to the floor. I swear I felt the blood whoosh back into my brain. *Thank you gravity.* I concentrated, counted the seconds for each inhale and breath blown back out, glad I'd mastered bio-feedback at an early age. It had been a lifesaver when dealing with freakish stuff that happened on set, and was coming in pretty handy now.

It didn't' take long for my system to settle and Lissa was crouched beside me when I opened my eyes.

"What happened?"

I groaned in frustration and with care, swung back halfway around, my head and legs on the chair's arms. "Panic attack." Not that I had any first hand knowledge of what that really meant, but it was the best explanation for the moment. I suspected that this new predisposition for loosing my grip had something to do with all the drugs they'd been pumping into me. "Is there any bottled water here?"

She rose and walked toward the fridge.

I shifted around to sit up properly in the chair, mindful of taking slow deep breaths and recognizing the name on the bottle of water Lissa handed me added to my settled feeling. I cracked the seal, drank deep, screwed the lid back on and tucked the bottle in alongside me. Kept my hand on it while the other woman searched my face for expression she could read but I gave nothing away.

"What triggered the panic?" she asked.

"Seriously? Let's see, kidnapping, drugs, lies, safe-house, loss of my business, that ought to be enough to freak out the average mortal.

"Something's changed," she muttered, then asked, "Why are you angry again?"

I could have been obstinate, but decided instead to give her something. "Up to a few minutes ago, because of the view out that window, I thought I at least knew where I was. Figured that somewhere along the line I'd get an opportunity to sneak out, hitch a ride.

"But then I noticed the sun was almost directly overhead, which only happens in southern Alberta in the summer. Therefore that," I pointed, "is not a window. And the landscape which looked so familiar is not actually outside this non-window. I could be on freaking Pluto for all I know and that pisses me off."

"You aren't on Pluto. We're still in America."

"Well hell, that narrows it down."

"Cass-"

"I have a home. A ranch to run. People on my payroll.

I have a life there, and I want to go back. Can you understand that? Or are you so up to your neck in freaking make-believe that you just don't get it?"

"Why don't I get us a cup of tea?"

Arrggh. "No. Do. Not. Drug me again."

"I'm trying to help you."

"Then tell me the truth. Tell me exactly why I've been kidnapped and if I'll ever be allowed to go home. Tell me my ranch and my family are safe. And tell me what the fuck I'm up to my blessed armpits in."

"Your family is safe. Your ranch is being manned by our people. And the horse that had everyone going around in circles, is also in a safe place."

Geez, I kept forgetting about Buck. That brought me back to earth. "He's being framed for murder."

She shook her head. "I'm not sure if that statement has any place in reality."

I explained about the horse being blamed for the deaths of three men, including my father and was reminded yet again, that the gruesome memory was never far from the surface.

Putrefaction of human flesh, its vile odor, was imprinted on my senses, as was the lifeless and rubbery texture. No warmth, no give.

I pushed up from the chair. Needed to move. Needed time, space and fresh air but wasn't allowed outside, so settled for the only other option. "I'm going to the exercise room."

"No problem." She smiled. "But do me a favor and don't try to find a way out."

My smile was no more genuine than hers. "No

problem," I echoed. And neither one of us believed me.

*

Making camp for the rest of the day, I tortured myself on a treadmill, an elliptical and a stair climber. Took breaks, sprawling on a mat and staring at the ceiling. Tested the punching bags and when I could move no more, sunk up to my neck in the hot tub. My mind still spun.

Back in my room, I took my time showering, drying my hair, and dressing. Wearing the jeans and white sweater someone had set on the end of the bed I made my way toward the distant murmur of voices. A group of five were gathered in the great room.

Lissa spotted me first, smiled and headed toward the kitchen saying, "Cass. Grab a seat, what can I get you to drink?"

I didn't answer, stood frowning, wondering where I fit into this cast of characters. A woman I assumed was Angie, was curled into one end of the sofa opposite Eve—her mirror image except for being quite a bit younger. Quinn looked relaxed in an armchair across from a man I'd never seen before.

His shaved head and thin linen shirt accentuated bulging muscles and a thick neck, while bushy eyebrows gave him away as yet another redhead. Something about him niggled at me. It wasn't that he seemed familiar in any way, just wrong somehow. I watched him out of the corner of my eye while Lissa handed me a bottle of water and I took a seat near the non-window.

It was a discrete movement but I caught it. He placed

his hands on the seat beside him, straightened his arms and shifted his weight to one side so there was room for Lissa to squeeze in beside him. But his feet stayed planted in the same spot. My gaze met his and he smiled as though to say, I did that so you'd know. He was introduced to me as Lissa's husband, Kyle.

Conversation swirled around me as, in spite of multiple urgings, I wouldn't participate. I was more interested in studying the group and their dynamics. Were these people actually related? Or was this entire presentation as farcical as the window? I didn't doubt that Quinn and Gage were brothers or that Angie and Eve were sisters. But there was nothing visible to convince me the women were related to the men. Yet I had to admit, there was an easy communication between them that smacked of closeness and understanding. The way family was supposed to be.

My head was starting to ache with the effort of putting all the information into the appropriate slots. Reminded me of a pile of papers on my desk at home, attesting my dislike of sorting and filing.

Disengaging from the others, I closed my eyes and imagined being in one of my favorite places. A meadow not far from my house, where Mule deer bring their fawns to graze when they're barely days old. I remembered a day last spring, when I'd watched two skinny-necked does in the belly deep grass. Jared explained that their necks were an indication that they'd given birth that year. A doe with a fat neck is what they call a dry-doe, without a baby to nurse. I'd eased closer and spotted two tiny fawns with big brown eyes, and white spots sprinkled over tawny backs.

The deer watched me, their huge mule-like ears wide, searching for sound as I'd backed away.

"Cass?"

I opened my eyes. Eve was leaning forward in her seat, studying me with a doctor's intensity.

"Are you okay?" she asked.

"Ah, sorry, just a fantasy moment."

There was a muffled snort from Angie and I caught the smirk and exaggerated wiggle of Quinn's eyebrows.

Geez. "I was fantasizing about being home. Alone." When I said nothing more, the conversation picked back up around me. I drifted again and the voices took on an odd quality. Distant and unclear, like a faint echo. My gaze moved from person to person, and the distance between us seemed to increase, leaving me isolated, separate.

"Cassandra." Someone was shouting. One of the women. Probably Eve. I knew she'd been studying me when she thought I wasn't looking.

"Cassandra!"

Oh for heaven's sake what was the problem? "What? Why are you all staring at me."

Lissa's voice was soothing, "Just making sure you hadn't drifted off to sleep." And there were several plastic, insincere chuckles from the others.

"Don't want you to get lost in fantasy world. Especially when Gage isn't here to rescue you." Quinn's attempt at a friendly teasing amused the others at least, but his gaze was intense, as serious as Eve's.

I considered the group, looked them over one by one. Their clothing was casual-expensive, cashmere, wool and linen. They all held thick glasses of various drinks, the men and Angie had beer, Eve and Lissa were drinking something dark, perhaps Coke, maybe they had rum or whiskey mixed in. They grazed from a tray of cut veggies and dip on one end table, a dish of dry-roasted peanuts, and a bowl of crinkle-cut chips plunked in the middle of a large leather ottoman.

Small talk had resumed and when I was asked a direct question, something weird happened inside my head. I began to unravel. Rather like what I've witnessed when a dog chews an old golf ball. Once the thick outer skin is off and it's nothing more than a hard mass of elastic strips, it takes on a life of its own, popping and pinging and jumping as the elastic snaps and unravels. That's how I felt as the words tumbled from my mouth in slow motion, but with gathering speed.

"What... is wrong with you people?" Silence settled over the room like skunk odor. I was perched on the edge of my seat, gripping the armrests as though preparing for lift-off.

"You are all sitting here making small talk like this is some kind of social event, while my life has been taken away from me. I didn't just drop in for dinner and drinks. I was kidnapped. Brought here without my consent. I'm not allowed to leave. I'm a prisoner."

Eve was making a bee-line toward me but Quinn grabbed her arm. Stopped her as I jumped up. Palms-out to ward her off, I stuck my arms in front of me, elbows locked. "Don't. Do not, touch me. Don't drug me again. Do not try to subdue me."

Voice low and compelling, she murmured my name and I heard Quinn tell her to let me be..

I backed away, shaking my head from side to side. "Do you have any idea how it feels when your life becomes nothing more than a series of bizarre events?" I began to tick them off on my fingers as I paced the room. "First, there's a dead man in the paddock beside my house. Then, when I'm in the mountains searching for the missing horse who is being blamed for said dead guy, somebody starts shooting at me. After that, I go for joy-ride on a panic stricken stallion, he careens up and down a freakin' mountain, stumbles and sends me catapulting into la-la land. When I come to, I get stuffed into a helicopter and drugged.

"I wake up in a strange place surrounded by people I don't-know-from-Adam, and a talking cat. But I don't get much time to worry about a cat that speaks English because someone drugs me again. The next time I come to, I'm in bed with Gage." I rolled my eyes. "I won't even go there, because more important than that, the room I'm in is a damned fine replica of my own bedroom, the one at home on my ranch.

"When all of this starts making me a little bit nuts, and I confront Gage, he informs me that I have to shut down what he insultingly calls my little hobby, my website, the one where people come to me, desperate for help because they've somehow lost a loved one. Not lost dead, just misplaced. Sort of." I waved my hands around as though it helped me discount all the confusion and move on.

"Anyways, he tells me that I'm endangering the lives of people he's hiding. That I'm helping the bad guys catch the good guys. Then, when the horror of all that is setting in, guess what? He DRUGS me again.

"So, enough already." I glared at them one at a time. "I've got the picture. This ain't Kansas, it ain't Oz and there's no white fucking rabbit."

I heard a distinct *hmmpph*, glanced over and saw the white, tail-less cat staring at me from Angie's lap. A slightly hysterical giggle bubbled up and out. Oh hell.

I closed my eyes for a sec, and took a deep breath as though to replace all the spilled fury, but I'd lost my momentum. "I will agree to giving up my ranch. I'll give up my identity, my website—which is not a hobby but a legitimate freaking Internet business—and life as I knew it. But I will not give up my sister, nor will I stop searching for my brother. Period."

"Maddy." The voice behind me was soft and low, but the hands that settled on my shoulders were firm. Their grip serious.

I stiffened, wondering where the heck Gage had come from. I refused to turn around. "Is Maddy my new name? My new identity?"

"If that's what you want. Would you like to be Maddy?"

I spun away. "Do not. Patronize me," I ground out. "It's bad enough that I let you screw my brains out the first time around. Drop the act and get on with the next step in this ridiculous process. You told me my sister was safe. I want to know where she is and when I can see her."

"She's safe."

Head, brick wall. The fight drained out of me. Left behind nothing but sadness. I wanted, badly, to step into his arms, let him comfort me. I backed away.

Lissa's well-timed announcement that dinner was

ready gave me the opportunity I needed. While the others made their way to the table, I escaped to my room. I couldn't sit with them and eat a meal. It was just too much normal in the middle of my personal chaos.

*

I stretched out on the bed and stared at the ceiling, marveling at the little stars glued there, just like at home. Tears slid from my eyes, into my ears. I shook my head and turned onto my side, drew my knees up and hugged them to me. I wanted to really cry, ball, wail out loud, but I'd never allowed myself such freedom before and now I didn't know how to let go.

The soft brush of fur against my knuckles reminded me of my cat Harris. He'd been there for me, warm and comforting, just like this for years. Always ready to snuggle in, chase the shadows away. Something else I suppose I'd lost. I opened my eyes to meet Merlin's direct golden gaze. He bumped his forehead against mine. I reached out to stroke his back and he snuggled in against me.

"What the hell am I going to do now?" I asked him.

Sleep?

"I'm sick to death of sleeping but what else is there for me to do?" Self-pity seemed like a comfortable blanket to wrap myself in—until my alter-ego kicked me in the butt. What the hell was I thinking, giving over all my marbles to the other team?

I felt new energy stir. Synapses began to fire as I thought about Gage. What he'd been like in Vegas. His voice when he'd found me on the mountain. His shorts when we'd fought earlier. Did I not have prince charming under my spell? Wasn't that my power?

By the time I'd worked out a plan, and done the bulk of preparation, the cat was asleep, curled into a headless lump. I gave him a gentle poke. He unwound and blinked at me.

"Hey pal," I said, "Time for action, and I need your help."

*

It was dark, save for tiny nightlights in the hallway and great room. Everyone had obviously turned in. Well, that was disappointing, although I wouldn't mind rattling a door to set off an alarm or something. First I'd wait.

In the kitchen, I scooped a sports drink from the fridge, guzzled half of it, carried the bottle with me to the living area. Tugged an armchair and ottoman around to face the big fake window and tossed down the rest of the drink. I'm sure my system was doing a happy dance, glad to have some nourishment because this morning's omelet was little more than a memory.

I slid low in the chair, stretched my freshly shaved, lotion smooth legs out across the stool, leaned my head back and stared up into the dark. I closed my eyes and contemplated my situation with a degree of calmness I hadn't had since arriving here.

If, I wasn't allowed to go back—fight back—then I'd have to find a way to make a new reality work for me. I'd have them set me up in a farming or ranching community. Even if meant moving me to another country, like Australia or New Zealand.

Or, perhaps I could have a tiny cabin on a mountainside in the middle of nowhere. I'd be happy to haul water from a stream, chop firewood, grow and preserve my food. Not that I'd mind an upscale home with geo-thermal heat and solar power.

I'd have a cat and a dog, for comfort, early warning and protection. That reminded me I'd yet to ask Gage if Blue made it back to the ranch okay. Though I had no doubt—he was ranch dog tough.

But what about Sydney? I sighed. She wouldn't want to live in an isolated place. She was city, right down to the bone. Would I be forced to give up contact with her for a while? Could I?

"Are you okay?" Gage's voice stole over me like the stroke of a kind hand.

"Just thinking." I watched, somewhat mesmerized as he sat on the stool, took my feet in his hands, and used his thumbs to rub gentle circles around my ankle bones.

"You have a lot to think about. Is any of it getting more comfortable?"

I chose to ignore his question and asked one of my own. "How did you know I was out here? Is my room wired? Motion sensors?"

"Merlin came and got me."

"The cat?"

"Came in and pawed at my face until I woke up."

"Turncoat," I muttered, while mentally grinning and giving the cat a big thumbs-up.

Gage's hands moved up to knead the muscles of my calves.

"How much control do I have in my relocation?"

"You'll be given several options."

"Like?" I prompted.

"I don't know yet. This is a process Cass. You were pulled in because of an emergency, so contingency plans hadn't been put in place. I thought you'd be safe for several months longer, I believed I'd have time to win you over, convince you to shut down your site, stop the searches and ease out of the line of fire."

I felt like he was being honest with me, so I hesitated, allowed him to lead, for now.

With my left foot between his hands, and his fingers making magic, he asked me for details about how I ran my searches.

As I answered all his questions, I willed myself not to let on that his hands were heating me up in all the wrong places, and when he moved his attention to my right foot, I'm sure the left whimpered.

"I understand why my business has to close but the disappearing? The relocating? That I don't get."

With a suddenness that startled me, his gentle grip on my foot became vice-like. Fierce and frightening. "There are things you need to know."

Chapter 9

My heart fluttered in my chest and a chill spread over my skin. "Okay. Now you're scaring me."

He spoke slowly, enunciated each word with care. "The dead man you found in the mountains above the ranch, was not your father."

I blinked. "The DNA tests--"

"Were cooked."

I needed to move. But his hands clamped over my knees.

"Altered to protect him. Your father is safe. He wants to meet with you but things are complicated."

My jaw went slack, my mouth dropped open, and struggling to get it closed was making me feel like a gasping fish in the bottom of a boat. My limbs were just as useless. I existed as a pounding heart, flapping lips and a single thought, *he's not dead*. Gaping empty craters occupied my mind where logic and reason used to live.

I blinked, consciously, as though to remind myself I did in fact, have control of my body, and everything snapped into place. With a great rush of energy I shoved Gage aside, slammed my feet to the floor and was halfway across the room before I turned back and ripped into him.

"How. Dare you." I snarled. "Do you have any idea how I felt when I found that beaten and bloodied corpse? Believed it was my father. Can you even imagine how horrible that was? And worse, what it was like, in the face of that horror, to hold out the tiniest smidgeon of hope that maybe, just maybe, it wasn't him?" I paced back and forth in front of the glass wall.

"But then the DNA tests came back, that official piece of paper, proof my father was really dead, and I lost him again." I stopped and glared. "Do you have any clue what that does to a person? I'd've been better off, in less pain, if someone had just reached into my chest and ripped my heart out.

"I had to face the pain of knowing he was not only dead, but after searching for him almost half my life, I'd been only a mile away when he was murdered. If I'd gone after him the day I arrived at the ranch, instead of waiting until the next morning, I might have found him in time." I shook my head. "Who the hell gets that unlucky?"

Self-pity threatened, hovered at the edge. Digging my fingernails into my palms, I shoved it back, stalked to the huge fireplace and stared in at the charred remains of the evening's warmth.

"Someone *decided*. Actually put thought into the alternatives and *decided it would be best* for me to believe he was dead." Thickness began in my chest and moved up into my throat. I battled it down, held my breath for almost a full minute, exhaled slowly.

I turned to study Gage where he balanced on the edge of the leather ottoman, fists clenched, legs tense and bent under him, ready to spring. Fast. The cords of his neck were taut like his jaw. He studied me with cold, flat eyes. This man was a warrior. Why hadn't I seen it before? His preparation, timing, watchfulness, calculated readiness. My hand came up to cover my mouth as another piece clicked into place. How could I be so stupid? When we'd met in Vegas, I'd acted like a freaking tourist while he'd worked me like an easy mark.

One of my Internet clients had requested a meet while I was in Vegas. Being a savvy woman, I'd set up a public meeting. Told her I would be in the Old West Casino, near the stagecoach display, between noon and one o'clock on the last afternoon of the Rodeo. We would each wear a polka-dot scarf, to identify ourselves.

She never showed up. But I'd stayed in the casino until three, playing a lively slot machine, paying no attention to passers by. Easy to spot, my ponytail fastened with a long pink and white spotted scarf, I hadn't even noticed the man beside me until he hit a jackpot, then I was the one who initiated our conversation.

"You bastard. You picked me up knowing full well who I was." Duh. Of course he did. It was too amazingly handy to be a coincidence yet my mind hadn't actually acknowledged the reality until now. Considering all I'd been through in a few short days, I cut myself some slack.

He remained very, very, still.

I shook my head. "I let you pick me up, wine me, dine me, dance with me and then screw my brains out. What was supposed to come next Gage? Get me in a car, drug me, put a freakin bag over my head? Arrggh. I'm so freaking stupid!"

"Stop it." His voice was cool, controlled.

"How long Gage? How long have I been spied on, studied, figured out, manipulated? You had a man in my house in the summer. I found my fath- I found the body months before that. How long have you been picking me up, moving me around and putting me back down in the appropriate place? Were you feeding me clues so I'd find him? Did you have someone killed so I'd have a body to find? So I'd stop looking?"

"I said, stop it."

Something inside me shook loose, like a little control mechanism slipping off and failing to protect. Left me operating on a weird kind of reflex. My furious gaze locked onto the heavy wrought iron fireplace poker. I wrenched it off the hearth. Hurled it at the glass wall where it ricocheted off. Clattered to the floor. And that enraged me more. Horrible angry noises were erupting from my throat while I heaved whatever I got my hands on. Kindling, tongs, dustpan, broom, anything that wasn't nailed down.

The clattering when they hit the floor, fed my fury, and I pitched lamps, baskets, blankets, candlesticks from the table, then I started on a stack of plates.

Finally. Finally the smashing sound of shattering china soothed the insanity inside of me. As the last plate exploded against obviously bulletproof glass, the pressure in my head eased. I stood in the middle of the carnage, hands shaking, chest heaving.

With his unwavering gaze locked on mine, Gage came to me, put his arms around me, and drew me in tight. Another one of those imaginary mind switches flipped and with absolute shock I heard myself crying. I never cry out loud. Ever. Haven't since I was about six. Until now.

He didn't speak. Didn't move. Just held until I slowed to hiccups and sniffling, then swung me up in his arms and carried me to my room. I recall seeing the rest of the people in the household standing together in the hallway but I didn't acknowledge them, neither did Gage. He kicked the door closed with his foot, lowered me to the bed and disappeared. He was back in a minute with a glass of water and a cool, damp washcloth. I drank the glass dry then mopped up my face with the cloth. I laid back. Exhausted.

"Feel any better?" he asked.

I grimaced. "Funny thing about tantrums, they knock all the fight out of a girl."

He smiled, pushed me over a little so he could sit beside me. "You've still got lots of questions and I'll answer them all when you're ready."

"When?"

"That's up to you."

"Nothing else has been up to me so far, why start now?"

"Because the secret's out, there's nothing left to hide."

"Bullshit."

He grabbed my hand and my stomach executed an Olympic sized backward roll, with a twist.

Our gazes locked and I imagined I could see a war going on inside of him.

He stood, still holding my hand. "You need sleep."

"Do you really think that I can shelve all this and drift off to dreamland? Besides, I've had enough sleep to last me for days." On top of that, I was getting a second wind.

"I can get you something—"

"NO." I wrenched my hand from his. "No more drugs, please. I hate being drugged."

"You could just take something light to ease the mental stress."

"No."

"Then move over."

I did. Made room for him without question. What is wrong with me? How can my body want him when my mind is appalled by what he's done?

I slid out the other side of the bed. "Go. Just go."

"Will you at least rest?"

"Sure."

But I would do just the opposite. I watched ten minutes tick by on the clock after he left, then headed across the hall to the gym.

Merlin padded in behind me just before the door clicked shut and perched on a weight bench while I pounded the man-sized punching bag that hung from the ceiling, and ranted about injustice. When the muscles in my shoulders were burning to the point I could no longer lift my arms, I moved to a treadmill, pushed buttons until it was moving at a good strong clip and settled into stride.

With the anger inside me still overshadowing the fact that my father was alive, my bare feet pounded the rubber surface. Mile after mile, I kept up an internal dialogue, working through the anger and the guilt. By the time I wound down, the faint light of dawn through the glass block wall was giving texture to the room.

*

Not exactly relaxed, but at least body-weary and freshly showered I headed for the dining area. Merlin was waiting for me in the hall. I crouched to greet him, rubbed under his chin. He responded by shoving his head against my hand and purring. Normal. This is what normal is. I smiled at the contented cat. "Thanks pal. Come on, let's get some breakfast, I smell bacon."

And somewhere in the back of my mind I could have sworn I heard a delighted echo.

Bacon!

I hesitated in the shadows of the hallway to take note of the players. Quinn, Eve and Angie sat at the table with Kyle. Lissa was tending to something on the stove. Gage stood away from them, and appeared to be staring out the window at a lovely sunrise over the ocean. Okay. Sunrise. Ocean. Well that was a little jolt to the system and the memory of the way everything had looked last night rattled me just a bit more. I shook my head as though to clear my vision and Merlin ribboned around my legs, grounding me.

I sucked in a big deep breath, stuffed my hands in the front pockets of my jeans, and cleared my throat. I'm sure they already knew I was standing there but now I was asking for them to acknowledge me. "Nice cleanup. Not even a hint of Hurricane Cassandra."

Several sets of eyebrows raised as they turned my way.

"I won't apologize for my actions last night, but I will say thank you to whoever disposed of the wreckage." Odd but I think I was wishing the mess was still there. Real. Not an illusion. No niggling worry that last night's meltdown had been a figment of my imagination.

125

Lissa spoke up first. "Orange juice or Apple?"

That almost made me smile. Some people dealt with the stress of uncomfortable situations in the old fashioned way—eat, or at least feed others.

Did I just hear that whispered word bacon again? I looked down at Merlin. He sat, shot a hind leg in the air and stuck his head up his butt to wash. O-kay, so it didn't look like he was the one breathing words into my mind.

I turned my focus to Gage and was met by a blank stare. Fine, I thought.

"Orange juice, but I'll get it, thanks." I retrieved the carton, and half-filled a water glass with sweet pulpy juice. When I glanced around to the others with a silent question about refills, they all shook their heads, no.

"Everything's on the sideboard, help yourself, Cass," said Lissa.

I glanced over at the chafing dishes, bowls and baskets filled with food, then at the table. The white of the china standing out against a bright Navajo patterned placemats, reminded me of the dishes I'd shattered last night.

Dammit I didn't feel guilty. Did I?

They'd brought it on themselves, lying, manipulating me, drugging me over and over again. Embers of anger still nestled in my gut. Geez. I looked at the plates on the table, all at least half-filled with food. I could make one hell of a mess this time. Colorful too, against the bright picture of morning at the seaside.

Gage's hand settled at the back of my neck, his fingers squeezing just hard enough to overshadow the caress in the gesture. He kept his voice low. "Are you going to sit down and eat?"

Instead of acknowledging him, I went to the sideboard, chose toast and bacon. Nearly stumbling over the cat winding figure eights around my legs, I joined the group at the long wooden table

I ate, and slipped bits of bacon to Merlin while the others made small talk.

Once my plate was in the dishwasher and the cat asleep on my lap, the conversation turned serious and scary real.

Lissa topped up everyone's coffee cups as I asked my first question.

"Is it true that my father's alive, and another man's dead in his name?"

Gage answered with a simple, yes. But when I shook my head and said that I needed more than that, Angie was the one with he explanation.

"Your father has been under the protection of Meyer Security, our family's company since he disappeared when you were a child."

That sounded simple and believable. "Why, exactly?"

Quinn answered, "Dean witnessed a gangland execution, and was spotted running away from the location. Two days later, your family's house burned to the ground. It's been assumed your brother was identified because your father took him to the police station to report what he'd seen and the Minnows were watching."

I couldn't help my reaction. "Like in a freaking movie? Gangsters burn out a family and threaten them so they won't talk? That's nuts. Hollywood."

Gage leaned back in his chair with a half smile.

"Where the heck to you think those illustrious writers get their ideas?"

"Next you'll be saying it's the Mafia after him."

"Definitely not. This is a group known as the Minnows."

"Baby fish? You're kidding, right?"

He frowned at me. "The Minnows are not a joke. They're a small but deadly serious group of poorly organized business men with really bad manners and they're known for making less than stellar decisions. They've been fighting amongst themselves for years."

"So because of these ill-mannered, murdering guppies, my family was split up and sent into hiding."

"Simply? Yes. But your father only agreed to give up his wife and daughters temporarily, in order to keep them safe. It was your mother's choice to make it, ah, permanent."

"No need to pussyfoot, I know she's a bitch."

Angie chimed in. "According to the history gathered at the time, your mother and father had to marry—being in a different era and all—when she was seventeen and pregnant. She was never happy in the marriage so when the offer of a new start came her way, she grabbed the ball and ran with it."

Nothing about my mother was news to me, nor was I interested in justification of her actions. "What happened next?"

"There was a staged accident, your father's car went through a bridge railing and into a large river where recovery was very difficult. When the car was eventually pulled out, there were no bodies inside, but being before the age of seatbelt laws, that wasn't unexpected."

"Your mother was set up in New York with you and your sister, your father and brother went to live on a farm in Kansas."

I couldn't resist adding, "And the names have been changed to protect the innocent."

No one smiled.

"Okay, cut to the chase. What happened to my father and brother?"

"Well, they went to a farm-"

I groaned. "I meant, what happened as in my father's most recent faked death and where the hell is Dean."

Gage took up the tale. "Several people associated with the Minnows, showed up in a couple of the small towns close to your father's ranch. Oh, on a side note, the ranch belongs to my family. Connie is our cousin and Jared was one of our security agents for years. They run the place and we use it and them as needed. When your father wanted to retire, we set him up there."

"I don't own it? Well of course I don't because my father's still alive. But he didn't own it either." It took a minute for my own words to sink in.

"Exactly."

Okay, well, color me disappointed and feeling even more cut adrift. A string of angry curse words bubbled to the surface but I clamped my jaw tight. No need to send people running to protect the china from the wrath of Cassandra. I forced myself to take three really deep breaths and let them out slowly through my nose. Better. Okay, where were we?

"So there's these small fish guys snooping around."

Angie snorted and Gage went on with the story. "Your father made the mistake of getting caught up in the rescue of the stallion being blamed for a local man's death which put him right out there in the spotlight."

"Damned horse," I muttered, "he'll be the death of us all."

"Jared called me when the horse went missing from the ranch and because of the Minnow sightings, we yanked your father out before he could go after it."

"And you put in another man to die for him?" My toast and bacon hit the spin cycle. "How could you do something like that?"

"We sent no one. Turns out, the dead guy was a Minnow."

Well, that was odd enough to be believable. But worse, the entire story made some kind of weird sense.

All of a sudden I couldn't sit still. Little things, ideas, bits of information started popping into my head. I could almost imagine the sound of clicking as the pieces fit together. I walked to the wall of glass—progress, I'd stopped thinking of it as a window.

I gave my shoulders a couple of exaggerated shrugs and circled them back to loosen the tension, tipped my head slowly from side to side, stretching out muscles tautened to an uncomfortable degree. Turning back toward the group at the table, I could see the expectation in their eyes even though they seemed to be maintaining bland expressions. Gage had turned his chair around to face me—waiting I'm sure for another ugly explosion.

Okay, I get it now. "It all started with my," I finger quoted, "little internet business." While I tried to find the right words, they waited. "I didn't just happen to find my father. It wasn't all my years of searching that finally turned up a clue. They fed it to me through my website. And that letter about a reunion was just another ruse. The fucking fish led me by the nose, didn't they."

Angie grinned, "I like her Gage, she's smart. And no pansy either."

Quinn added, "Whoever has the remote, I suggest changing the screen. Chances are she sees a fish jumping out there she'll start throwing things again."

Okay so they were trying to ease the tension, sort of. But the facts and questions kept humming in my mind. "Why? Why did they want me to find him?"

Gage answered, "It's your brother they want. Dean saw the execution, heard the conversation before and after. Even though dozens of years have gone by, Dean has information the Minnows want, need. We believe they were leading you to your father, hoping that Dean would be drawn into the family's gathering."

"But he was a boy of ten. Would he even be a useful witness in court?"

"This isn't about going to court. It's organized crime, Cass. They have their own rules and protocols. When a Minnow was killed that night, their group was split down the middle and both sides can only speculate as to what exactly went down. Dean has the answers, saw the faces. So not only do the Minnows as a group want him, individuals want to be the first to get to him. They will do just about anything to find him, including using you as bait."

The next thought hit me with a wallop, nearly doubled me over. If they couldn't get me, they'd go for my sister.

My subconscious treated me to a snapshot of Syd's smiling face, quickly followed by a flash of the beaten body I'd found months ago.

My stomach clenched and rolled, as my breakfast made for the exit. I bolted for the nearest bathroom, dropped to my knees and heaved until I felt like the soles of my feet were coming up next. I was drenched in sweat, my vision was blurred by a fine mist of sparkling lights and my skin tingled from lack of oxygen.

Someone held my hair. The cool dampness of a washcloth swiped across my forehead. Tiles were cool under my hands as my senses began to clear and my focus expanded past the white toilet someone had kindly flushed. I sat back, plunked on my butt, stretched my legs out in front of me and shimmied backward to rest against the wall.

Gage crouched beside me, put a damp cloth in my hand.

"Empty," I said. A damned pointless comment but the best I could manage for a moment. Merlin would hate that I wasted bacon. My head cleared a little more. And then a groan erupted from my throat as I managed one more word. "Sydney."

From the look on Gage's face, I knew my thoughts had been dead on. My sister was the target now that I was out of reach. Oh bloody hell, my stomach lining was headed up my throat. I swallowed the burn, struggled to my knees and went for the ceramic bowl face first. Dry heaving is damned painful.

"Water." I gasped between retches and looked up to see Eve in the doorway. "No Drugs. Please no drugs."

She disappeared and returned with an empty glass,

handed it to Gage and he used the tap at the sink to add water.

I swallowed a couple of sips. Who knew lukewarm water could burn like that? I sighed. Would life ever be normal again? I could feel the water settling my stomach. Okay, so this would be the time to test it. "She's not safe. Is she?"

"I don't know."

My stomach squirmed. I took another sip. "What do you know?"

"Wesley went to pick her up. He's been out of contact ever since."

"What the hell does that mean? Give me a break here Gage, I don't know about this cloak and dagger stuff. Do you have suspicions? Assumptions? Fears? Give me something."

"Are you ready to get out of here?"

Not caring if he meant the bathroom or the house, I said yes and hauled myself off the floor, neatly avoiding his helping hand. My view of the room tipped sideways just a little, but hell, my whole life was on tilt now, so no biggie. I kept moving forward until I was in the hall. His hand settled on my shoulder, slid down to grip my elbow but I wrenched away.

"Two minutes. I'll be back in two minutes." I looked him in the eye. "You disappear on me this time and I'll tear the entire house apart. You have two minutes to get some answers ready." I didn't wait for a reply but headed for my own bathroom where I knew my toothbrush was calling me.

Unlike Vegas, I took no time to primp. I squirted a double-dose of toothpaste on the brush, scrubbed my teeth, gums and tongue at warp speed, rinsed, washed my face, ran a damp cloth around the back of my neck, over my throat and my chest, was back in the great room in less than two minutes—or darned close to it.

"Okay," I said to the group now seated on the leather couches and chairs, "Tell me what's going on with my sister."

Angie spoke first. "She's been on my watch since Wesley."

"Dumped her?" I finished.

"It's more complicated than that. He was supposed to be doing recon but got more involved."

"You mean he was only supposed to gather information but helped himself to everything else. Then he dumped her like cold coffee." I gave Gage a killing look.

"Let's just leave this part and move on," he said.

Angie did a fast forward. "Sydney disappeared the same day you landed in Vegas.

I was gob-smacked. "You are just telling me now, that my sister has been missing for --" I went blank. "I left for Vegas on the first and now it's?" I looked at Gage for help. "What the hell day is this?"

"December sixteenth."

"Seriously? My sister could have been in the hands of some very nasty people. Fish. For more than two weeks?" I'm sure my eyes were bugging out of my head. "We have to do something, find her. She's all the family I've got."

"You're forgetting your father is alive."

I rolled my eyes so far back I'm sure I saw hair follicles from the inside. "A virtual stranger. A man who walked out of my life, left me behind and never looked back. My voice thickened as I fought for control. My sister is my person. My everything important three hundred and sixty-five days a year."

The room stayed silent for a beat too long. And then it dawned on me what nobody was saying. They weren't making any attempt to reassure me that Syd was okay, that they'd find her and bring her back. Fear clawed at my throat.

Chapter 10

"What aren't you telling me?" I felt Eve's gaze, she was probably just waiting for me to dissolve into a blithering heap so she could harpoon me again. Lissa and Kyle had left the group, probably while I'd been off hurling. I glanced from face to face.

Tension drained from my muscles and my mind cleared. These people weren't the enemy. In fact, they were all that stood between me and the bad guys. The concept of a group of bad guys out there trying to hurt me was too vague. Even the danger my sister was in, was little more than a dark murky image. My panic at the thought of losing her had dissipated.

Perhaps I'd finally run out of adrenaline and with fight, flight, or puke no longer options, there was room for clear thinking. This was better. This was more like the me I'd known and lived with all my life. That reactionary emotionally driven woman I'd been channeling for the past day or so was an uncomfortable stranger—fun in a spooky sort of way but mostly scary and exhausting.

They were all staring at me. Had I grown a second head? I smiled at the thought of keeping them off kilter with more unpredictable behavior but didn't have it in me to lie or play games.

"I want to know everything. I need details." Gage had skeptical written all over his face. He wasn't buying the sudden transition. I did a mental shrug. For the moment I was lucid, maybe all the drugs were out of my system. For whatever reason, my brain clicking on all cylinders and I had to make use of it.

"I need paper and a pencil, pen, crayon, whatever— something to write with."

Eve went to the faux suede wall, pushed her hand against it at shoulder level and a panel about six feet square, slid up and back rather like a roll-top desk.

Cool.

In the now-exposed office alcove, I saw shelves, computers and cupboards. Eve dug out a legal-sized notepad and a pen.

"Thanks," I said when she handed them to me. "Now, lets start at the beginning so I can get this all sorted out in my pea-brain. First question, how long have I been under your watch?"

The corner of Gage's mouth twitched. "In some form or another since you were five."

"O--Kay." Not. How the heck was I supposed to swallow something like that? I've been watched all my life? "Maybe you could give me a little overview."

He sighed and I'm sure Quinn's sudden interest in the scene on the glass wall was to hide his amusement.

"I'm only going to tell you this stuff once because in the face of Sydney's disappearance, it just isn't that important."

I held my hand poised to take rapid notes.

"Your brother Dean accidentally bumped into Sydney about eleven years ago, when he was in Vegas to ride in the Rodeo Finals.

I remembered Syd talking for weeks about that Vegas trip. "She was modeling, on a big shoot for a major jeans manufacturer. Lots of horses and cowboys involved but she never mentioned anyone in particular."

Gage nodded. "Growing up with a shadow over him the way he did, Dean developed pretty good radar. Something about Syd was familiar but he didn't know why until one of the group jokingly asked if there were 'anymore like her at home' and she talked about her sister."

"Amazing coincidence," said Angie.

I shook my head. "No, I'd call that Fate. They were meant to meet. We belong together. That's why I've spent so many years trying to find Dean and my dad." I swallowed back the emotions.

Angie went to the kitchen. Puttered about making coffee and setting a tray.

"So, what happened?" I asked Gage., but Quinn answered

"Dean contacted our father, asking him to arrange a meeting with his sisters. Dad immediately headed for Vegas to meet with him, taking Angie and I along, for camouflage, you know, family trip and all. He talked Dean out of the reunion he wanted." He leaned over to put his hand on my shoulder. "If it helps at all, he was a mess. He kept saying that he'd made a promise and meant to keep it but my dad pointed out that if he really loved his sisters, he'd stay away from them to keep them safe. Said that's what a man would do."

Tears pooled and blurred my vision while I fought back the pain I felt for a young man facing by such a momentous decision. "And he'd be about what, early twenties?"

"He was devastated," said Angie as she set a tray of coffee and fixings on the table beside me. The cups rattled.

"To put it mildly," added Quinn.

I looked at Gage. "So he did the manly thing, sacrificed his own feelings for our safety, and then what, your family helped him disappear again?"

"No. We'd only been in Vegas for a few days when there was an accident-"

My heart thumped hard against my ribs and for a split second I had a conscious thought about the human body and its ability to produce adrenaline. "What happened?"

Gage shook his head. "Not Dean. There'd been a helicopter crash back at our ranch, in Texas. But we couldn't find Dean before we loaded up, headed for the airport and we never saw your brother again. My family was caught up in the aftermath of the crash for months. Our cousin was in hospital with second degree burns and a spinal cord injury.

Another piece clicked into place. Kyle, Lissa's husband.

"Dad and his company continued to watch over your father but couldn't find Dean."

"Ever?"

"Nope, after we left Vegas, he rode two no-scores in a row then skipped town. Sports medicine reported torn shoulder muscles as the reason he'd dropped out."

"Coffee?" Angie was in front of me, holding out a cup. As I reached for it, I was momentarily distracted by an odd look on her face. Then she said, "You probably should put some food in your stomach too." She hurried to the kitchen, returning with a cookie jar shaped like an apple. She lifted the lid and held it out toward me. "Plain sugar or double chocolate."

I pulled out one of each and bit into the sugar cookie. Yum. I savored the cookie and waited to see how my stomach felt about it while the others were getting their coffee.

I licked crumbs from my fingertips and watched Gage's eyes darken.

"Okay, so there was no more contact with my brother. What happened next."

Quinn took up the tale again. "Over the next year or so, once my cousin was well on the road to recovery, we all went our separate ways. I joined the military, wanted to be special ops like my big brother Gage. Angie went off to flight school and Eve decided to specialize in spinal cord injuries—even though she'd just finished her surgical residency. Oh, yeah and Kyle seriously hated his physiotherapist right up until he married her. Long story."

"All very interesting. But what about my family?"

"Things were quiet for a few years," said Gage. "Your dad continued working for a big cattle company in Alberta and volunteering at local rodeos until we set him up for retirement on the Washington ranch. He's been relocated several times since and none of us know where he is. We make contact through a string of complicated addresses."

Quinn grinned. "That's so we don't have to worry

about big brother talking in his sleep." He winked at me while Angie snorted a laugh and Gage scowled.

I forced myself not to squirm. I wasn't comfortable with all the innuendo. It just felt too weird to suddenly be treated like part of a couple, let alone this family group. See, that's the old grass is greener thing. I'd always dreamed of having a family but this wasn't what I'd had in mind. I wanted the warm fuzzy stick together through thick and thin kind, not this - I love you and I've got your back but man it's gonna cost ya—group.

"The last time I talked to Syd, she was waiting for her flight to Tahiti. Tell me what you know." I held my pen over the still blank page, determined to take notes, make sense of their information and find my sister.

"Tahiti?"

"She didn't want to be in Vegas during the rodeo because of Wesley. She decided to go to Tahiti instead. Figured there'd be no reminders of cowboys there. Said she was going to flop on the beach—under an umbrella of course because she's religious about her skin—and wallow in atmosphere. She went to one of those five-star places where they wait on you hand and foot and give you hot rock massages and mud wraps and all. She could only afford a week. That's why she'd be getting home before me."

"Well," said Angie. "Sydney didn't change her tickets, never went to Tahiti. She landed in Vegas about an hour after you, just like the two of you originally planned. We have video confirmation that she left the airport in a rental car-"

Instant relief washed over me. "Sydney doesn't

drive."

"Wesley was driving."

The words hung. Suspended. In air thick with tension.

I gaped at her in disbelief. Syd would have told me she was meeting Wesley. She wasn't a sneaky person. She'd never lie to me. I know my sister. I opened my mouth to tell them this but nothing happened. Mouth movement, no sound. I'm sure I may have blinked but for the most part I felt frozen in place while pictures, like flickering bits of film flashed through my mind, as though all the stuff from the cutting room floor of my life had been spliced together and stuffed back in, out of context.

A single word popped into my head and sat there, waiting for my attention. I nearly smiled. The first time I saw this word was in a *Nora Roberts* novel that is still my all time favorite read. The word was used just once and so very well that it had stuck with me for years. I'd always wished for an opportunity to use it, but now that I had one, the only good part was the word. "Clusterfuck."

I must give Angie credit, she managed to nearly squelch her snort, then grinned and said, *"Birthright."*

I nodded. "My favorite book, all-time."

"Had a happy ending."

"You think I'll be as lucky?" I asked.

"Hey, anything's possible."

So she dodged the question, I would've done the same thing in her shoes. And funny, but the little side-trip about a book had given my insides a chance to settle again.

"There's been no sign of Sydney or Wesley since then?"

Joining in once again, Gage answered, "One message,

a week ago."

"And?" I prompted.

"It was a simple 'all's well'. Standard Procedure."

Sure he was going to leave it at that, I gave him a *don't even think about it* look and he continued.

"We have certain company protocols. When an agent is staying out of contact for whatever reason, there are a dozen ways for him or her to leave a message of A-okay or SOS."

"So a simple, uncomplicated message."

Angie shook her head. "Not exactly. They're texts or emails. Each word in the message means something specific. The messages say a whole lot more than ok or not. There's a full set of codes built around the family's beef business so the emails look like standard inquiries. We also have dozens of other codes, just like real spies." She winked.

"Computer generated?"

Angie laughed. "Nope, they use my kid. He's ten. We tap into his adolescent thought process on a regular basis so anything we incorporate has roots in kid logic and adults have a hell of a time connecting the dots."

Fascinating as this was, I pushed back to the important questions. "So, you're telling me you're not worried that Wesley vanished and took Syd with him?"

Gage nodded. "He was assigned to her. His job was, is, to get her into one of our safe houses." As though anticipating my question he added, "No. She won't be coming here. This area is being watched. That's why nobody is moving in or out for a while."

"Just for the record, where the hell is here?"

Gage gave me that long serious stare I was starting to interpret as him wishing he could read my mind and/or trying to decide if he should trust me.

"Come on Gage, it's not as if I'm about to call up all my girlfriends and share my vacation adventures with them." Like I had girlfriends. Geez, having spied on me for so long, I suppose he knew that. "If I at least know where I am it will help to give me a sense of stability, ground me. Right now I'm in limbo, kind of like when I was a kid in New York." I sighed. "We lived on the twenty fourth floor and sometimes the fog would roll in and I'd feel like we lived in a cloud. There's something disconcerting about not being able to see the ground."

"I think we can trust her Gage."

"Thanks Quinn." At least I had one brother convinced. "Gage?"

"Canada. British Columbia, just north of the ranch."

"My ranch?" A peculiar excitement filled me.

He nodded and I watched the subtle changes on his face. His brows lowered, deepening the line between them. His mouth thinned, jaw tightened. I was pretty certain he was already regretting telling me the location. That in itself hinted I wasn't as defenseless a captive as I'd thought.

There must be a way for me to get out of here. But why would I want to? What was there to gain? Oh hell, this prisoner thing was getting weirder. I longed for the days of solving all my problems by jumping on horseback and heading for the hills.

Buck. Jiminy-H-Christmas where was my brain?

"What happened to Buck? Where is he?"

"Safe."

144

I gritted my teeth, so damned tired of that word. I could almost feel a condescending hand pat on my head every time I heard it.

I kept my tone neutral, even. "Unless you'd like another meeting with the crazy woman from last night's demolition event, I suggest you give me a little more than your stock answer." I kept my gaze fixed on his as I reached for my cup and took a long swallow of lukewarm coffee. Had there been a clock in the room, I'm sure the ticking would have seemed loud and exaggerated against the backdrop of silence.

Something changed in his eyes. I'm not sure if the color darkened or the black centers dilated but there was something deep and compelling there now. I dropped my gaze to his mouth. Dammit why did I do that? The thin line of his lips softened and moved ever so slightly at the corners, suggesting he was hiding a smile. Warm slid over me like a down filled comforter, even before he began to speak in a low persuasive voice.

"When the helicopter picked you up, they dropped me a saddle and bridle for the horse. I rode him," he hesitated and I was pretty sure he was doing a quick edit of the story. "To a safe place where I could load him on a truck and bring him here."

Hold it. That didn't fit. Had he ridden here? Was Buck here and was the ranch close enough for me to ride home? If he was lying to me, he'd just given me ammunition to catch him this time. "You said we're in Canada. You can't ship a horse across the border without health papers and a negative Coggins test which takes something like four days to process."

He sighed and Angie snickered. I glanced her way and saw she was smiling at Gage with a look that asked, how you going to get around this one bro?

"Forged papers."

I rolled my eyes at him and shook my head—nearly making myself dizzy. "Government seals and stamps and all? Get real."

He pursed his lips and leaned back. Propping his elbows on the arms of the chair, he pressed his fingertips together, making a steeple with beautiful masculine hands. "Have I mentioned that our agency does security work for both governments? Bringing a horse into Canada to keep him secured indoors at a remote location and then return him to the US without having contact with any other animals, is not going to be a problem for the departments of agriculture on either side of the border. And of course, all his paperwork and tests will be complete in the next day or so."

He was bluffing. In my gut I knew he was bluffing. Well, I've always heard that turnabout is fair play. So, "I hadn't thought of that," I said.

His eyes narrowed.

"If Buck's here, I want to see him." And I wasn't about to back down. I only had to see the horse to know for sure if Gage was lying. Buck was a bad shipper—would lean his weight against the trailer hard enough to rub himself raw. If he was loose inside a rig, he'd stand with his butt against a side panel. If he was tied and couldn't sit back, he'd lean a shoulder or hip against the side. I always covered him with a special padded canvas blanket for protection. Gage wouldn't know to do that.

146

"Aren't you even surprised Gage had no trouble handling the supposed man killer?" quizzed Angie.

"No, because he's not a killer. He's been abused by men. Aggressive, abrasive men acting in anger or fear. Horses have great instincts. Buck wouldn't sense anything threatening from Gage because I'm sure his approach would be the same one he uses on women." I tried not to smile. "And it's very effective.

Eve spoke for the first time in ages and I realized that I'd pretty much forgotten she was there. "So you think the last victim was actually attacking the horse?"

"No I think he was killed, then dumped into the pen."

Gage was nodding, but frowning. "We got confirmation this morning. No ties to the Minnows. Feds suspect he was a mule using the job on the ranch to get established in the area." He looked at me and started to explain. "A mule is-"

"Someone being used to transport drugs." *I wasn't born yesterday.* "And on that note I should mention my damaged, make that destroyed, line shack." I told them about finding the building torn apart by a chainsaw, or two.

Quinn stood. "Something for me to check out." I watched him leave the room, head down the hallway and I'd swear he walked right through a wall.

Chapter 11

I turned back with what I'm sure was a stupefied expression on my face which Gage ignored. He held out his hand. "Let's go see your horse."

Confused and not certain what to say about what I thought I'd seen, wondering if I was losing my marbles, I went along with him.

The route we took was intriguing, to say the least. He led me through the pantry to a door—which opened with a key fob like I used on my truck—to a long narrow stairwell. I counted the steps as we descended. Sixty-two. A long blessed ways down to a small hexagonal foyer with five doors.

Gage's hand was in his pocket when I heard the lock snick on the door to my right. I pushed it open to a dark hallway with plywood walls and dim ceiling lights to guide us. It was cold, making me glad I was wearing thick woolly socks. We trudged on in silence. But it was comfortable. He was still holding my hand and it was such a warm, real connection that I let my mind wander back to the strip in Vegas.

As though his thoughts had gone down a similar path,

he lifted my hand and touched his lips to the back of it. Warmth suffused me and I glanced up, startled. There was some kind of question in his look and my heart gave an answering thump. Our pace slowed until we were standing still in the shadowy hallway, in the middle of God knows where, and nothing mattered but meeting the mouth that was lowering to mine.

I was sandwiched between him and the wall. Reduced to senses and nerve endings, vaguely aware of some internal happy dancing. I heard myself moan then gave up trying to focus until chilled air came between us when he pushed me away.

With his hands on my shoulders and his elbows straight, he kept space between us. I still saw heat in his dark, hooded eyes and I wanted him too. Bad.

Luckily, my thinking brain shook free. For if it hadn't reminded me this was the man who'd been manipulating and using me, I'd've had him down to his boxers by now. A shudder ran through me as my body protested the lack of fulfillment—in the most literal sense.

"Pheromones."

"What?" he asked.

"I don't trust you, I'm not sure I even like you. So it must be pheromones driving this bus."

"You couldn't kiss me that way if you didn't like me."

"Huh. A lot you know. Didn't you do the facts of life in biology class? We all exude pheromones to attract the opposite sex. They're what start an attraction that is meant to culminate in procreation, which guarantees the future of the gene pool."

"This isn't about saving humanity."

I could feel his amusement. I backed away, couldn't afford to let him touch me again. Not right now when my resistance was at such a pathetic low. "Are we getting close to the stables?"

"We've a ways to go." He turned and resumed walking, watching me over his shoulder as I kept pace. "You're going to give me a kink in my neck. Come up here. I promise I won't crowd you."

I stepped up alongside him and wished I couldn't smell his scent—that something male mixed with soap and coffee. I needed my wits about me so I could find a way out of this prison. Even if it meant I had to disappear for a while. I'd learned a thing or two about hiding while in the business of tracking missing people.

All I needed was one clear shot to get to one of a dozen contacts I had. They'd help me access my secret bank account and establish a temporary identity. Then I'd be set. Sydney knew where to look for a message from me.

Setting up an escape plan had been a bit of a lark, many years ago when I wanted to get away from my mother, permanently.

She'd laughed at me when I told her I was going to leave because I didn't want to model anymore. Her response had been, 'You wouldn't dare walk away from me. You're a minor, fifteen years old, in my custody and I'll drag you back by the hair if you ever try such a stupid stunt.' I'd yelled back that I was smarter than her and she'd never find me. The fight had gone on and on. In the end, I'd simply hidden out in my room for a day, but the idea stayed, like a flea nipping away at me. Her words echoing, taunting, saying I was too stupid to pull it off and that's when I'd decided to prove her wrong.

Being in the adult world of modeling, I had exposure to people and places most kids would never imagine even existed. And I made friends easily. I was at a shoot in Miami one day and said to Mike, who was my age and seemed to have a mother like mine, "I just wish I could run away and hide from her."

He'd suggested we run off together, said he had connections. Fascinated by the word connections, the two of us spent months researching and planning our liberation. Of course it never happened.

But a few years later, when I did leave my mother and the business, I *was* afraid of her. That's when I used the names that Mike and I had researched. I set myself up an escape hatch, complete with ID cards and hidden money. A way to go to ground, just in case.

On top of that, I'd used the off-shore bank account as a good way to save money, by keeping it out of my own easy reach. If it wasn't in my American account, it wasn't available for impulse shopping. No falling for a horse at a sale and spending thousands from the savings account.

Gage put his hand on my arm to stop me in front of a door I'd been about to pass. It opened to reveal yet another hallway. This was getting boring. Plus, I had lost all sense of direction as we hadn't been going in straight lines. My gut told me we'd traveled in a half circle but I couldn't be sure.

We rounded a corner and there was nothing but a blank wall in front of us. Gage reached up and touched a button near the ceiling and the wall lifted up and back like a garage door. In front of me was a row of hooks on the wall where warm outdoor clothing hung and I spotted my own Carhartts, with my boots on the floor below.

When I raised my eyebrows he chuckled. "Put them on, it's cold out there."

While I climbed into my gear, he donned a one-piece version of the same brand and I was reminded of my friend's story about accidently peeing in her hood. I hadn't seen her in a long time, but she was someone else I could rely on for help if I needed it.

Once Gage and I were bundled up, he led me through one last door, into an indoor riding arena. It was an interesting design. Wooden walls went up about ten feet and from the top edge, metal arches rose to form the skeleton for the dark green fabric roof. The six stalls along one long side looked sturdy, with high plank walls and Dutch-doors.

Buck was watching us from the fourth stall over, where the top door was swung open. I wanted to run right to him but it was more important to observe every detail of my surroundings. I could hear music.

"Tunes?"

Gage nodded. "Satellite radio. Thought he could use the company." He opened the top and bottom door of the first stall and walked in. I struggled to keep my mouth from hanging open in surprise. I'd noticed a roof on the stall and assumed as in most barns this would be the tack and or feed room. What I hadn't been prepared to see were a dozen flat screens showing security footage, and three computers.

My system hummed as I searched the images for an exit door, then, realizing Gage was watching me, I scurried away, and headed for Buck.

Most horses would have at least nickered when we came in but Buck had never been much of a talker. Didn't stop me from holding up my side of the conversation though.

"Hey pal, how's things?" I rubbed my hand on his forehead and he leaned into the pressure. I smiled. "Miss me?" He used his nose to check my pockets. "Candy-hound." I stuck my hand in and found there were still some peppermints in the plastic bag. I gave him only one, as I may need them later.

Gage came up behind me. "You happy with his accommodations?"

"Very nice." And it was. The wall between two stalls had been removed so he had a double sized space to move around in. "But what's with the blanket?"

Buck was covered from neck to tail in a green, brown and beige, camouflage blanket. Which pissed me off because now I wouldn't be able to tell if he'd been trailered. But then again... I could change tactics.

"What are you hiding under it? Is he injured?" As in big rub marks from behaving badly in a trailer?

"All I was hiding was his bright coat. Made it harder for a shooter to spot him in the woods."

His story made sense, but I needed to know for sure if he'd ridden him to a trailer, or all the way here. Unlatching the bottom door, I swung it open. "Back, Buck," I said and ducked under the rubber coated door chain. "Want to get these pajamas off for while big guy?"

I eased behind him and unsnapped the hind leg straps one at a time, stepping forward to clip them to the d-ring at the wither, giving me ample opportunity to check the back-half of the blanket for rub marks. Nothing. I unbuckled the belly straps and slipped under his neck to his off side to swing them over his back, seeing no marks on the shoulder areas of the blanket either.

Once the chest strap was undone, I slid the blanket off over his rump.

By now I'm sure I looked like an anal idiot, but at least I was next to certain Buck hadn't been trailered recently, which meant he'd been ridden here. I recalled the fleeting look of regret on Gage's face when he'd said we were just across the border from the ranch.

I struggled to hide my grin. I had everything I needed. A fair idea where I was and transportation. But damned if I wanted to get on him again without a bridle.

"He needs exercise. Is there tack to ride him?"

Gage gave a directional tip of his head toward the second stall. "Saddle and bridle, everything you'll need's in there. Help yourself."

I took my time brushing a glow back into the stallion's golden coat and combing the tangles from his inky black mane and tail. I was hoping to bore Gage with slow actions, while I worked out a plan.

*

Gage studied the way she handled the horse and his blood heated with the memory of those same hands on his skin. He shook his head, shut down that kind of thinking. Couldn't afford to be distracted again. He'd already screwed up once.

He knew better than to get caught up in wrong

thinking again. Especially since Quinn pointed out how it had happened. How watching her for months, learning her habits and figuring out her thought patterns had set him up to falsely believe he knew her intimately before they'd met in Vegas.

Cassandra on the other hand, had no such background to build on and viewed Vegas as nothing more than a one night stand. So now, how could she see him as anything but a kidnapper, a villain and a stalker?

That she continued to kiss him back when he made a move gave him hope. She wasn't immune. But it didn't take genius to know that if he pushed, she wouldn't hesitate to shove back.

According to Quinn—his brother the psychologist—Cassandra needed time to catch up. To learn to trust him. And although Quinn's specialty was men suffering from PTSD, he knew what he was talking about from a personal level. Because he was still waiting, believing his own wife would trust him enough to come home.

Gage shook off the heavy thoughts and left Cassandra with her horse. Inside the office he studied her on the security monitor for a minute or two before pulling out a chair and plopping down in front of a computer to stare at the screen saver—an aerial photo of his family's Texas ranch. Thousands of acres with more than a dozen homes, where they raised the next generation of Meyers, Prime Red Angus Cattle, and Champion Cutting Horses.

Gage spent time going through various files and websites, checking in on business in general, stats from sales and shows, then correspondence.

Checking for requests for semen on the AI Cattle

operation, he hoped to see a coded message from Wesley but there was nothing and that set Gage on edge. To distract himself from his brother's current status of missing, he glanced over at the screens to watch Cass ride.

WTF? Buck stood alone. The punch of adrenalin catapulted Gage out of the room. The horse didn't move. Gage stopped, did a full visual sweep. Nothing. She couldn't be gone.

He bellowed her name. Ran for the door they'd come in through. Closed, still locked. He hit the fob, wrenched open the door and stared into an empty room.

He wheeled, ran to the far end of the arena, pounded a post and a panel of wall swung outward. He scanned for movement, saw none, raced out, along a trail in the undergrowth and was nearly into the forest when her shout came from behind him.

He spun around and there she was. Standing in the open doorway, grinning at him. With fury and relief at war, he marched toward her. He needed to chill. She'd hadn't taken off. Hadn't left him.

"Where the hell were you?" He wanted to grab her but didn't trust himself. Not yet. She'd scared hell out of him. God knows, if he laid his hands on her now, there'd likely be no stopping him until he'd either rattled her bones or jumped them. Fucked her blind. Proved she was his.

He fought to get his emotions in check. Didn't want her afraid of him when she needed all her fear, all her defenses to keep her away from the men who called themselves, Minnows—about as tongue in cheek as a biker gang with a Gerbil mascot.

"Were you going for a run in the woods?"

The hint of laughter in her voice had him gritting his teeth. "Just needed a little exercise, fresh air."

She did laugh then and it unexpectedly curled around him, somehow easing the tension in his body. "You thought I'd run off." She headed for the horse still waiting for her, but Gage snagged the back of her jacket.

"Hold it right there." She half-turned toward him. "Where were you?"

She smirked and tilted her head toward the stalls. "I drank way too much coffee today. Didn't see a bathroom anywhere so I used the empty stall at the far end, hoping you didn't have a camera in there."

Gage stuffed his hands in his pockets, and turned his attention to the stallion in the middle of the ring. "Most horses only stand and wait like that if they're ground tied."

A smile lit her face as she backed toward the horse. "He panics if his lines touch the ground. Looks at them like a couple of snakes. Yet step off of him anywhere, anytime, and he'll wait all day if you loop his reins over his neck or the saddle horn. He's a bit of an unusual dude. Maybe that's why we get along so well. Not like I'm exactly normal." Her smile faded into something sad.

He couldn't help himself. "Come here."

She shook her head. "Not a good idea."

"Maybe not, but it ain't goin' away." He closed the distance between them as though stalking a skittish deer. "You scared hell out of me just now." He just needed to touch her, hold her for a minute. He held out his hand and when she laid hers in it, he pulled her into his arms. He'd thought that just holding her would be enough, but the bulky clothing put too much distance between them.

He slipped a hand into her hair and cradled the back of her head while he lowered his mouth and took possession of hers. Took everything he needed, then more.

*

My bones had liquefied by the time I came up for air, dazed, still hungry. But the scary part was the peculiar sense of belonging sweeping through me. I am not a stereotype. I am not some dime store heroine. I'm a strong, kick-ass, save myself kind of woman who doesn't swoon or go limp with desire and get swept off my feet. I don't need anyone.

But I couldn't seem to catch my breath as I stood with my forehead pressed against his chin. Must be something to do with elevation or the cold or whatever. Maybe the drugs they've been pumping into me.

I sucked in air, hoping for a big blast of oxygen to help my brain cells sort themselves out but instead I was filled with his scent. *Ohmygod*. I wanted to press my face into his throat, taste his skin, feel his heartbeat against my mouth.

Stop it.

I pulled away as fast as I could, kind of like removing a Band-Aid, get it over with before you can think about it too much. He let me go easily and some little contrary being in my head was offended that he hadn't tried to keep me in his arms. *Arrggh.* I took several deep breaths while giving myself a pep talk about pheromones and how they were influencing me, trying to convince my body to ignore common sense.

His voice vibrated under the skin on the back of my neck as though he were standing against me, not six feet away. "Why don't you ride for a while, I'll be in the office, working.

Good, great, that's just the opportunity I need. This time, I'd head out the door I'd watched him open.

"Sure, good idea. This guy still needs his exercise."

I checked the snugness of the cinch, gathered the reins in my left hand, stuffed my left foot in the stirrup and swung up. Buck was a good boy and stayed still until I nudged him with my heels, asked him to move forward.

We walked a few laps of the ring, his hooves making swishing sounds as he dragged his toes in the deep sawdust footing. I pressed him into a slow rolling jog and circled the ring a bunch of times while my mind worked on the escape plan.

I rode for about a half hour, then led him past the office where Gage was working at a computer and asked, "Is it okay if I take some time to give him a good rub down?"

He smiled and the first little niggle of guilt edged under my skin. "No problem, I've got plenty of work I can do here. Take your time." Wishing I hadn't seen the warmth in his eyes, I took Buck to his stall, left the reins looped over his neck and pulled off the saddle. After stowing it back in the tack room beside the office, I grabbed the basket of grooming tools.

I rubbed the sweaty saddle-mark from his back with a soft towel, then I used a plastic curry to scrub his coat and loosen any matted hair. I picked up his feet and cleaned out the bits of sawdust, then finally put the blanket back on him.

This was it. Time to make my move. Hoping to appear nonchalant on camera, I sauntered to the office door, closed it and slid the latches in place.

I ran to Buck. Swung up on his back. Tried to ignore Gage's shouts as I jabbed the horse in the belly with my heels and rode straight to the place where I'd seen Gage stop earlier. I slapped the post with the heel of my hand and the door swung open in silence.

I froze.

Chapter 12

There, on the precipice of freedom, with the horse under me not only willing, but eager to make a break for the hills, I freaking froze.

As though someone had wrapped heavy arms around my chest, I felt great pressure on my heart. My lungs seemed empty of air. I held the reins tight and set my heels against the horse's sides, preparing to launch us out of the barn, through that open doorway to freedom, and I couldn't do it. The panel swung closed.

I don't know if I'd been affected by the fear in Gage's voice, his earlier concern, or something else I didn't recognize. My shoulders slumped. I couldn't do it. I moved my hand so the reins pushed on the left side of Buck's neck, turning him, riding him right into his stall. I slid off his back and removed the bridle.

The pounding and shouting had stopped. Gilt and worry ate at me. How the hell was I going to open that door and face him now. I leaned my forehead against the horse's neck for a moment. Then, resolved, determined to face the proverbial music, I turned to leave the stall.

And walked into an immovable object.

161

I reversed a step or two, glanced first at his angry expression, then past him at the remains of the office door, and of all fool things, a giggle escaped me. *Oh shit, oh damn.* He strode away.

Before I sagged in relief, I checked both the hayrack and water bucket to be sure Buck was well supplied, snapped the stall chain in place and swung his door closed.

Without so much as a word or glance between us, we shed our outer wear in the mudroom and marched back through the maze. We came to a stop in the great room, stood rigid, one on either side of a large leather couch—his move, not mine—not that I thought it was a bad idea.

When the silence between us stretched to a critical breaking point and I felt like something was about to shatter, I spoke the truth. Good or bad, smart or stupid. I had to be honest. "I can't say yet, that I'm sorry for what I did—and didn't do. But I am sorry for upsetting you."

He sported the grimmest look I'd seen from him, ever. Not that our ever had been a long journey but this was indeed, a milestone. His voice was so low it was like a secret between us. And his anger, well, I'm sure if I dared to inhale deeply, I'd be able to taste it.

"I want to pick you up and shake you until your brains rattle for even contemplating such a stupid, fucking, move. I want to kick myself around the block for letting you lock me in there like a goddamned rooky." He shook his head. "And I want you way, way, too fucking, much."

He turned and stormed out of sight. Down the hallway, somewhere past the exercise room, a door slammed, and if there'd been real windows in this place, I'm sure one or two would have fallen from their frames in teeny tiny little pieces.

I sat. Right there. Landed on the floor with a thump. I crossed my legs, leaned forward with my elbows on my knees, rested my face in my hands and stayed there for god-knows how long until Merlin brushed back and forth against my knees.

I pulled him into my lap and cradled him. His purring helped to ease the pain in my chest. I stopped hearing the air move in and out of my lungs. "Thank you."

He reared up, slid his cheek across mine and I could have sworn, buried in the rhythm of the purring, when his breath touched my ear, I heard, *you're welcome.*

An hour or so later, I was parked at the breakfast bar, sipping a cup of the coffee I'd made, and trying to nibble on a slice of toast. My stomach was giving me hell, refusing to settle. I dumped the coffee down the sink and rifled through the fridge and cupboards until I'd found soup crackers and ginger ale.

Lissa came into the room and stopped in front of me. "You okay?"

"Sure."

"You don't look much better than Gage." She poured herself a coffee, added sugar, and milk from a gallon-jug I'd seen in the fridge.

Wait a minute. "Fresh milk. You have access to a grocery store. Not so isolated after all."

Lissa smiled as she climbed up on the stool across from me. "Our last supplies came in by helicopter about ten days ago. We try to get a drop-off every other week." She tipped her chin as I raised the half glass of pale amber soda for another swallow and nibbled the cracker in my other hand. "You pregnant?"

I nearly spewed ginger ale across the room. I swallowed hard, coughed and said, "NO."

Her eyes narrowed thoughtfully. "You sure?"

"Yes."

"You were sleeping with Gage in Vegas."

"Hey." I was getting a little defensive and felt a whole bunch of pissy-attitude coming on. I mentally squashed it. "Look. What happens between Gage and I is our business. But just for the record, condoms were used and all swimmers died a timely death without finding a comfy place to roost. Okay?"

She continued to study me. "Gage doesn't make mistakes."

"So why do you suspect I'm pregnant?"

"No." She waved her hand in dismissal. "Not the condom thing. I was in the control room with Kyle when you went to the stables. We watched what you did. I hadn't figured you for the femme fatale type but I must say, you had him by the short hairs." She smiled. "My husband called it when you went into the end stall and hid. He said you were setting him up and I defended you, said you wouldn't do that.

"Then, after he kissed you—and let me say, that was unexpected, and felt intrusive—Kyle was going to call him, warn him, and I talked him out of it."

"Why?"

She shrugged her shoulders. With a little half smile, she said, "I'm a romantic. I want everyone to be happy and in love like I am. Corny, I know, but true. I thought you might be a good match, a strong enough woman for him, but--"

I grimaced. "But now you don't think I'm worthy."

She frowned and it occurred to me I'd seen little but a passive face on her before today. "I don't like seeing Gage upset, in turmoil. He was a Green Beret. The kind of training he went through, the job he did for years before he joined the family business, isn't the kind of background that produces a soft man." She looked away, then turned back to meet my gaze, head on. "I don't like that he's allowing you to get him all twisted up, and I really hate seeing him unhappy."

A second voice chimed in from behind me and I just about fell off my perch.

"I, on the other hand, am kind of enjoying watching you rock his world a little. Game-on girl." Angie pulled out the stool beside me and slid onto it.

"Look, I'm not," I made air quotes, "playing games with him. We spent a night together in Vegas and you know how the saying goes about what happens in Vegas... well, anyways, it was pure escapism for both of us, a one night fantasy. But now, this whole other level of confusion has taken over my life. Turned it into something bizarre and frightening."

"So you're leaning on him, understandably." Angie may have made it a statement but her eyebrows rose in question.

"No, I'm not." Or was I? I groaned, planted my elbows on the counter and dropped my chin on my fists.

"I don't want to be leaning on anyone, least of all him. My life is in the freaking toilet, I don't have a home, I probably have to give up my name—again—my sister's run off with a guy who can reduce her to a whimpering idiot with a single look, my dead father is alive and my missing brother is—crap—I can't remember what his status is. See? My life?" I held out a hand, mimicked pushing down on a lever and made a swooshing sound through my teeth. "There it goes, swirling off into some distant pit."

I stuffed a whole cracker in my mouth and chased it down with a swallow of ginger ale. Then finished off the rest of the glass.

Angie was watching me. "Are you pregnant?"

"Arrggh!" I thumped my fist on the counter.

"Hmm. Soda crackers and ginger ale are classic cures for morning sickness," she said to Lissa.

I rolled my eyes. "I. Am. Not. Pregnant. Perhaps I should have that tattooed on my forehead for the next person who walks in here."

Gage of course arrived at just that moment. He looked at me, the cracker in my hand, then at Angie and Lissa. When he opened his mouth, about to add his two cents worth, I hopped off my chair and headed for the hallway that led to my room.

"What's she pissed off about now?" I heard him ask, and to my utter astonishment, both women, in stereo, answered, "She's not pregnant."

For a flicker of an instant I wanted to spin around, go back and qualify their statement, but it just wasn't worth it. I needed to stay away from Gage and get my mental marbles back in all their appropriate places. I needed a new plan.

*

Gage's mouth dropped open and the two women grinned at him. WTF? He ran a hand through his hair, still wet from the shower he'd taken after spending an hour on the cross-country running machine.

He had to clear his throat of what felt like an army of frogs before he could ask what the hell was going on. When they explained, he said, "Not possible."

Angie's eyebrows went up. "Jeez, I said the same thing about eight months before Dustin was born."

"Hey little sister, you can't compare me to Brandon."

"I've told you a hundred times, Brandon is not Dustin's father."

"Fine, keep covering for the guy. But I certainly didn't get Cassandra pregnant."

She giggled. "No, she was Maddy in Vegas right?"

He grunted. "Did she tell you she wants to be pregnant?"

Angie grinned. "You volunteering to help her along?"

"No. I'm just curious that she'd say something like that. It's out of character."

Lissa sounded like she was talking to a slightly slow child. "Gage, you haven't spent all that much time with her. I'm not sure if you'd have such a good idea about her character yet."

He scowled. "True enough. But we actually talked about kids and she seemed to be very open and genuine about her plans to never have any. Said she was more comfortable being a terrific caretaker and nurturer of animals instead of humans." And he hadn't mistaken the shudder that had run through her when she'd said that babies and children scared the beejeezus out of her. "I really find it hard to believe that she's wishing she was pregnant."

The two women exchanged a look. "What are you talking about?"

Gage shook his head. "Okay, pay attention. I asked what she was pissed off about. You both said, 'she's not pregnant'."

Angie and Lissa stared at each other for just a moment, before Angie snorted and they both burst out laughing and each time they nearly regained control, they'd meet each other's look and start all over again.

Gage went to the fridge, pulled out a soda, popped the top and guzzled half of it down. He finished it off, released a manly belch and tossed the can in the recycle bin while they wound down to gulps, wheezing and mopping of tears from their faces.

"You two done?" He asked, fighting to hide a smile.

Angie hiccupped and nodded to Lissa to do the talking.

After she'd recapped the entire soda cracker scene, Gage shook his head at them. "It's her standard method for dealing with a nervous stomach."

"She told you this?"

"No. But we've had her under surveillance since Wesley put a camera in her kitchen last summer."

Angie shrugged. "Well, hell, that takes all the fun out of it."

"How was her state of mind before you two messed with her?"

"I resent that."

"Resent away sister dear. How was she emotionally?

Mad, sad, resigned? What?"

Lissa replied, "I'd say she's down, Gage, kind of treading water, not knowing which way to shore, you know? A little resentful, yet resigned." She sighed. "I feel bad for her, yet I don't like that she's messing with your head."

He put his hands on her shoulders and planted a kiss on her forehead. "Thanks." He held her at arm's length. "But you don't need to worry about me." He turned to Angie. "Same goes for you brat, stop speculating, worrying or rubbing your hands together in glee."

"Payback's a bitch isn't it?" She grinned.

*

While standing in the shower shampooing my hair, I was somewhat thankful for the bright colored cartoon fish that filled the lower two thirds of the curtain. Merlin sat on the counter, listening to me, while I talked through my problems.

There was a solid knock on the door and I yelped before answering. "What?"

Of course it was Gage, and he cracked open the door a couple of inches. "You okay in there?"

"Yes sir, learned how to do this all by myself a few years back."

"So you don't want my help?"

"No." I glanced at the cat and I'm sure he winked at me. I frowned as the door began to swing open. And I'm sure the word semantics, moved through my mind. Shit. "I mean, yes that's correct. I don't want your help." The door closed with a click.

Ten minutes later, stepping into my bedroom wearing only a robe as my clothes smelled like the inside of a barn, I wasn't surprised to see Gage there waiting for me.

"Now what?" I asked.

"How's the stomach?"

"Fine. I assume they explained?"

He didn't smile. "I told them to back off. Give you a little breathing room. We're going for a walk after you get dressed. Maybe I can help you feel more settled here, less inclined to consider bolting." He tilted his head toward the bureau and I saw that once again, a little pile of neatly folded clothing had been left for me.

I frowned and tried not to grit my teeth. Since he was trying to play nice I figured I'd best make an effort to help myself, as well. "I have to tell you that this little clothing thing, doling a wardrobe to me one outfit at a time isn't helping. I might feel some measure of control if I had a few things in the closet or bureau to choose from."

"You don't like my choices?"

"They're fine. But just that. Your choices."

"Okay. Come on." He took my hand to lead me from the room.

Used to walking around a set in only a robe, it didn't bother me to go down the hall to the huge wardrobe room while dressed in so little. He stopped just inside the door. "I've been getting your clothes from that area." He pointed and I went there.

Ten minutes later, with an armful of shirts, sweaters, jeans and leggings, I headed back to my room with Gage in tow carrying shoes and socks. Over the last few days, I'd grown used to going commando so didn't bother with underwear.

Once my new things were packed away, I chose, to wear the sweater and jeans Gage had originally picked out, which earned me an exasperated shake of his head. I simply smiled. It was all about choice and control. But I didn't expect him to understand.

Our walk was to be outside. He took me into a room lined with cupboards full of outdoor wear, saying, "It's just a little below freezing so dress as you see fit."

Quick learner, I thought, and startled him by pressing a quick kiss to his cheek while he was half in and half out of his parka. All of a sudden I felt warm inside. Not heated like horny but warm like home. I blinked and sucked in a quick breath, waited for uneasiness to follow such a telling thought, but nothing happened.

Before we left, Gage unlocked a cabinet containing a huge selection of weapons and I was surprised for just a moment to see my own rifle. "Annie Oakley."

He looked over his shoulder. "What?"

"My thirty-thirty. I call her Annie Oakley."

I could tell he was trying to think of something to say besides, 'you've got to be joking.' Appreciating his effort I explained that as a kid, I'd done a commercial where I was supposed to be a child pretending to be Annie Oakley. I'd been set up in the full cowgirl outfit including a big long rifle. So whenever I took my dad's old gun out of the cabinet at the ranch it reminded me of being Annie Oakley.

He smiled. "Well, Annie can stay on the rack. I'll just take something else along for safety sake." He pulled out a weapon that looked kind of serious, not that the other's weren't, just that this one had a big scope on it and was plain dull black, no fancy carved wood or polished brass. A little shudder ran up my backbone. This was no varmint gun.

"Do you think the Minnows are out there?"

"No activity on any of the sensors or cameras, but no point taking chances."

"Yet you're willing to take me outdoors just to ease my mind."

He sighed, reached out a hand as though he was going to touch me but pulled it back. His eyes darkened and there was a sudden tension in him.

I waited. Not certain what I wanted, I was willing to wait for him to make up his own mind. When he did there was both relief and disappointment for me as he took my hand and led me out the door. I guess I'd been dreading, yet hoping for one of those mind altering kisses.

Instead, I was outside. Finally. No walls between me and the forest, and nothing pulling me back this time as Gage was beside me instead. We followed a path leading steadily away from the exit we'd used.

The path narrowed into a trail climbing upwards, under draping firs. Our feet crunched the tiny seed cones littering the barely frozen ground. It smelled so good. The cool fresh air pumped life into me.

"I can feel you changing." His voice was quiet and even, showing no strain from the climb. And it reminded me.

"Angie told me you were Green Beret. That's Special Ops, right?" My gaze fastened on the weapon. "Is that the kind of thing you're used to?"

"I'm comfortable with all weapons. We're trained to handle anything."

"What was it like? The training, the job?"

"Intense, consuming. Total commitment for those who survive training. My team worked in all corners of the world. We did whatever jobs needed doing."

"Like what?"

"Special reconnaissance, counter-terrorism, hostage recovery."

"Why? Why did you even think about joining Special Ops?"

"Tradition. Since the Second World War, there's always been a Green Beret in my family. My dad retired before I was born, but my uncle and cousin were still in when I was growing up."

"How long does it take? The training?

"About two years from enlistment to first mission."

I stopped then and looked at him. I wanted to ask, even though I knew the answer. I'm not sure why I needed to hear him say it, whether it was something I could use to keep myself from falling for him.

"Have you ever killed someone?"

Chapter 13

His gaze was steady on mine. The blue of his eyes seemed brighter somehow, probably just the natural light.

"The guns, the weapon training, it's all for a purpose Cass."

I stayed stubborn. "Have you?"

"Yes."

"What does it feel like?"

He shook his head. "I'm not going there with you. I did a job. A necessary job. I've saved far more lives than I've taken. And I can live with that." He waited a heartbeat. "Can you?"

He watched me. I felt like he could see into my mind and hoped that he couldn't see what was in my heart. Because at that moment. There was a strange pain there. A scary good and comfortable pain. Like the scream of muscles nearing the finish line.

My heartbeat quickened. *Oh god, oh god I can't let this happen. No. I can't fall for someone who lies, kidnaps people, kills...*

I resorted to snapping at him. "I don't get to decide anymore what I can and can't live with." I scurried up the path with him hard on my heels. Climbed at a grueling pace until I was forced to stop, to brace my hands against my knees and gasp for air. He stood beside me. Silent. Annoyingly stoic.

Overheated, I unbuttoned the coat, and tugged the woolly cap off of my still wet hair.

"Put your hat back on."

"In a minute, once I cool off."

"Turn around then, and take a look."

I did and immediately frowned. We'd been travelling in pretty much a straight line, uphill. I should be able to see the house right below. I frowned. "Where is it?"

"Right in front of you, halfway down to the grassy valley bottom."

I could see the long meadows of dried summer grasses, but no building in between.

"It's invisible," he said with a smile.

"Huh?" Heaven help me I was ready to believe him.

He took pity on me. "When we designed the compound, we hired a Hollywood scenery designer to mock up the outside so it would appear to be part of the natural setting. He used standard photography of the area as well as satellite photos taken before we broke ground."

I was staring at the place where I was fairly certain the house, compound, whatever, was. I couldn't see a single hint of it. Wow. Amazing. Freaking unreal.

"Considering how much it feels like my life is being scripted, it fits."

He dropped an arm around my shoulders, led me to a big flat rock and we both sat down. "Just enjoy the scenery and don't worry so much about what's happening."

"Easy for you to say."

He drew me into his side and kissed the top of my head. "No, it's not easy for me either. I don't like putting you through all this."

"Then why?" Jeez what was I thinking? "Never mind." I didn't want to hear about duty and criminals and keeping me safe because it's his job. Damn. Wasn't it just what I needed to settle these mixed up feelings? Didn't I need to remind myself that I was simply a job to him? His family business hard at work. Yes. That's exactly what I needed.

"You're not just a job to me Cass."

Oh crap, oh hell, sonofabitch that was the wrong thing to say. My mind screamed while my flesh sank happily into him and my head nestled against his shoulder.

"Don't." My voice squeaked and I'm not sure the word was even loud enough for him to hear.

His arms wrapped me up tight and all resistance fled. "Are you through fighting me?"

Like a ping pong ball. That's what I felt like. One minute on his side of the net, then whack and in a single sentence he's sent me rocketing back to my own.

I sighed and pulled away. Stood and wound my slightly iced hair into a knot so I could pull the cap over it. I buttoned my coat while he waited in silence. I cleared my throat to make sure the squeakiness was gone. "I have to keep fighting for myself. Whether it's against you, or the Minnows, or whatever tomorrow brings. I won't ever stop fighting. I'm just not made that way."

He took my arm and turned me toward him. With a hand on either side of my face and his thumbs under my jaw, he forced me to look up, meet his gaze. His eyes had darkened like a night sky. There was a wealth of thought and feeling there that I didn't dare try and decipher.

"If you run, from the compound, you will be foolishly putting your life at risk. I need you to bear with me for another week or two and things will get better. We'll get you moved somewhere that you can be outdoors whenever you like, safe and happy. You can have a life again."

"A week or two. Last I heard it was a day or two. What will it be next Gage, months? Years? No. Put me on a plane and send me to the Arctic, or Russia or somewhere ridiculously remote. I'll learn a new language, customs, get on in whatever way I have to. But don't expect me to sit here on my hands." I gripped his wrists and tried to pull his hands away.

Instead he slid them down until they were wrapped around my neck. "Do you have any idea what a frustrating woman you are? I'm in a constant battle with myself. Should I kiss you? Or just wring your fucking neck and be done with the aggravation called Cassandra?"

He ran his thumbs up and down the sides of my windpipe and for the tiniest of moments, it occurred to me that I should be afraid. But I wasn't.

"Then let me do something. Maybe I could help find Sydney or Dean. Let me help Kyle in the security room or on the computer with whatever it is he does. He's your techno-geek, I can help him. Anything, something. Christ, let me be laundry woman, or look after Buck, keep his stall clean, exercise him."

The thumbs that had felt just a little scary, were now caressing the line of my jaw, moving toward the soft

177

sensitive place below my ears. I'm sure I held my breath for a moment or two before I wrenched away.

"Look." I cleared my throat. "Let's get the elephant out in the open." I took a big gulp of air. "You want me, I want you. There's no need to keep making your point—yes, you know exactly how to push my buttons. Yes you can make me whimper like a needy trollop. No point going over and over the same ground." I swallowed hard and went on. "The sex in Vegas was over the top. You're the best I've ever had, or been had by. But that was Vegas. In the real world, I'm just not that kind of girl. I don't let my hormones overrule my head. So you can play your little games, lighting my body on fire and making me a little bit crazy but I'm not going to jump your bones. Period. So get over it and quit torturing us both."

"Hell of a speech."

I glared at him, then headed down the trail just as fast as I'd come up, driven by the smirk I'd seen on his face. I don't think he got the message.

Perhaps I could convince my heart that it didn't get a vote in the whole ugly mess. I may have to resort to Eve's offer of a sleeping pill tonight. Because the way I was going, I didn't think sleep was going to be an attainable goal without help.

And the kind of help Gage was offering was not going to happen.

He reached my side just as I found the doorknob in the fabric of the camouflage canvas he'd left slightly parted. We were both silent, hung coats, stripped off the boots and he stowed the weapon. I'd forgotten my hat. He plucked it off, grabbed a handful of hair and pulled me toward him.

Lowered his mouth until his lips were brushing mine and said softly, "There's a hell of a lot more than sex between us Cassandra." And then he was kissing me.

It wasn't the passion, fire, or demand for surrender I'd expected, admittedly wanted. Instead I was devastated by tenderness and my heart rose up my throat. Tears pooled, and when he stepped back, turned and walked away, they tracked silently down my face.

*

I found Lissa in the kitchen and helped her get supper set up. There were two crockpots on the sideboard, one contained thick, rich, chicken stew. When I lifted the other lid, the aroma of spicy chili permeated the air. We filled a beautiful willow basket with homemade buns and there were small lidded containers with everything from sour cream to shredded cheese and pickled jalapenos.

I removed warm, deep-sided plates and soup bowls from the oven and stacked them alongside the cutlery baskets on the table. I was curious about the first buffet style meal since I'd arrived here and asked.

Lissa waved a hand toward the hallway. "They're all working and who knows when they'll come out for food. I set it this way and anyone drifting out will follow their noses. By seven, if there's no action, I'll go in and roust them."

"That works?"

"Sometimes, or I fill bowls and take them in."

"What exactly are they working on?"

"Not my story to tell. Why don't you go in and ask

them? Come on." She touched my arm and lead the way.

Lissa put her hand on the wall at waist height, directly under one of the tiny night light fixtures and pushed. I heard a click and a panel swung open. She smiled over her shoulder and whispered, "Welcome to the inner sanctum. Go ahead."

I took a couple of steps forward and stopped. Did a slow visual sweep of a room that looked a little like the inside of a movie set. Walls were lined with flat screens and monitors. The desk-like counter running the circumference of the room, a dozen keyboards, plastic file boxes, several coffee cups coffee cups, and a couple of ceramic bulls? A huge table spread with maps filled the center of the room.

Gage, Quinn and Angie were seated in three of at least ten black leather executive chairs, Kyle occupied one of those cool wheelchairs like the cars that unfold to be monsters, *Transformers*. The chair was in a standing position and the man was vertical, closely studying a satellite map on one of the screens at shoulder level.

I went to his side, scanned the fancy piece of technology, then looked up, way up—who knew he was over six feet tall—into his smiling face. I couldn't help but grin. "Cool accessory."

"You're easily impressed." He winked.

"You don't know the half of it. What are you looking for?" I tipped my chin up at the map.

"Don't know yet."

"Oh, well, that must be fun. When will you know?"

"When I find it." His gaze narrowed as he studied the bottom left corner. "We've had more action than usual on the motion sensors. So we're trying to find a reason for it."

"What are you expecting to see?"

He turned his head and studied me for a minute. His fingers flew over a keyboard, then he pulled a tiny laser pointer out of his pocket. I followed the red dot as he pointed out the tiny blotches on the screen that represented wildlife. Then he clicked some keys and the map blinked. "There's a twenty minute update. Now look for the game again, see how far they've moved."

I searched, found some of the dots with ease, others, not so much. I felt Gage's presence when he came to stand beside me but I didn't waver from the task. Each time I found a new animal, Kyle made some kind of notation on the computer.

"Okay," I said, "I think that's all of them."

"Nice work." He glanced at Gage. "We can use her help. She just cut my tracking-slide time in half."

"Tracking-slide?"

He pointed to the screen on the left of the one I'd been studying. There was a series of dots, with lines between them. "Homemade term for searching movement patterns for something other than animals. Game rarely walks a straight a path."

"But humans follow game trails in the woods, not roads and walkways," I added.

He smiled. "True, but here," he worked the keyboard again, "look at the screen on the right. The dotted line in yellow, is a moose. The one in red, is a man. They're on the same path. Now check the dots because they represent twenty minute intervals."

I saw the difference immediately. "The human is obviously going somewhere while the moose is wandering along, grazing."

"Right. The moose was traveling at a quarter the speed the man was." Kyle added.

"How can you be sure it was a moose, not an elk, bear, deer, whatever?" Seemed a little over simplified to me.

"We have motion triggered cameras." The image on the right changed to a split screen of a moose, and a young man wearing summer clothes and a knap-sack. "We get the odd traveler passing through. Or in this case, drug smuggler."

"If you've got the cameras, why the need to track through satellite?"

Gage joined in. "Because not everything or everyone is obliging enough to walk past a camera." He changed the subject. "You want a dinner break Kyle? I can run this station with Cass while you go eat with your wife."

The chair made a humming sound while he lowered to a sitting position. "Thanks, I'll be back in an hour. Anybody else coming?" Neither Quinn, nor Angie looked up from their work, so Kyle wheeled out on his own.

Gage pulled a chair over beside me and sat down with the keyboard in his lap. He handed me a little pointer gismo and showed me how to use it. Pretty much, point and click on any thing that looked like it didn't belong to the landscape.

We worked in silence until I felt I'd finished the frame. "Done," I said. While I waited for him to change the picture for me, I glanced at the plotting map to the left. Most of the dots were in yellow, a few were red and there was one pink one.

"Ready." Was all he said to indicate that there was a new photo up for me to work on.

I stared at it for a minute, and frowning turned my attention to the man at my side. He'd been waiting, and smiled. "It's dark out. This one uses a new technology that is not quite night-vision, or heat-seeking. Start by scanning it for a while. Once your eyes adjust, you'll find it easy to read."

He was right. I soon settled in and started clicking dots into place. I barely noticed Angie and Quinn leaving and I lost track of time. Kyle returned with Lissa who said, "We'll take over while you two grab a bite."

Gage touched the back of my neck. "Come on, I'm starved." He turned his wrist to look at his watch then grinned at Kyle. "Must be good grub."

They both smiled, but neither said a word.

Quinn and Angie were in the kitchen when we got there. I hadn't seen them in hours.

"We were just coming to rescue you two, figured Kyle and Lissa were down for the night," said Angie. She looked at me and qualified. "They're still newlyweds."

Gage asked, "You two need to catch some sleep? Once I get some food I can go back in and stay until you're up."

"That works, thanks bro." They were rinsing their dishes and putting them in the dishwasher by the time we'd filled our bowls with chicken stew. They left us alone.

With one look at the hard back chairs beside the table, I gathered up my meal and made myself comfortable in a big armchair in the dimly lit living room. Gage followed and sat across from me.

He looked comfortable balancing the bowl in one hand and eating with the other. I felt a smile in my mind. Probably one of the things he learned in Special Ops training. Not that they'd have a class called how to eat standing up, but I'd bet they were taught to make themselves fit into any situation or culture. *I wonder...*

"Do you speak other languages?" I asked.

He nodded and kept eating—not quite shoveling his food but it was obvious the man was hungry.

We ate in silence. He polished off three bowls of stew and as many buns before leaning back to rest his head on the chair, stretch his legs out in front of him and close his eyes.

I followed suit. And promptly fell sound asleep.

When I woke up it was dark, something was tickling my cheek.

"Hey, sleepyhead, time to go to bed." Man o man that's a sexy voice to wake up to and his tender side was really hard to resist.

I struggled to sit up, found him crouched in front of me and realized I'd been asleep in the armchair. "No. I'll come and do the shift with you in the work-room. I just needed a cat-nap."

His chuckle vibrated through me. "Cass, it's four in the morning. My shift is done and I'm going to bed. Come on, I'll tuck you in first." He stood and held out his hand.

He tugged me to my feet, draped an arm around my shoulders and we walked to my room in companionable silence. At my bedroom door he turned me to face him. "You okay?"

I nodded because I was afraid to speak. If I opened my

mouth right now I was probably going to ask him to stay with me and that wouldn't be a good idea. I swallowed hard to get rid of those wrong words.

He wrapped me in his arms and held on for a minute. His breath in my ear and his whispered words, "I'll always have your back," nearly undid me.

Lucky for me, or maybe not, he opened my door and gave me a little push. "Go, get some more sleep." The door closed behind me. The nightlights were enough to help me find the bed. I pulled off my clothes and crawled under the quilt, hugging a pillow against me.

Chapter 14

Gage couldn't sleep. He pulled on sweatpants and paced the halls for a while then stared at the white cat when it appeared near Cass's room. "Piss on it," he muttered, walked past Merlin and closed the door with a soft click.

He woke up with a groan. He'd slept, fully dressed, on top of the covers with Cass snuggled into him, spoon-fashion, trusting and vulnerable. He wanted to bang his head against a wall and rail at his own stupidity. He couldn't afford to get wrapped up in her. She was a job. Period. He had to keep her safe, get her reunited with her family then walk away.

With a sexy little moan she shoved her gorgeous ass right into his morning hard on and he held his breath, heart pounding, sending all the blood intended for his brain, south. Hell. Special Forces hadn't prepared him for this. A strange woman? No problem. One he had genuine feelings for? Not.

He forced himself to think about the details of this mess he'd gotten himself into.

He'd been watching over her for so long, he was fucking invested. He'd become her personal shadow when she arrived at the ranch. Then with the motion sensor cameras installed, watched her every move. Like lurking in a blog or chat-room, feeling as if he was a part of her life somehow. And that's why he was too stupid to leave before she woke up.

The sudden tension in her muscles gave her away before her breathing did. He stayed very still, waited.

She took his hand and held it between her own. He pressed his lips to the soft skin where her neck curved into her shoulder. She made a sweet sound deep in her throat and lifted his hand to her mouth, nibbled on his fingers until he groaned and pulled away.

"Darlin, you're playing with fire." He swallowed hard. She was willing for Christ's sake. Yeah, but she wasn't quite awake. Hadn't exactly invited him to her bed. His thoughts teased him.

"Poor sport," she mumbled and he felt a laugh building in his chest.

He pulled her in tight and buried his face in her hair, inhaling her scent, wishing they could stay this way, easy and familiar. This was the woman he'd dreamed of waking up with, forever. But she'd be fully awake soon. And when she remembered the last forty-eight hours, her mood would likely be as shattered as the dinner plates.

"That was a hell of a mess I made the other night." Spooky how closely linked their thoughts were.

"It was." He kept his voice neutral, gave her shoulder a playful nip and waited for her to make the next move.

When she tipped her head to allow him more access, his teeth made a trail to the base of her ear. He worked his way around the edge, nibbling, tasting. His tongue slid toward the center and his hand across the soft skin of her belly.

*

My insides began to hum.

What the hell am I doing? Stop. Now.

I sat up fast, scooted my butt to the edge of the bed and bolted for the bathroom. Leaning both hands on the counter I stared at my image in the mirror. "Are you crazy?" I asked. I slid a hand over the ear he'd been devouring... wanted to cross my legs hard and whimper.

"Pathetic," I growled. "I'm flipping pathetic." And then I did something I'd only read about in romance novels. I took a cold shower. *Brrrr.* It worked. Took my mind off of my heated parts for a minute or two.

When I walked out of the bathroom wrapped in a big turquoise towel—just like the one at home—Gage was gone, and the bed was made.

I dressed and headed down the hall for breakfast—assuming it was morning. I'd come to realize that the lights behind all those outer walls of glass blocks were set at varied intensities, programmed to give the illusion of daylight. And so, with the light pouring through the glass, I believed it was morning and that was good enough for me.

The kitchen was empty. I rifled the cupboards until I found all I needed for a light breakfast of tea, toast and yogurt. I washed up my dishes by hand, something felt right about putting clean things back in the cupboard and wiping down all the counters even though I'd only used a small area myself. Perhaps being left alone, to fend for myself, gave me a sense of belonging. I shrugged. *Whatever.*

Merlin showed up and wound himself around my legs in happy figure eights. I crouched, gave him a good chin scratch, and his purring stepped up a decibel level. So simple to please some creatures. I ran my hand down the length of him and stood. *Time to go to work.*

Not if you're a cat.

Hmm.

When I touched the right spot to gain access to the tech-room, palpable anxiety poured out at me. Tension rode the entire group and not one of them bothered to acknowledge my presence.

I checked the monitors. One displayed odd squiggly lines, another had what appeared to be Asian symbols. And one sported a world map with colored dots on it.

"What's going on?" I heard my question but apparently no one else did. I touched Angie's shoulder . Her body jerked in surprise as she wheeled around in her chair and pulled tiny ear buds from her ears.

"Hey," she said stretching a leg out to kick Gage's chair. He looked around, saw me and frowned, said something that I couldn't hear but all the others responded, so I assumed he was on mic.

Lissa asked, "Can I get you some breakfast Cass?"

I shook my head no. "What's going on?"

They did a little group meeting of the eyes that was followed by barely perceptible nods. A shudder rolled up my spine.

Gage stood and motioned for me to sit in his chair. He spun me toward the screen, rested one hand on my shoulder and reached out with the other to click the mouse a couple of times. A three word email message appeared. 'NOT IN TROUBLE'

"Ok-ay"

He clicked through two more messages. 'NOT AT HOME' and 'NOT WITH HER'

Gage then explained. "The messages are blatant fakes. One of our rules for authenticity is to avoid threes."

I nodded. "This is different than the code using the AI bulls."

"Right. But on that note," he did more clicking, "here are the requests that we're trying to track. They mention both past and present bulls, which again, goes against code." The screen filled with some sort of hieroglyphics. "In several different languages."

"So from the outside, looking in, as an uneducated guess, I'd say someone is bluffing."

Angie grinned. "My thoughts exactly. The women and men are split down the middle."

I frowned. "The women are seeing it one way and the men another? I don't like that. It feels wrong." I regarded Angie's cheeky grin and added, "I know men are from mars, etc. But doesn't it add something to the puzzle anyway?"

Lissa spoke up. "Perhaps it was engineered to keep us busy trying to figure it out and take our attention away from something else."

"Intentional misdirection," I said.

In a smooth wave of action everyone turned to different work stations. With the clicking of keys, the pictures on all the screens and monitors changed.

Gage was leaning over me to work. I tried to slip out

of his chair but he kept me still with a hand on my shoulder. I protested. "You need to sit and work. Let me stand."

"You want to go through maps like yesterday?" His mouth was too close to my ear.

"Yes." I pushed against the counter so my chair would slide back into him, force him to move. He gave in, let me stand, and he sat. Then with total nonchalance, he took my hand, brought it to his mouth and ran his teeth across the knuckles.

My heart did a double thump and I felt like a fish on a hook, being reeled in. He released me before I could pull away.

I stared hard at the satellite photo, but saw nothing. No place to put a dot. No living creatures. "That's just wrong. There should be something."

"It's an anomaly, but not unheard of," Gage said as he moved to the next photo.

By the time we'd covered photos from a seven hour stretch and found nothing, everyone in the room was getting antsy again.

Angie, flipping through motion sensor photos, suddenly hooted. "Woo hoo! I've got it." Everyone gathered at her screen to look at the picture of a scrawny mountain lion. "Here's the hungry bugger that's run off all the game."

I understood. Remembered well. Commenting to Jared one day that I hadn't seen any deer on my daily rides for over a week, his face had blanched and he'd given me a lecture about cougars. From that day forward when a day went by that I didn't see wildlife, I kept close to the ranch. The wildcat in the picture that Angie had on her screen, did look thin and hungry. That would make him twice as dangerous, willing to take down anything he encountered.

I shuddered at the thought of Gage and I out there yesterday, paying little attention to our surroundings as we fought our emotional battle. Gage's thoughts may have been going the same direction. He wrapped an arm around my shoulders and drew my back against his front while we watched a series of pictures flash on Angie's screen. So right. Comfortable. He was beginning to feel like home.

Lissa spoke into the silence. "I'm going to start lunch. Should be ready in about an hour."

I pulled away from Gage and followed her, had to get away from the intensity. "Can I help?"

"Sure." She glanced over and her gaze narrowed. "You okay?"

"I think so. Not really sure though."

When we got to the kitchen, she asked, "What's wrong?"

"Nothing, everything. I'm scared, mad, stupid with feelings I don't understand."

Her smile grew. "Love's confusing if you pick at it. Just enjoy being together for now. It's sure making a difference to him." She laughed. "Funny how regular sex takes the edge off a man. Be like him Cass. Enjoy what you have."

My jaw dropped open. I was speechless. There's a good chance spit was running down my chin but I was incapable of movement. Half a dozen thoughts bounced around in my head, vying for attention. I wrestled one to the ground and held on to it.

"If he's having regular sex it isn't with me." I held my

hand out as though swearing a pledge. "I swear it's not with me. Not since Vegas."

Lissa frowned, "Well, that's just too amazing. Stupid really if you ask me. You're both adults and the chemistry between the two of you is scorching—or it feels that way from an observer's standpoint. Who knows how long you'll have together."

Flabbergasted was the best word I could think of to describe how I felt. Up until now, Lissa had struck me as a sweet, mind-her-own-business kind of woman, but in a matter of minutes she's rendered me speechless, twice. New ground for me. I heard a giggle and turned to find Angie coming across the room. I did a mental eye-roll. Great. They were going to tag-team me again.

Angie was the first to speak—of course, it was her turn. "Preaching again Lissa?"

Flashing yet another dimension of personality, she stuck out her tongue and grinned. "Can't help it. You know what born-agains are like."

Angie leaned a hip against the kitchen counter. "I'll give you the condensed version of her story so you'll understand when she's meddlesome like this. At the ripe old age of ten, she fell in love with Kyle—that was the first time her mother used him to occupy Lissa, so she could have a quickie with his dad." I'm sure I looked confused after this sentence because she added, "Can you say sidepiece? Her mom, doing his dad. Don't worry, it'll all make sense in a minute."

Lissa was at the fridge, pulling out food, piling it on the counter. I watched for a second, then picked up the carrots, and a knife. "Slice or dice?" I asked.

"Fine dice."

While I decimated the carrots, Angie continued, "The affair—one parent of each—lasted for years but while Kyle knew about it, Lissa was blissfully ignorant of anything but her own eye-crossing infatuation."

"Exaggeration Angie. Penance, you do the garlic and onion." Lissa handed her both and a tiny rubber tube.

Angie swung hard and hit the garlic against the counter with a resounding thunk, to dislodge the cloves. "Fact. You had no clue about the affair. Fact. You were infatuated. Okay, so your eyes weren't crossed." She dropped a clove into the tube and rubbed it between her palms. "Anyway, I promised the short version so, Kyle and Lissa finally hook up just before he heads off to the air force. While he's gone, she finds out about the affair her mother is having with his father, when *her* father files for divorce. She's devastated, her world is crumbling, she writes a letter to Kyle and he *stupidly* confesses that he's known about the affair for years."

Lissa handed her a knife and ordered, "Fine chop." Took my diced carrots and tossed them into a frying pan, handed me a couple of celery sticks and said, "Same."

Angie continued the story with a sigh. "Lissa was so messed up by all of the going's on that she turned on Kyle, called him deceitful like his dad, and she ran off to a culinary school in France of all places."

"Oh." I turned to Lissa. "Didn't someone tell me you were a physiotherapist?"

"She is. But before that she became a chef." She sighed. "Then walked away from a promising career because she found out Kyle's dad—you know, the villain of the story—had secretly financed her education. That was when she went to my mother, asked her to co-sign a loan at the bank and trained to become a physiotherapist."

"Wow," I said. "You've lucked into a life where you can use all your skills."

Angie looked like she wanted to give me a thump on the back of the head. "Sorry, just saying, things work out and all." I stopped short of wedging the other foot in up to my knee.

"Lissa had barely graduated—again—when Kyle had his accident. That's another whole story we won't get into." She scooped the garlic into a little bowl and started on the onion. "My mom had to bully her into working with Kyle and then it was him digging in his heels, said he wouldn't be a pity fuck."

"Hey!" Lissa held up a knife. "Watch your mouth while I have sharp tools at hand. We're not talking sex here, we're talking relationship."

Then of course, my foot slipped out of my mouth. "No you were talking about Gage and I having sex."

"But you said you're not. And that's what I'm trying to point out with Lissa's story. She didn't go with her feelings and trust Kyle. She fought the sex and the love and then he did and then years and years of good sex were wasted." She looked so triumphant that I couldn't help but laugh.

"Okay, I get the message. But we're nothing like Lissa and Kyle. We can't look forward to having an amazing future together."

Lissa held up her hand. "How do you know? And besides, who cares? How do you think I would've felt if

Kyle had died in that crash? The rest of my days would have been spent wishing I hadn't been such a ninny. I'd have missed out on feeling loved and cherished." She held her hand up when I was about to interrupt. "I get it. You're not buying into the loved and cherished part yet. But there's lots of argument for multiple orgasms too."

I heard a choking noise and the three of us spun around to see Quinn struggling to keep a straight face as he commented. "Now there's a hell of a sentence to arrive in the middle of. But I see lunch isn't on yet so I'll just go back to my computer for a while." He spun on his heel and disappeared while the three of us dissolved into a puddle of laughter.

*

Gage looked up when Quinn came back into the room wearing a grin. "What's so funny bro?"

"Ah, just something I overheard. Out of context I'm sure." He kept chuckling, shaking his head.

Kyle looked over with a quirked eyebrow. "Must've been good."

"Apparently you are." Quinn ran his hand down his face as though to wipe the smile away, but it didn't help. "I stumbled into girl talk in the kitchen and got my ears singed."

"Eavesdropping is so below you." Gage teased while wondering if he wanted to hear this.

"Our girls talking dirty?" Kyle shook his head. "Hard to believe."

"Hah," said Quinn. "Not just our girls, but your sweet

innocent—well apparently not so innocent—wife was doing the talking."

"Saying what?" Kyle looked comfortable until Quinn went on to tell them that Lissa had been commenting on the value of multiple orgasms and sounded like she was an authority on the subject.

"It's always the quiet guys." Quinn back slapped him. "Our hero."

Kyle smiled and shrugged. "Hey, you know what they say, you lose one sense, the others get stronger to compensate. Same goes with being dead from the waist down. Everything from there up is honed to near perfection."

The door opened and Eve stuck her head in. "Anybody up for a little exercise before lunch?"

Gage coughed. "Ah, maybe Kyle." And the laughter followed.

Chapter 15

Siting at the table to eat, I caught the glances back and forth between the men and I figured Quinn must've shared what he'd heard. And who knows how much he'd heard.

I shrugged it off because there were much more serious thoughts rumbling around in my head now that I'd learned about Lissa's background. These people were family, beyond DNA, with understanding and genuine caring for each other as their foundation.

"Where's Eve?"

"Exercise room."

"Want me to go get her?"

Angie shook her head. "Leave her be. She's been holed up in her lab for hours so it'll take her a while to work out the kinks. She'll come looking for food when she's ready."

Sipping on soup I'd helped prepare, I was finding it hard not to watch the interaction between Lissa and Kyle. With a look or the slightest of moves, they seemed to communicate everything from 'pass the salt' to 'I want you naked'. I saw the slightest flush run up her neck when she caught him staring at her mouth. When she winked at him, I turned my attention to Angie and Quinn, who also seemed to know each other's thoughts, but in a less intimate way. Not unusual I suppose, for siblings working so close together as adults. Interesting though, Gage didn't seem to have as tight a relationship with the two of them.

I felt disconnected from the entire group, as though I was floating around with my feet not quite touching the floor. Pushed and pulled in whatever direction the current went. Except when Gage touched me. Then I'd heat up like water in a microwave. Sexual attraction, or chemical reaction, bottom line, I didn't know him any better than I knew the others. And I had no choice but to trust the entire team to help me find Syd before I could disappear.

"Great soup Lissa." Gage's compliment interrupted my thoughts.

Angie piped up. "She had rookie sous chefs to work with and still pulled off perfection. Not bad for an old married broad."

Lissa was smiling. "Old? Hah. Kyle's the fossil of the house."

Quinn and Gage guffawed theatrically.

Kyle grinned and winked at her. "The boys here will be masters eventually. But all skills require regular practice."

"Nice shot," Angie muttered under her breath.

The banter between them reminded me they were all making the best of a bad situation. My bad situation. They were being held hostage because of my problems. They'd saved my life at least once already and I didn't deserve more than that.

*

I spent a quiet afternoon searching satellite photos for intruders besides the cougar, and conveniently, we were alone in the room when Gage enlarged a map, pointed out the compound, and had me track outward from there.

"Even knowing they're fake, I find it hard to believe those aren't real tree-tops I'm seeing. How on earth did you manage such detail?"

Gage was reading emails on the small desk monitor, but still answered me. "Photographs transferred to fabric. Hand painted over that, textured and shredded so that even snow will look natural. Same basic technology as printing on t-shirts. But kicked-up a notch or ten with special fabric and paint tough enough to survive the elements. In some places we used military style camo netting.

I used my little pointer. "This is the exit we used yesterday."

He glanced up. "Yep. Good to watch for the cat there because our scent is pretty fresh.."

"With only a fabric roof on the arena, the cougar could pick up Buck's scent. Heaven help us if *he* catches a whiff of a predator.

"Enlarge the bottom left of that frame by two hundred."

I clicked.

He pointed to the center. "There's the barn. Keep an eye on the area outwards from there. I'll pull up the security video on one of these other monitors so you can watch the horse as well. Use him as an early warning system. He gets edgy, we'll know something's up." He reached for my hand

and gave it a squeeze. "We'll keep him safe, Cass."

"Thanks." It was the best I could do with a lump in my throat and a guilty conscience gripping my insides. I forced myself to scan the wall screen, tracking the area for deadfall, cliff edges, anything that could be dangerous when I made a run for it on horseback. My leaving wouldn't affect Syd's safety. She was with Wesley so the Meyer's group would continue to search for her. Make sure she was safe.

I glanced at the monitor to my right, noted Buck was standing with his head over the stall door, apparently dozing. I switched my big screen to a new area and continued scanning for movement of game or humans.

When Kyle and Quinn came in, Gage pulled up emails on a wall screen. "You guys want to do a quick run over these, just in case something jumps out at you?"

Quinn groaned. "I hate email duty. Never any good pictures."

"Just one quick run through content for me. I've already done the standard searches."

The email's appeared, one at a time. I scanned each one while they did, hoping that I'd see something that would give me a clue. Right, like I'd know a clue when I saw one.

Ohmygod.

Words jumped off the page at me. It was a code that Syd and I used as kids.

My heart thumped against my ribs, and I must have made some kind of sound because Gage turned toward me. I stared hard at my screen, enlarged it and moved my cursor.

"See something?" he asked.

"Hmm?" I zoomed in, then without looking his way said, "guess it was nothing."

"What did you think it was?"

"Just a flicker, like light, probably a reflection when you were changing pages on your screen. Nothing there." I turned and smiled. "Kind of cool the way the adrenaline kicks in so easy though."

He smiled and an odd warmth ran through me, like recognition. I shook it off best I could, rolling my shoulders and tipping my head from side to side as though working out kinks.

"You need a break. Hit the hot-tub or take a hot shower to loosen up those muscles."

"Hmm, yeah. Sounds like an idea." I stood and stretched. "Back in a half hour or so."

"Want help?" he teased as I opened the door.

"Would your eyes cross if I said yes?" I scooted out before he could answer.

My heart nearly stopped when his hand landed on my shoulder and his breath in my ear. "Not as fast as yours would."

Gulp. Okay so my pulse went from zero to a hundred in less than two point three seconds. Fight fire with fire, I thought. "Think so?"

He grabbed my hand and dragged me through another one of those freaking doors that's invisible until you tap just the right place.

With a wall at my back and him against my front, I no longer had a brain. My head lolled to one side while his mouth did something magical to my throat, my neck, lingered at my ear, and then ... I think my eyes crossed.

Through a haze of the most delightful, unexpected, mini step-off-a-cliff orgasm, I could hear chuckling. *Don't care. Having trouble caring about anything.* The pressure of his thigh pressed against me in just the right place was causing the most exquisite aftershocks.

"Open your eyes."

I shook my head no.

"Look at me Maddy."

My eyelids parted and I was impressed to see more than my own nose. Really impressed to see that the bright blue eyes in front of me had no laughter in them.

"Want help in the shower now?"

"Um."

"Yes or no?"

Crap. There I was, up to my earlobes in afterglow, with him hard against me—go figure—and I wanted to say yes just as much as he needed to hear it. But I had to say no. *Arrggh.*

"You're a hard man to say no to."

He chuckled and stirred the heat by pressing the evidence against me in a way somehow provocative, instead of sleazy.

My circuits were about to fry. "The answer is a definite, although painfully regretted," I fought to keep my leg from climbing up to wrap around his waist, "no."

*

I bypassed the shower for a visit with the stair-climber. Not an easy feat considering the rubber legged state I was in but I needed something intense. I set the machine for a half hour workout but gave up after ten minutes of climbing while thinking about some of the things Gage and I had done in the shower in Vegas that first night. Damn skippy.

I switched to the weight machine where I'd need to count reps. Lost count twice in the middle of calling myself a barrage of nasty names that referred to my serious lack of control. At which point I began to fantasize about how hot the man was when I left him and what I could do about that.

My knees gave out, nearly slamming me in the chin as the stack of weights came down with a resounding crash. That's it. I give. I marched to my room, grabbed cargo pants, a thin silk turtleneck and oversized flannel shirt, plunked them down on the bathroom counter, locked the door and turned on the shower—full cold.

I walked into the spray face first and sucked in a gasp of air so hard I almost drowned myself. I bent double and spun around, coughing and choking and sputtering until the cold water hit me in the ass and I nearly drove my head through the tiled wall. *Crap.* I crumpled and lay on the floor in a pathetic heap, feebly pounding the tiles and cursing. I used every word I could recall from smarmy to outright foul—until I realized the whimpering sound was me crying. I don't cry. Ever. Well, I didn't used to, but that seems to have changed in the last day or two.

The man could not only make me forget I had a mind but he could make me cry. I had to get away. At that thought, I went from crying to outright balling and I was appalled by my own behavior.

By the time I wound down to hiccupping, and

snorting, I was ice cube cold. With considerable effort, I got the water shut off and dragged myself out of the shower.

The image I grimaced at in the mirror bore tiny square tile impressions down one side from cheekbone to hip. Stupid, stupid place to have a mini-breakdown. I sighed, wondering how long it would take for the pattern to fade.

On the upside, the cold water had prevented a swollen, ball-baby face. My sister Syd was a crier and I'd spent a lot of time mopping her up when she'd had to go on set after a crying jag. *Have to tell her how well this cold shower thing works.*

I don't know if a knife in the gut could have hurt any worse than the pain that shot through the middle of me when I remembered that I couldn't tell Syd anything right now. I took several long, deep breaths, and reminded myself I knew where she was and only had to get to her, so we could disappear together.

Her email message had looked like your garden variety scam in rambling sentences and paragraphs that essentially said. 'I'm a prince from Kenya, my family is being held hostage, you will become rich if you send me two thousand American dollars to pay the ransom for I will pay you back in diamonds worth ten times ...yada, yada...'

But what I saw, was a game Syd and I played as kids, making up secret messages we could leave in our overbearing mother's plain sight, by using the second word in each paragraph. The hidden message in today's email read, 'not, hostage, island, house'. The signature line was the clincher because she'd used our old code. We'd write our names backwards, and bookend them between our initials—which, before I'd changed my name, were both,

S.A.M.—forward and backwards. The email was from Samyen Dysmas, which I recognized instantly.

Now all I had to do was get to her. Simple stuff. Hah.

*

I poked my head into what I now thought of as the 'war-room'. Gage looked up and I fought a smile, gritted my teeth against the warmth that flowed through me.

"Hey, you real busy?"

"Nope. What can I do for you?" He wiggled his eyebrows comically.

"I'd like to ride Buck again today." I left it at that, waited.

He glanced at his watch. "Give me an hour."

"I'll be in the kitchen pilfering treats when you're ready."

And I was. My pockets filled with apples and carrots I'd stolen from the fridge. Well, not exactly stolen as Lissa *had* said to help myself. I'm just not sure she meant—go ahead and take five pounds of carrots for the horse. I'd cut up 6 apples as well, and put them in little baggies so they'd slide into the gazillion pockets of my pants. The carrots, fit neatly in the leg-side pockets.

Almonds from the big jar on the counter were squirreled away in various pockets as well. My shirt hung over my middle so the bulging pockets wouldn't be too obvious to the casual observer.

I was just grabbing two bottles of Gatorade from the fridge when Gage came to find me.

He raised an eyebrow and I responded with a shrug.

"Eve's been going on about hydration and electrolytes, figured I'd keep her happy."

"It's her job to fuss over our health." He was staring at my bulging pockets. "And yours to fill that spoiled horse with treats.

I glanced up at him. "You don't miss much."

"You weren't quite so lumpy before."

He chose a much shorter route to the arena today, and I was surprised to find Buck wandering loose instead of in his stall. Gage explained that it was because of the cougar. If by some remote chance the hungry cat got in here, at least the horse wouldn't be cornered in his stall. He'd be able to look out for himself until help arrived.

I nodded—impressed by his concern—pulled out a carrot, and broke it in half. Buck's head came up sharply, and he headed right for me. I fed him bites as I walked toward his stall and he followed. Gage opened the tack room door, brought me a halter and lead-rope, as well as the bridle. Then stayed with me as I haltered the horse and hooked the rope through the ring on the wall outside his stall.

Continuing to be helpful, he pulled the camo blanket off as soon as I had it unfastened, passed me brushes as I groomed. When I was ready for it, he retrieved the saddle and set it on the felt pad. From the off-side he passed the cinch underneath.

Sending a frosty glare across the suede seat of the saddle I snapped. "You gonna ride him for me too?"

He stepped back and held his hands in the air as though I'd just jerked a red paisley bandana up under my eyes and snarled, give me your money. "Sorry. Backing-off now." He wheeled and went into the office beside the tack room.

I let out a tense breath and rolled my head to loosen knotted neck muscles. I switched the halter for the bridle, snugged the cinch a little more and climbed aboard. Buck was eager to please once he knew I had treats and boredom probably played a part in his responsiveness as well. We went through a pretty light workout, walked, jogged and loped a couple of times each direction of the arena. I should have been loping for endless laps and then working through a couple of reining patterns. Fortunately nobody knew that but me.

Gage hadn't so much as peeked out at us, although I'm sure he watched the video feed. So when I packed the saddle back to the tack-room, I peeked into the office and said to his back, "Just gonna rub him down for a bit, then we can go back up." I was surprised that he never even moved. I looked a little closer and saw he had ear buds in place. My heart gave a little pitter-patter and I backed away.

Maybe now, not later? My plan had been to stash the food and sneak back but…

I scurried to brush the horse off, slip on the camouflage blanket and get all the buckles and snaps properly fastened in spite of my shaking fingers. I slid the bridle off so I could put his halter on. Slung the lead-rope over his neck, slipped the bridle back over his ears while my heart pounded hard against my ribs. Did I have the balls to close that door on Gage again?

And what if this was a set up and there was some kind of alarm in place this time. I went to the doorway and looked in again. Gage's attention was glued to the computer screen, his fingers flying over the keys. I closed my eyes against the tears that were pooling, tried to blink them away.

I have to do this.

I didn't want to. But I had to. *If I stand here any longer I'm going to either hyperventilate or do something that will make him turn around.*

I closed the door, backed away slowly until I reached Buck. I wiped my eyes with the backs of my hands and forced myself to do what I had to do. I swung aboard, spun him around and dug my heels into his sides. We skimmed the wall, I hit the button and the panel swung open.

Chapter 16

Bent low over Buck's neck, I rocketed into the forest with my heart pounding as hard as his hooves, longing to close my eyes but didn't dare. I had to find my way to the trail I'd studied on the satellite map. Needed to keep my wits about me while urging the horse to maintain a fast pace.

Forest flashed by, branches whipped and stung. The smell of pine was sharp and cold air bit at my skin. Frost sparkled around us. With reins and a proper bit for control, I was able to bring Buck down from the initial dead run to an easy lope for a mile or so, then a jog.

When I finally eased him to a stop, I slid to the ground slipped the bridle off and used the rope to lead him at a walk until we both got our breath back and he'd cooled down.

He nudged my arm and I reached into my pocket for one of the last peppermints.

He lipped it off my palm as I muttered to myself that running away from a safe place was idiotic. Like one of those too stupid to live bimbos in horror flicks.

I shook off the thought and got on with checking

Buck, making sure the leg straps on the blanket hadn't rubbed on him during the gallop. He was fine, no marks.

After putting his bridle back on, I remounted and prodded him to continue along the forest trail, knowing there was every chance that they'd send the Steed up after me. I checked my compass, took a swallow of Gatorade and tried not to think about what I was leaving behind.

*

The roar of blinding fury inside Gage's head could probably be heard in Kansas. And then it burst loose.

"Mother-Fuckers. You set me up!" His gaze tore through the group blocking the doorway. "All of you."

It took every ounce of control he could muster to stand there immobile while what he wanted more than breath was to plow through them and go after Cass. Barring that, he'd gladly smash his fists through every lying monitor in the room.

"Gage." Eve's voice was smooth, low, and her hand was tucked behind her back.

He got in her face and growled. "Don't, fucking talk to me. You fucking dare to spike me you'd better put me in a cage before I wake up."

He looked into each and every face. People he trusted, family. He'd go to the wall for any one of them. "Fuck. Me." He stormed right through the human barricade, and all the way over to stand at the open panel where daylight flooded in. Where she'd ridden out while they'd distracted him with an emergency call, and fed him footage from her earlier ride.

She was out there alone. Great, they'd implanted her with a tracking device the first time they'd knocked her out, and the horse had one as well. Fucking good for nothing but retrieving her body.

Not a fucking thing he could do about any of it now. He slammed a fist into the rubber- padded post of the doorway, heard Eve's sucked-in breath behind him and whirled on her. "Go. Away."

She held up the syringe. "You have a couple of options here big brother. I can stab you with this now, or, you can go pound on a bag in the weight room for a while. Third option, I can get the tranq gun and dart you from a safe distance. And for the record? You slam that hand into the wall again, I'll be damned if *I'm* gonna fix it."

"Talkin' pretty tough for a hundred pounds of nothing but spit and red hair."

"Hair color's the important part." Her voice softened. "Please, Gage. Go upstairs."

He felt self-control edging into place, surrounding the rage. Attempting to assess the situation, he looked past Eve to the group of people he'd loved forever. Thought about the woman he'd only loved for a little while. Knew his life would never be the same, no matter how it all unfolded. Things would always be different because they hadn't trusted him to choose.

He sucked in a breath and didn't allow his shoulders to sag, marched past them. He'd beat the shit out of a bag or two. Regroup. Plan. Chances were they'd all be smart enough to keep their distance at least for a while.

*

Gage walked out of the bathroom, still rubbing his wet hair with a towel. He pulled on clean clothes and checked his watch. It had taken him sixty-five minutes to get his shit together. He should be embarrassed by the time he'd wasted on useless emotion but Cass did that to him. Or rather, he heaved a sigh, he did that to himself when she was involved and it had to stop. She was a mission. Period. He used his fingers to comb his hair as he strode off to meet the others.

They all looked up when he entered the tech room. His jaw clenched, then he forced it to relax. He let go of the anger and it must have showed on his face.

The immediate looks of relief were telling. He'd bet they'd hated going around him, tricking him.

"You made a team decision for the good of the mission. No sweat. Now, bring me up to speed. Leave out nothing, or I won't be held accountable."

Kyle nodded toward the screen on his left. "There's the email that set her off. Just happened I was turned toward her when it first came up on screen. Watching her eyes, I believe I saw recognition, then concentration as her gaze hopped down the page. You heard her indrawn breath, asked her about it and she claimed she'd seen movement on the other screen."

"And I bought it."

"No reason not to, unless you'd witnessed her initial reaction and what she'd focused on. She covered with a believable excuse."

Gage maintained a bland expression. "Why did you decide to leave me out of the loop."

"You two left right after that so there was nothing I

could say without her knowing. Quinn and I studied the email, put it through the code program and only got back what the two of us had already seen."

"Which was?"

Kyle used the laser pointer to show him. "Their names. The repeated letters jumped out. A fairly simple code."

Angie added. "Kind of a kid thing I'd say. And if you follow that logic, and look at the first and last words of sentences and paragraphs, there were a hundred different possibilities." She shrugged. "So we decided to give her a little rope."

Gage understood their strategy, even though he'd have handled it much differently.

Eve spoke up. "We need to find Wesley and Sydney before the Minnows do. And we believe Cass can lead us to them."

"If she survives." Gage had to add. He studied the rest of the wall screens where he saw the pink dots he assumed showed Cass's route so far. He pointed at the map closest to him and said to Kyle, "Cut the zoom here in half."

Quinn came to stand behind him. "What are you seeing bro?"

"She studied these. Said she was looking for the cougar. What the hell did she really see? Move east about twenty miles and zoom back. No, wait, pull up the history instead. Show me everything she did, yesterday and today." Gage took the coffee cup Lissa held out, inhaled the aroma.

Kyle's fingers flew over the keys. "We did that already and saw nothing specific. Seemed she was just looking at the trail she eventually followed. But maybe something will jump out at you. I'll set the images to thirty-second intervals."

Gage scanned each frame as it came up, noted she'd zoomed in and out a couple of times. The wall clock counted off the seconds.

Relief washed through him when he saw where she was headed, and for just a fleeting moment he considered not sharing. He slapped back the thought, glanced around at all the computer monitors. "I need a file."

Eve clicked keys. "I'm open here."

Gage rattled off a bunch of numbers and after Eve entered them, and passed him the keyboard, he sent photos from the file to the wall screens.

"This is her friend Delia. She works fire-watch in the summer months, right here." He pointed to a second screen and zoomed in to a cottage perched on the mountain top. "Cass spent a week there last August, and if I'm right, that's where she's headed now."

"Hmmm. Even a pen for the horse. That works."

With minimal discussion, they split up, worked communications, maps, direction and timing. Phone conversations were in code and emails likewise.

Gage shut down the rising fears and drew on years of training and discipline. He'd track Cass's progress with GPS while utilizing satellite snap shots to watch for Minnows.

*

The air grew colder, snapped at my cheeks and burned the insides of my nostrils. Nightfall hovered, with blackness impatient to pounce while I scrambled to make a place to curl up and sleep. I burrowed under a pile of deadfall, scraped dead pine needles and leaves in around me.

I'd considered taking the blanket off Buck to use for myself but didn't dare. He'd heated up and broken sweat under it a couple of times. He'd lose too much body heat if I uncovered him now. So I made do. He was my only means of transportation. I had to keep him healthy. Bad enough that he had little to eat. We'd shared the carrots and half the apples so far. Now he'd have to make do, nibbling what grass he could reach from where I'd tied him. With the blanket on he'd need less fuel to keep warm, plus, the canvas would be good for initial protection if the cougar happened by.

Unable to bring Annie Oakley with me for protection, I had to make do with the paring knife I'd used to cut the apples, then stuffed in my pocket.

I'd grown more comfortable with my decision to run. The plan was solid. I knew where I was going, but the niggle of worry about how easily I'd gotten away had grown claws.

Acknowledging that Gage had turned his back and let me go was hard, left an emptiness in my gut that I had to ignore because I couldn't let self-pity interfere, distract me from my mission. It would take another day at least to get to the Lookout. I just hoped there'd be no more surprises waiting for me.

*

The night I spent burrowed under the deadfall was

good incentive to make it to the cabin the next day. I'd woken half-frozen, with muscles cramped, and my stomach inside out hungry. I drank half the second bottle of Gatorade to see if I could get my system up and running. Talked myself out of staying under the pile of broken trunks and branches, and going back to sleep, and split a baggie of apples with Buck. Once he was done munching, I slipped the bit in his mouth and the headstall over his ears, looped the lead-rope around his neck and tied it. Pretty certain I was too stiff to swing up, I dragged him alongside a stump and clambered onboard like a greenhorn.

We trudged on for several hours, the horse no more enthusiastic than I, but there was a desperation growing in me that thankfully drove me on. Whenever we came upon grass, standing dry as it was, or water, I stopped Buck and let him have his fill. By the time the sun was straight up—well as straight up as it gets this time of year which is actually a fair distance to the south, I spotted the trail that traversed the side of the mountain to the lookout. I thought about stopping to rest before tackling the long climb but decided to just get on with it. Go as far as I could before resting. Otherwise, I'd not get started at all.

About halfway up the switchbacks, Buck began to strain under me. I slid off and led the way on foot until the screaming fire in my leg muscles forced me to stop. Refusing to give in to the pain, I tied the reins to the lead rope, slipped it through the d-ring of the blanket so it lay across the horse's top-line, and wrapped it around my left wrist. If I fell, he'd have to stop. I braided his tail, twisted the end into a knot, forced my right hand into the woven hair and hung on.

When I chirped, and urged Buck to move, he put his head down low, and plodded forward while I coached. "One step at a time, pal, one step at a time."

Every now and again, he'd stop, and rest. I'd catch my breath too. I contemplated sharing the last handful of apple pieces but decided they'd be better as a reward when we reached the top. If we ever reached the top. I grew to hate switchbacks because each time we reached the turn and I'd feel like celebrating, two steps later there was a new stretch upward in front of us.

My thoughts drifted to Gage. To what I'd left behind. From the minute I met the guy, I was comfortable with him, as though I'd known him for years. Yet, he constantly surprised me. He was a good man, and I had no business wishing he could be more than the proverbial ship in the night. He had a big happy family and a job that made a difference in the world. He was an all round good guy, so much more than eye candy. The perfect illustration of a real man. If I could have kept him *and* rescued my sister, my fate would have been sealed.

Dragging behind Buck now, struggling to keep my feet under me, my quads and shins burned, my knees and ankles hummed, plus the fire inside my boots meant blisters. I'd glued my focus to the horse's butt for so long that when he stopped, I just draped my left arm over the top of his ass, rested my face on his hip and let my whole body sag against him for a few minutes. Horse-scented steam wafted from under the blanket.

When he slouched a hip to rest, I lifted my head and was too exhausted to be surprised or elated by the sight of the quaint little cabin.

On auto-pilot, I freed my hand from his tail, led him around the cabin, past the outhouse, and into the corral beside the lean-to. Sliding rails into place, I pulled his bridle, then rummaged in the small storage area for supplies.

Lucky for Buck, I found both hay and grain. Scattering some hay on the ground, I headed for the cabin with a water bucket.

Hopefully the luck held, and not too many hikers and hunters had been by, so there'd be water, food and fuel.

If I hadn't been so bone weary, hadn't wanted so badly to just I lie down and shut down I probably would have grinned at the sight inside the door—about a dozen collapsible containers full of water, three propane tanks plus two shelves stacked with tinned food and juice.

I popped the top off a can of vegetable juiced and forced myself to sip slowly while I got water for Buck. Once he'd been tended to, I nibbled on cold beans, put soup on the stove to warm, and pulled a sleeping bag from a clear plastic bin on the bed.

Only then did I go to the table in the corner, where I found the note I'd expected—held in place by two bright blue ceramic coffee mugs and a fat red candle with gold sparkles that looked like a Christmas leftover.

The note read, 'Welcome. Take what you need, replace what you can and leave something for the next tired traveler.'

Tears welled but I blinked them away. No time to be sentimental. Instead I went to the lone cupboard and found mason jars containing staples, and other goodies. I couldn't resist. I opened a jar of homemade beef jerky and the rich punch of teriyaki aroma nearly took me out at the knees. I gnawed on a strip, squeezed the rest into the empty apple baggies and stuffed them back in my pockets.

With nutrition and hydration already sharpening my dulled wits, I studied the food tins and planned what I'd take with me tomorrow. Heavy on the protein and liquids. Had to keep my weary muscles fed. Ready for whatever came next. With that in mind, I drank a full cup of water, then opened another juice.

It was getting dark by the time I'd finished my soup and gone out to check on Buck. I topped his water and gave him a big armful of hay with some oats sprinkled over it, glad to see he seemed no worse for wear.

Heading back inside, I was ready to make my next move. I'd given myself a couple of hours. Maybe stupid but I'd needed the time to eat and recover. Now I was ready to find out whether I had any shot at help from Delia—and a ride out of here—or if I would be on my own, on horseback again tomorrow. I refused to even think about the man, the family I'd run from. My only goal, the only thing that mattered was getting to my sister before the Minnows did.

I lit the fat red candle, went to the wooden trunk in the opposite corner, said a short prayer, really short as in, 'Please God' and lifted the lid, releasing a stale mustiness. My heart beat erratically as I wrapped both hands around a heavy metal box, heaved it out, and set it on the floor.

Kneeling, I unlatched the lid and—glory hallelujah. The radio was there, just as it had been when I'd visited Delia in the summer. And her radio handle was on the side, felt pen on adhesive tape. Thank the heavens above, she'd shown me how to work it by cranking a handle.

Within minutes, I had the radio up and running but Delia didn't respond to my call out. Afraid my location could be tracked if I stayed on the channel too long, I sent a simple message I could follow up on, in the morning.

"Important message. Delta -3-4-7-Fox. Blue mug. Red candle. Note. Morning. That's. Delta-3-4-7-Fox."

I set the radio back in it's box, crawled into the sleeping bag, and fell into blissful oblivion.

When my eyes popped open to inky blackness hours later, I caught myself wishing I could hear Gage breathing beside me, and gave myself a mental head slap. The guy had held me prisoner. Drugged me. Yeah, I thought, but in the interest of my safety. Everything he'd done fell into the category of good intensions. Plus, he acted like he genuinely cared about me and my family.

Still, I didn't regret not telling him about Syd's message, that she was at the cottage we'd secretly bought years ago when we were getting tired of being tabloid fodder. We'd needed a place to hide then, to just be ourselves. I hadn't been there in years though. Neither had Syd.

We'd laughingly called it the island mansion but in fact, it had only one more room than this cabin. The one room being critical though as it was a bathroom, complete with a soaker tub. Tucked away on a hillside on Mayne Island, not far from Vancouver, a few of hours west of here.

I smiled in the darkness, to make myself believe that this was the day I would find Syd and everything would change.

.

Chapter 17

Dawn had begun to light the sky when I made the dash across frozen ground to the outhouse, dropped my drawers and swallowed a scream when frigid air sunk its teeth into my naked behind.

Buck nickered a greeting from his pen as I stepped out of the tiny wooden building. I tossed him some more hay and banged his water bucket against the ground to break away the lump of ice on the bottom then scurried to the cabin and back, getting him fresh water before dealing with the radio.

After cranking it up, I put out one call to Delia, waited a full minute, then shut it down. It was early yet, so I boiled water for coffee, added a handful of grounds and left it to simmer, shrugging at my own ignorance of this sort of thing. I opened another can of beans, and put them on the stove to warm.

When I tried the radio again, I nearly squealed like a girl when Delia's was the voice that answered. I didn't do small talk, just repeated the message I'd rehearsed. "blue mugs, red candle, note, scared." I was pretty certain Dee could put the pieces together.

Her answer came back within seconds. "Gone out. Call back in two."

Yes. I shut down the radio and carefully stowed it back in the trunk. She hadn't asked questions, just responded in single words, enunciated carefully. I assumed she meant she'd be here in two hours.

I set my breakfast on the table, sat down and ate although my stomach said it was still full from last night's meal. When I dumped sugar into the coffee and stirred, I had to wait for the grounds to settle again—lesson learned. Impatient, I sipped from the top, straining coffee through my teeth and could almost feel individual brain cells sitting up and saying good morning.

After heating water in the soup pot, I washed my dishes, wiped down the table, counters, and stove. Knowing rodents were enough trouble without unnecessary encouragement, I gave the floor a thorough sweeping then took the sleeping bag outside to give it a vigorous shake before sealing it up the way I'd found it.

Buck was next. I puled off the blanket and gave him a good brushing. Once I was done, I leaned my forehead against his, and hooked my hands over his neck. "You're gonna have to find your own way home this time pal."

Thinking about the journey in front of him, I scooped him some more oats. Dumped them in the water bucket that was still about a third full.

"Extra groceries and a good way to get more water into you." I explained. It was quite true that little thing about leading a horse to water. However, mix water with oats and it's a pretty good bet you can make him ingest it, thirsty or not. And as much as I hated to think about it, left to his own devices here on a strange mountain, he might not find water for a day or two. There wasn't even any moisture in the summer-dried grasses he'd find to graze.

Oh god, how can I do this? He's innocent, saved me, packed me here...

I whirled around and went to the shed. Dragged out the trash bin the oats were stored in, and used the scoop to empty them into an old sack. Setting the bin below the edge of the porch, I dragged a plastic water jug out and opened the spigot so it ran into the container. When it was empty, I repeated the exercise. The third, I put in place but didn't open. I figured if worse came to worse and Buck did stay around, and did run out of water, he'd mess with the spigot until it either opened or broke off. Back at the ranch he'd been known to turn on taps and open latches if they didn't have safety snaps on them so I didn't doubt his dexterity.

I felt a little better now, knowing that if he was in trouble, and came back here, he'd at least have water. Horses could go a long time without food, but require about ten gallons of water a day. If he didn't show up at the ranch, I'd make sure that someone came up here to look for him. I ignored the little voice in my head pointing out that the water was going to freeze tonight and be useless to him.

Halfway back to the cabin, I was startled when the mountaintop silence was broken by the sound of a revving engine. I scooted behind the shed and waited. It might not be Dee. And if it wasn't, I was going straight down this mountain. On foot.

But I had nothing with me. *Shit.*

Listening intently, I decided that the vehicle was laboring up the mountain from the opposite side I'd approached from. I sprinted to the cabin, grabbed a big knife, stuffed my pockets with the jerky, a can of beans and the two cans of cola I'd resisted the night before. I was about to run out the door when I doubled back and scooped up the stove lighter. Fire could save a life just as easily as take one.

I shot out the door and over the side of the switchback trail. Stopped two levels down near a turn, and snuggled into some brush at the base of a tree, my golden-brown clothing would be decent camouflage among the dried leaves, grasses and dirt. I concentrated on slowing my breathing while I waited. It calmed me, helped me feel ready for whatever I'd have to do next.

I could no longer hear any engine noise. Was it because I was over the edge and down the hill? I contemplated the possibilities. Dee would have been approaching from that direction. If it was her, I'd look like an idiot cringing under this tree. But, what if it wasn't?

A huge crashing noise decimated the quiet, ended my thoughts, forced me to look up just in time to see Buck come barreling over the edge of the hill, drop to his haunches and ride his hocks down the vertical slope until he hooked to the left and disappeared from sight. Then the roar of an engine swung my attention back up the hill and—

Holy crap.

A man on a motorcycle catapulted over the edge. It might have been what they call a dirt bike, but the guy flew it like a plane. Sailed right off the first ridge, missed the next, and making a one point landing on the front wheel, sent the pilot cartwheeling through the air, dropping another level or two before landing in a heap with a gut-curdling thud.

My stomach lurched into the back of my throat just before I heard the bellow from above.

"YO, JACK!"

A guy dressed in black, came down the mountainside, jumping and sliding his way to his fallen partner, passed about twenty feet away from where I was hidden and I silently thanked whatever god had convinced me to choose this spot. Just before he reached what looked to me like a dead guy, I scooted from my hiding place, eased further to the side and out of his line of sight while working my way back up the hill. There was a chance that Jack had just demolished their only transportation. But there was equal or better chance, figuring in that they wanted to take me with them, that there was a second bike.

I circled around until I was behind the privy, and could see a motorcycle parked near the cabin. Now that, I thought, is something I know absolutely nothing about. Did I dare to try and start it? There must be a key or something, and I was sure I'd heard somewhere that the gas pedal and brake are operated within the handlebars... somehow. But I didn't want to set sail like that Jack fellow had. Cripes, I've just seen a guy die, probably, and I'm not feeling anything but panic for myself.

"Pssst."

Huh?

"Pssst ... Cass."

Holy shit. Delia. I swung around, my eyes searching until I saw a fingers stick out the top edge of the outhouse where air holes, in the shape of stars, had been cut out of the wood.

She was in the privy. "Dee."

"What happened?"

"One guy went over the edge on his bike and crashed ugly, the other one's gone down on foot. We've only got a few minutes to get away."

The door creaked as she slipped out. "I've got an ATV hidden back there." She used her thumb to point over her shoulder. "You want it or the bike?"

"ATV, I've never been on a bike."

"Straight line, about a hundred feet. Follow the trail, I'll catch up."

I took off one way, she ran the other. I threw my leg over and cranked the engine as soon as I heard the motorcycle start up. Turning the machine, I headed down the trail, praying she was right behind me. I couldn't hear anything but the motor I was virtually sitting on.

When the dirt track swung sharply to the left, I had a chance to glance back and relief nearly overwhelmed me when I saw Delia on the motorcycle. I chanced a big fat fist pump but clamped my lips on a loud wooo hooo!

The trail widened so I waved at Delia to come past me and lead the way. She slowed down as she pulled alongside and with a grin on her face yelled, "You got some explaining to do woman!"

I nodded and smiled, thought better of an eye-roll— we were probably going about as fast as a person dared on a mountain trail and I needed to keep my eyes on the job. Not that we were on the edge lookin' over, but it was still a steep rocky path in the middle of nowhere.

We traveled in line for close to an hour, I'd guess, before we reached a clearing where Dee came to a stop and hopped off the bike. "My truck's in there." She pointed.

I saw nothing and watched in awe as she grabbed a rope that was tied to the back side of a tree and pulled, hard, letting her whole body-weight hang against the rope. A branch and moss covered net raised up in the air and off of her shiny blue truck.

"Holy Hanna. Nice trick."

She tied off the rope, slid into the driver's seat, swung the truck around beside me, jumped out and slid a loading ramp from the cargo bed. I stood back and watched like a useless idiot as she drove the four-wheeler, then the motor-cycle up into the truck, closed the tailgate, hopped in the cab, backed the truck under the camo-net, jumped out, lowered it over the bikes and cut it loose from the pulley hidden in the tree branches. I was so impressed by her skill and smooth moves that I stayed rooted to the spot for a second or two after she waved at me to get in.

"Ready to rock," she said.

I clambered into the pickup and we were pulling away before I could even get the words out. "You're freaking amazing."

Her grin was filled with excitement. Green eyes sparkled and white teeth flashed, highlighting her almond skin. Little bits of kinky strawberry blonde hair stuck out the sides of a brown wool cap. She worked the stick shift like she'd been born with it in her hand.

"Practice makes perfect."

"Why in hell would you practice a quick getaway like that?"

"I work fire-watch, alone, from the top of this mountain. Someday, a fire could make me run for my life."

She gestured toward the back of the truck with a tip of her head. "High-tech camo-net's made out of fire resistant material, the branches and stuff are coated with retardant."

"Wow. Practice or not. Just wow. That was damned impressive work. You saved my life, Dee. Thanks."

She shrugged, "You'd do the same for me."

"Sydney's in trouble."

"So are you. Who were those guys up at the cabin?"

"Good question."

"That's what I thought. How about an answer seeing as I'm up to my neck in this now." She spared me a quick glance while we careened down the barely visible mountain track. "Is it still about searching for your Dad's killers? And who was the guy who called me?"

"I don't know. I just sent out a message to tell you I'd be on the radio in the morning. By the way, nice pick up on the clues, you didn't even hesitate."

She glanced out her side window for a sec, then back at me before she returned her focus to the path in front of us. "I got the message last night when you put it out. What I was asking about was the guy who called the day before."

I frowned. "I was in the bush, on horseback. No clue--" Shit. "What time of day?"

"Late afternoon."

"What did he say?"

"That you were in trouble, could be headed for the Lookout, asked if there was a radio there. Told me I might be under surveillance and to be extra careful."

"So he knew where I was going, who I'd call. Means he must be tracking us now." And that should piss me off. But instead it gave me a ridiculous sense of warm.

229

"He said he'd try to watch over us but couldn't guarantee. Told me to keep my head up and try not to get followed. I guess I blew that." She muscled the truck around a sharp turn and down a nasty drop onto a dirt road.

"You were followed?" Of course I did the stupid thing and looked behind us.

"Those two guys on the bikes. I assume they belong to the grey pickup that passed me halfway between here and home. They must have figured out where I was headed and jumped in front of me. Good thing they parked at the trailhead while I drove past to my secret back-route."

I was beginning to realize just how lucky I'd been to have all the little things come together.

"Thank the gods of nature that Buck didn't like those guys and busted through the fence."

Dee swung a look at me. "One guy was in the pen trying to catch him. I suspect that's how they planned to get you out of hiding."

I felt a little bit ill knowing that it would have worked. Now I had to wonder if they actually knew me that well, or were making assumptions about silly women and their horses.

"He'll be fine Cass."

Yeah, I thought, the way he was moving, chances were he'd be halfway home by now. I shook off the things that didn't matter right now. "So, do we have a plan Dee?"

Her eyebrows shot up. "I was hoping you had one. Mine ends about a half hour from now when we make it to the highway."

"Mayne."

She swung around to stare at me. "The freaking East

Coast? For real?"

The truck lurched through a big pot hole. "You wanna watch where we're going?"

She returned her attention to the road. "You sure you need to go that far? I know somewhere you could be safe, of course I don't know what you're running from but I think it would be good place to hide. Pretty secluded and no hunters around, this time of year. One's fully set with wind and solar power so no smoke to give you away. We'd have to stock up on food because once the snow comes it will be inaccessible for about three or four months-"

She was babbling. In a corner of my mind, a note was shoved into a file. "Not the east coast. It's in the Pacific. One of the Gulf Islands just off the coast near Vancouver."

She deflated instantly. "Oh. Well. That's much easier to get to."

"Just a few hours, right?" I was hoping I wasn't wrong about how far away we were. My mind was a little muddled by the adrenaline hangover.

Delia laughed, "With our wheels on the ground, we're still a bumpy thirty minutes to the highway, then four hours to Vancouver. From there you choose, ferry-boat, water-taxi or chartered float plane. Of course, if we're staying off the radar, we'd be better to rent ourselves a boat but we'd have to use cash, no traceable plastic and wear disguises too. This could be fun."

Tension drained and I sank back against the seat. "Thanks."

She looked over in question.

"For taking this mess from panic to adventure. I'm sure glad you're here."

"Okay, good. Now," She tipped her head to indicate the little storage area behind the seat. "How about getting us some coffee and a snack while you're explaining what the hell I've gotten in to."

Reaching for the thermos and insulated tote bag, I remembered the food I had stashed in my pockets. I pulled out the can of beans and held it up. "I brought rations too."

"Yuk, I hate those things."

"Then why the stash in the cabin?"

"Visitors, wayward hikers and hunters. Everyone but me seems to like them—good protein and all."

I showed her the jerky and smiled. "This was my first choice for protein."

Dee held her hand out for a strip. "Now you're talking." She ripped off a bite and hummed with pleasure. "My Uncle makes this by the bushel just for me."

I must confess that gave me a twinge. I didn't have anyone to do something just for me. I delivered an immediate mental head-slap. No point feeling sorry for myself, lots of people had even less than I did. I had Sydney. Okay so it appears she's chosen Wesley over me, but she sent the email, asked for my help. And I'd do anything for her. Apparently.

I poured coffee into pretty pink travel-cups I assumed were made of some kind of environmentally friendly material, knowing Dee. "You take sugar right?" I asked as I searched for some in the food bag.

"I knew you did too so it's already in the coffee. Could you grab me half an egg sandwich, they're cut in square halves. There's cheese in triangles and chicken salad in square quarters."

I set the mugs in holders between our seats and dug for the sandwich. "Quite the method."

"One of the forest rangers taught me that trick a few years back. Makes it easy to dig and find without taking my eyes off the road. He was a great old guy, had a wealth of useful little tips like that to share with us new kids."

I unwrapped the waxed paper, handed her half a sandwich and it smelled so good that I took the other half for myself.

We munched, and sipped coffee between potholes while I filled her in on the crazieness that had been my life for the last week or so. She made few comments, but Dee was a thinker and would take the time to sort and file before she shared her thoughts.

Once we were on the paved highway, I fell asleep, not raising an eyelid until we were pulling in to park beside a Dairy Freeze sign.

"Pit-stop," Dee said as she jumped out and went inside. I couldn't help but grin when she came back out with two chocolate-dipped ice-cream cones. She passed them to me and climbed in, escorted by a blast of frigid air.

"Not exactly ice-cream weather."

We devoured the treats while watching traffic go by. Mostly pickups with dogs in the back, a few with livestock trailers attached. Everyone going into the drive-in smiled and waved a hello at us as if we were old friends.

"Should we be sitting here, I mean out in the open like this? With so many people noticing us?" I shook my head. "Friendly people for such a bleak looking place."

"Damned pretty in the late spring, early summer, when it's all green." She chuckled and used her ice-cream to point. "I sat at a restaurant down the street once and watched six deer, Muley does, wander right through the middle of town, some in the street, others on the sidewalk. People just waited until they were out of the way to pass by. Amazing." She shook her head. "Gotta keep your eyes pealed for people here too, when you're driving. It's like they consider crosswalks sacred ground. Folk step right out in front of you." She laughed. "On the flipside, if you're on foot and so much as look at a crosswalk, locals come to a screeching halt to let you go by. Damned nice, friendly people."

"Sounds like you've spent time here."

She nodded. "there's a Fire Suppression camp just outside town. Did three weeks training about five years ago."

She crunched the last bit of her cone, wiped her hands on a napkin, started the truck and pulled out onto the highway. A dusty red pickup with two big guys in it pulled out behind us and I watched the mirror, my heart in my throat until they turned off into a pub parking lot.

Four hours later, we were in a sailboat, crossing from the mainland to the Gulf Islands. We'd lucked out, finding an old friend of Delia's willing to shuttle us to Mayne.

I still didn't get how you could put up a sail and make progress heading into the wind, but I refused to try and wrap my head around anything right now, stretching out instead on a big flat cushion on the front deck. With my eyes closed to savor the contradiction of the sun's heat and the ice cold wind on my face, I sucked in huge volumes of ocean air. It was a glorious respite from the insanity that had been my life for a while.

It was late afternoon by the time we'd reached the island, dropped anchor, dragged in the dingy, rowed to shore and hiked to the cabin. The sailboat puttered away, slowly raising the rainbow colored sail before we'd even crested the hill.

Chapter 18

The cabin looked deserted.

No friendly wisp of smoke from the chimney, no curtains pulled aside to let in the winter sunshine. But I didn't lose hope. I went around the back, dug the key out of the garden and marched up to the door looking for all the world I'm sure, like I was confident and not the least bit afraid of what I would encounter next.

Huh. I was scared spit-less, afraid to put the key in the lock. What if this was a set-up? What if the bad guys, Minnows—what a stupid name—had someone inside waiting for me. Or what if Sydney was in there. Dead. *Stop it.*

I took a long slow breath while I inserted the key and turned until I felt the click. Exhaling slowly, I twisted the knob. Pushed the door open just a little. To darkness. Silence.

And the smell of bacon?

"Syd?" I whispered, pushing the door open all the way, letting in the light while I cleared my throat and called out, "Sydney?"

Muffled sounds greeted me, slightly familiar. Syd

crying? Or was that... giggling?"

"Sydney!" I shouted and marched into the cabin to the sound of a muffled shriek.

And there I stood, in the middle of the room, staring somewhat stupefied at the moving lump under the pink comforter on the bed. My eyes were drawn to the four feet sticking out the end. One pair pointed up the other pair down.

"Oh for cryin' out loud. I'll be outside." I wheeled around and stormed out, grabbing Dee by the arm and dragging her with me.

Once in the garden, I knelt and buried the key back in its hiding place, glad the ground rarely froze here. Then I looked up at Dee and a heartbeat of silence hung between us before we burst out laughing. I tipped back on my heels to plunk my butt in the wet grass while Dee dropped to her knees. Tears running down our cheeks, and howling with laughter until we could barely breathe, it's a wonder we didn't wake up every Minnow in the Pacific.

Still hiccupping and bursting into short fits of giggles, we looked up when Syd stomped over. I was glad to see she was fully dressed but when I noticed her bare feet, I cracked up all over again, pointing at them like an idiot. I'll never again see her feet naked without getting a mental picture of them tangled with that bigger, masculine pair.

Hands on hips, she scowled at me. Best I could manage for a minute or two was an expressive shrug. I tried for an eye-roll but apparently that's physically impossible while laughing. *Okay, a deep breath.* I tried to look her in the eye but noticed her hair was pulled tidy around her face, with the back still flat and knotted. Yup, lost it again, so did

Dee. Sydney stalked back into the cabin.

My stomach ached from laughing and my fingers tingled from lack of oxygen. Through the tears I could see Delia was gaining some control so I fought for my own by flopping onto my back and staring up at the endless sky.

Minutes of silence were interrupted by the occasional gulp. I turned my head toward Dee, found her stretched out as well. "Spose we'd best go and be social?" I rubbed my aching stomach muscles.

"You got a grip?"

"Yeah, thinking of Wes tromping around my house planting spy cameras is helping with that." I sucked in a big lungful of air then sat up. I was soaked from the wet grass. I reached out a hand and pulled Dee up.

We stopped in the open doorway and peeked inside. "You two decent?"

"Ha ha," replied Syd from the kitchen area. "You want coffee?"

"Sure." Dee sat at the table while I gathered the mugs, sugar and milk. Syd stood by the coffee maker, watching it drip and tossing side glances my way. Never one to give things time to settle, I prodded. "What?"

She looked up with tears in her eyes. "You're mad at me."

"Oh Syd." I wrapped my arms around her. "I've been so scared that something awful had happened to you."

She sniffed. "You're not mad about Wesley?"

"I never said that." I squeezed tighter for a sec. "I'm mad as hell that he used you to get to me and then made you miserably unhappy. I could kill him for breaking your heart."

"I'm okay now."

I pulled back and looked her in the eye. "Do you trust him?"

Her gaze slid away from mine and I sighed. "Never mind. Everything's bound to work out somehow." Even if it took a little sisterly intervention with Romeo.

At the clearing of a distinctly male throat, we both looked his way. I was stunned. The man standing there, wasn't Wesley. Crikey, that hadn't even occurred to me. What the heck had I missed?

Sydney walked over, hell, she glided, over to the very hot guy wearing a thin washed out olive green t-shirt and equally faded black jeans. Naturally my eyes tracked down and I was pleased to see he wore socks and I wouldn't have to look at his naked feet—again.

His pale blue eyes were steady on mine, his mouth, hell his whole face, was expressionless. The only thing giving anything away, was the thumb of the hand holding Syd's as it slid back and forth in a way that looked both soothing and possessive.

I huffed out a breath when still no one spoke, and asked the guy with something spooky familiar about him, who he was.

"Donald Duck."

Sydney's snicker was accompanied by her feeble attempt at a poker face. Okay, so it was to be games. Whatever. I think the exaggeration of my shrug was more mental than physical but I'm not entirely sure.

"Anyone for coffee?" I asked, as I pulled the finished pot out from under the drip filter and took it to the table. I poured a cup for the silent and watchful Dee, one for myself, then in a fit of pissiness, I slipped the pot back onto the heated burner. They wanted to play games? Fine. They'd be on their own.

I sipped my coffee while Syd whispered with her mystery man. I was steamed that I'd been shot at, kidnapped, chased by evil minnows—okay so now I had a comical mental image of a goldfish with a fake shark fin strapped to his back—worried sick about my sister's broken heart and her safety, when in fact she's off having a romantic runaway, boffing some new guy. And all she's worried about is birth control—hopefully.

Once I was finished all the shouting and complaining in my head, I asked Sydney to go for a walk with me. We left Delia and Mr. Duck, behind.

We headed into the woods, following a trail that would take us to a small clearing where there was a bench to sit on, with a glorious view of the Pacific.

We'd gone about halfway, when Syd touched my arm and demanded to know what I was so steamed about.

At first I was stumped for an answer as there was too much to choose from. I gave her one of those, 'what are you, stupid?' looks and watched a range of emotions cross her face.

She seemed to reject angry and settle on dumbfounded, saying, "Look. My mind reading skills are shot all to heck these days so you'll have to just spell it out for me."

Squelching eye-rolls was beginning to annoy me but I managed, again. "Gee Syd, maybe it's something about your declarations of undying love for that cowboy you met last summer? Yet today I walk in here and find you doing a mattress dance with Bachelor Number Two. Or is it Three?

She shot me a look that would scare the pants off most mortals. "For starters," she said in the deadly quiet tone I recognized as her—I'm furious and just barely in control so don't interrupt me or I won't be responsible for what happens tone. "I don't do mattress dances. What you walked in on was me making love with the man I'm *in love with* and would be willing to die for."

I opened my mouth to say god knows what, but she held up one finger with an expression on her face that made me swallow the words so she didn't have to shove them back down my throat.

"That-" she tipped her head in the direction of the cabin "-is Wes. The same Wes I fell in love with last summer."

Okay, maybe I'm an idiot but I had to add my two cents worth. "Wesley Jackson the bull rider, has his Mexican mother's coloring, and he's five foot ten and a half," I said smugly as though what I wanted to say was, 'I may not have met him honey but I ran his plates.'

Her little smile warned me that I probably wasn't going to like what she was about to say. "You're absolutely right." The smile grew cocky. "But Wesley Meyers is six foot two, and has his *Scottish* mother's red hair and blue eyes."

"So, you're trying to tell me that I'm not only acting like an idiot, I am an idiot."

"Must say it looks good on you for a change, instead of me." And in her usual forgiving way, she pulled me into a hug.

I held on for a minute saying, "I've had a really crap

week Syd." Then pulled away quick before I started to wallow. "Let's keep walking for a while."

As we wandered up the trail, she told me her side of things and that she'd been told Gage had gone to Vegas to rescue me.

Then she said, "I was shocked you showed up here without him. Wes was afraid to use his usual email codes and routes after we had a Minnow-encounter in Seattle. He didn't want them to get wind we were headed across the border."

Okay, so the blocks were all lining up in perfect order and I was feeling more than pissed off. I'd been used by all sides assuming I'd make the expected moves.

"Why did you think I'd bring Gage?"

"That was me."

Startled, I spun around to glare at Wes. "Do. Not. Do that again. You scared another freaking year off my life and the way things are going lately, I'm running low on spares."

Syd snickered. "Gee, usually I'm the drama queen."

My nostrils flared. "I've had a busy week." I held out my hands and counted off on my fingers as I went through the events. "I got shot at, spent a couple days riding in the mountains on a slightly psychotic horse without a bridle, got *rescued*, tossed into an invisible helicopter, drugged, taken to a safe house, drugged a few more times between fits of fury, ran away, got tracked down by the fish, then Dee rescued me and helped me make my way here so I could save your ass from the dastardly Minnows." I'd run out of breath.

Syd zeroed in on the one part of my adventure I hadn't shared. "What happened in Vegas?"

Heat shot through me and an invisible hand reached in to squeeze on my heart like a dry lemon. I closed my eyes and waited for the pain to ease, while I ignored the curiosity I could feel emanating from Syd. I was surprised by the lump that formed in my throat and the involuntary crinkling of my chin.

"Cass?" Syd sounded worried.

What the hell. I managed a flippant, "You know what they say Syd, what happens in Vegas..."

She frowned. "But Gage was supposed to meet you. What happened."

"Oh, he met me there all right, neglected to mention that I was his mission and I left without him."

Wes was squinting at me and I longed to stick out my tongue. It was the Syd influence. When the two of us were together, it brought out the childish in us. Like the eye-rolling thing. It had been our entertainment when dealing with our mother and directors, photographers and such. We'd made our own fun with signals and visual comments behind their backs. We were working kids for the most part, and good kids but hey, girls will be girls.

Delia came into sight around the bend of the trail. "Geez guys, I thought you'd been kidnapped."

"Sorry Dee." I gave Wes a glare. "I didn't realize dickhead here was going to leave you behind, unprotected."

Syd put her hands on her hips and snapped. "I don't know who shoved the stick up your ass but it wasn't us so why don't you just back off with the attitude."

"Fuck you Syd. Oh, no, that's his job." I sent a snarl Wes's direction and stormed off toward the overlook, muttering to myself all kinds of vile things I wish they'd

243

do, places they could go. I was so angry I couldn't stand myself. I wanted to let out a furious bellow but had just enough sanity left to know that I shouldn't attract attention. I hated the world right now. And my sister's, happy in love, attitude was pushing all the wrong buttons. I stomped my feet and swung my arms trying to work off the frustration.

I could hear my mother's voice chanting in my head, 'poor little girl, you're just so hard done by aren't you? Nobody likes you, everybody hates you, go to the garden, and eat some worms'. Jesus I was humming the ditty in my head. I needed to get a grip and I didn't have the luxury of time on my hands. I sucked in air, then more, then more, until I felt ready to burst with it. I exhaled, pushing it out slowly through barely parted lips.

I repeated the slow breathing exercise a few more times, then did some shoulder rolls and deep knee bends. I wasn't any happier than I'd been a few minutes ago, but I had some control.

I stared out over the ocean and willed myself to employ a few brain cells before I turned to face the threesome approaching.

Dee stepped up beside me. "Nice view." She nudged me. "Wishing you were back out on the sailboat?"

"Nah. Just wishing life were simple again. But I guess it never was simple. It's hard to accept that I've been deceived by everyone I've ever cared for."

She gave me a gentle poke in the ribs with her elbow. "Hey, I haven't lied to you. I told you right up front about the phone call from that guy."

I draped my arm around her shoulders. "Sorry Dee. This whole thing is making me a little crazy."

I heard Syd's voice behind me. "You've always been mmurfmumph."

I wheeled around to see Wes had his hand over Syd's mouth and a smile directed at me.

"Sorry. Almost too slow," he said while he wrapped his other arm around her middle and pulled her back against him. The indignant look in her eyes almost made me laugh.

"Okay, thanks, needed that."

The four of us stood facing the steady give and take of ocean waves for a few minutes, just taking in the beauty and brute strength they embodied. The power of it seemed to dull the animosity, and the harshness of reality that hung in the air between us, so by the time we tromped back toward the cabin we were reasonably behaved, if not exactly best buddies again.

I had learned the lesson well. You just never know who might turn on you next. Oh, I know Syd didn't turn on me, but she did choose to keep me in the dark about her relationship with Wes. True, she'd believed that his safety was at stake, but it still felt like deception. Still felt like she'd chosen him over me. Did that mean he was her soul mate? Life mate? I suppose it could.

Being unable to let it go, and I admit I'm a bit of a glutton for punishment, I asked her to give me a minute before we went inside.

"What's wrong now, Cass?"

"I want to know what he means to you. Why you chose him over me." There was that squeezing feeling around my heart again.

She sighed. "I hadn't seen him since summer, when he disappeared and left me miserable." She looked me in the eye. "He showed up at my apartment the day I was supposed to leave for Vegas, I'd decided to surprise you and just show up, instead of going to Tahiti. And there he was. He told me that we were both, you and I, in danger, he would keep me safe and his brother was looking after you."

I felt the pressure ease. "Thanks. I needed to know you hadn't been keeping secrets from me since you two met."

She smirked. "And I forgive your spying and checking up on him."

I smiled back. "Okay. Even."

I followed Syd into the cabin and nearly knocked her over when she stopped without warning. I gave her a gentle shove while I pushed past and froze, my heart thumping hard against the ribs holding it in.

Chapter 19

Gage's face gave nothing away, his eyes were as expressionless as I hoped mine were. He stood statue still, coffee pot in one hand, cup in the other. Angie appeared at his side, took both pot and cup from him and set them on the counter. He didn't move.

But I did. Wheeled around and bolted through the doorway like startled rabbit. Didn't stop until I'd reached the water's edge. Stared out to where the sailboat had anchored earlier. Today? Mere hours ago? My concept of time was all screwed up. I couldn't seem to wrap my head around the fact that just this morning, I'd woken up at Delia's mountain lookout. Yesterday morning I'd been Gage's prisoner.

I heard him come up behind me, felt him, and my heart pressed the back of my throat.

"Maddy."

Oh lord how could he breathe out a word like that and make me want to just sink into him. Lose myself in his scent, his sound. Climb into his skin.

"Maddy, please." Pure masculine control on a plate. No demand, no plea. Nothing but a genuine, heartfelt request that left me more needy than I'd ever been in my life.

He seeped into my bones. The embodiment of pain and pleasure.

God help me, I've never wanted anything so much. My body vibrated in recognition of the reward so close. My mind screamed in protest.

And I simply turned. Threw myself into arms that folded me in. Held me with a hand cradling the back of my head while I drowned, his mouth at my ear murmuring words, his need as great as mine. My fingertips dug into his back, holding hard as our hearts pounded in one place.

"Damn you," I whispered into his throat, my mouth tasting him. "Damn you to hell for letting me go."

He rocked me, held me. Grenades could rain down around us and I'd not move a muscle. Right this moment. I was where I belonged. A shudder almost rattled my bones and I felt the echo in him.

I lifted my head and looked into those eyes that could shut down, turn cold as ice. And saw something different. Something new.

Breathing my name as his mouth lowered to mine, he devoured. Took. And gave. My soul shifted, lifted as I took what I needed from him, gave back.

His hands framed my face, thumbs stroking my jawline, grazing my throat—and I may have forgotten to breathe. If I could just crawl inside of him, be a part of him.

He lifted his head. Stared into my eyes. "You scared hell out of me woman."

"I expected you to stop me." And I hadn't admitted that to myself, until this moment.

His mouth twisted up on one side. "They tricked me so you could get away and lead us to Wes and your sister. I nearly took the place apart when I found out." He sighed. "I did everything I could to try to keep you safe while they tracked you. I guessed you were headed for Delia so I sent her a heads up to be ready to help you."

Something niggled. I gave it a minute to grow substance. "Tracked me?"

I hadn't heard Angie's approach so her voice startled me. "Hate to be a party poop Gage, but we need to get a move on. Bird's been on the ground nearly an hour."

He stared into my eyes while he answered her with a question. "Where's Wes?"

"Off-loading equipment. Cabin's clean, set for scenting."

He closed his eyes and leaned his forehead against mine. "We have to go." He pressed his mouth between my eyes and I felt tears well.

His hands pushed on my shoulders until I let go and my arms dropped away from him. He turned to Angie. "I'll go help Wes. You two can catch up." He jogged off toward the cabin.

I hurried after him, ignoring Angie as I passed her. But she had other ideas. She grabbed me by the arm, forced me to stop and face her.

"You got a problem with me Cassandra?"

I'm sure my nostrils flared. "I don't like being lied to, and set up."

She snorted. "Said the pot to the kettle."

"Excuse me?"

"You started it honey."

"The hell I did." I hate conflict and physical aggression but with my emotions all over the board, I did the unthinkable and pushed her, hard. "My life was on the line because you wise ones decided to let me lead you to my sister and Wes. You set me up and put your brother's neck ahead of mine by a country fucking mile."

"Why you bitch. All you had to do was tell us when you got that message from your sister. If you'd shared the information, your sanctimonious ass could have spent yesterday morning screwing my brother blind while Quinn and I flew out here to retrieve Wes and Sydney."

I had mouth movement, but no sound.

Just as well when she seemed to be working up such a good head of steam. "And further more, right now, I wouldn't have to fly out of here without my brothers, leaving them to face god knows what before I can get back to pull their asses out of here." She flung her hands in the air. "Your lie has endangered everyone including Delia. She rescued you and for that, her life will never be the same. You exposed your friend to the Minnows, Cass. Painted a target on her back. Nice going."

Okay, so hit me with a brick. She was right. Not that I said the words out loud, but in my heart, my mind and deep in my bones I knew. So I sucked it up. "Now what?"

She stared off across the ocean as though trying to get a grip. Shook her head. "Come on, let's get this done." She turned and hurried after Gage.

The spooky looking, dull black helo seemed otherworldly, crouched among the rocks.

I stared in through the side door, my feet planted and hands on hips as I bucked the system one more time. "No."

Their plan hadn't been intentionally sexist but Syd, Dee and I were supposed to ride out with Angie. We'd be zipped off to a safe house, while Wes and Gage took to the water in scuba gear and made their way to a pickup point on a neighboring island.

"Cassandra," growled Gage, "Get in or I'll put you in."

I backed up a step.

Angie, black helmet in place, was busy doing pilot things, with Dee strapped in beside her.

Syd was behind them, buckled in next to the empty seat that was supposed to be mine. She'd pasted that perfect model's smile on her face, but her eyes gave her away, locked onto Wes as though she feared she'd never see him again. Her chin wobbled. *Shit.*

I followed her gaze to where the apparent love of her life waited near the pile of scuba diving equipment they'd pulled from the helicopter.

Not so often a person gets a chance to right a wrong. I confess, I would also be getting what I wanted. And I didn't have time to consider the risk benefit ratio.

I stepped around the pile of gear—something I knew absolutely nothing about unless you counted what I'd seen on television—and grabbed Wes by the forearm. "Go with her."

"Cass." Gage's voice came from over my right shoulder.

"Wes, she needs you with her." I waved a hand at the pile. "I'm good with this."

"Cassandra." Gage's tone was low, a little mean and said, listen to me NOW.

"Wes. Go. Don't make her suffer like this. She's been through enough because of you disappearing once already." I lowered my voice. "Besides, I need some one on one time with your cement-headed brother."

His glance moved from me to Gage and back again before he marched to the Steed, jumped in and slid the door closed. Gage grabbed my hand and pulled me away from the kicked up sand and dirt. Once at a safe distance, we leaned on each other in silence until they were airborne, had done a quick pass low over the cabin, then lifted and disappeared into the evening sky.

He turned me to him and planted a quick kiss on my mouth. "That was a good thing you did for your sister. Not so good for you though. We've got a couple hours swimming ahead of us." He reached down and started gathering up a huge armful of stuff like wet-suits and tanks and flippers.

My arms filled with everything I could scoop up, I followed him to the beach where I'd come ashore earlier.

He set things out in a neat, orderly fashion while I watched and began to doubt my wisdom—one more tedious time. I gave myself a mental shake like a wet dog. Can't be that hard to learn can it? Kids do it. Sure but kids can program computers before they learn to walk too so that's no comfort.

Gage handed me a wetsuit and grinned. "Too bad you don't have a swimsuit, guess you'll just have to strip down to your skivvies."

"We have bathing suits in the cabin. I'll just run up and-"

"NO. It's been brushed, you can't go back in."

"Brushed?"

"A family term for swept of all trace that we've been here. Wes made sure there were no fingerprints, opened up both doors and the windows, then treated it with mildew scent and the final step was a fly-by to send dust and debris everywhere."

"Mildew scent?"

He nodded. "Special capsules of scent and diffusers used to mutate existing odors. Neither scent-hounds nor computer devices can find anything recognizable but mildew afterwards." He smiled. "So you can't go back in there."

Ever. I'd heard what he hadn't said.

So, instead of going back for a swimsuit I'd be stripping down to my underwear—if I'd been wearing some. Oh hell, not like he hadn't seen me naked before.

He turned away, maybe to give me a little privacy or simply to concentrate on donning his own gear. I watched and tried to copy his moves while he kept up a one-sided conversation.

"I don't remember seeing diving on your resume. Not that I'm surprised, of course, considering you seem to know something about everything. Where did you learn?"

I grunted as I pulled the cold rubber torture chamber up over my starkers derriere.

"You take a course on the Bahamas trip? Or Hawaii?" He reached for items one at a time and strapped them to his body. I wasn't keeping up and wondered if I should tell him this was a first for me.

As if on cue, he turned. Caught me twisted like a pretzel, while I tried to get the stupid tank to stay in the middle of my back and fasten the straps around my middle. The look on his face made me pretty sure, I probably had it upside down.

"Been a while?" he asked.

"You could say that. Maybe I need a refresher course before we get started." If I'd been adept at eyelash fluttering, this would have been a good moment to utilize the skill.

His lips thinned and his nostrils widened. "You've never done this before?"

"Well that depends on your definition." Oh, why was it so hard to be honest these days? I swallowed. "No. The closest I've ever been to a wetsuit and tank would be watching Jacques Cousteau reruns on Saturday mornings." No point adding it had been ten or fifteen years ago.

He turned, and stormed along the water's edge, like a ridiculous cartoon-character with the big flippers. I cracked up.

I was fighting to stop, gasping for breath when the tips of his flippers touched my toes. I looked up into his angry eyes and sobered instantly.

He grabbed me by the shoulders with such force that I expected him to make my teeth rattle. Instead he growled, "You will be the death of me woman." He shook his head. "I can't believe I just said that." He let me go and turned away. "I guess I'm lucky we didn't need a pinch hitter to fly the fucking bird, chances are, you'd have volunteered."

He spun back toward me with his jaw clenched as hard as his fists. "You can't just *pretend* to scuba dive. What the fuck were you thinking?"

"That you could teach me. I'm a quick study. Heck, I

got into this getup didn't I?"

He reached over and undid the buckles I'd struggled to fasten. Stripped us both of everything but the wet suits and his flippers, hooked all the gear together and said, "Stay." He swam out a long ways towing the gear, let it sink in deep water, pulled off his fins and swam back.

When he came out of the water, he was calm again. "Look me in the eye and tell me if you've ever been in a kayak. In water."

I'm sure my smile was grim, not that he'd notice. "Nope, not ever. But I'm sure that's about to change."

He grabbed the waterproof bag we'd both stowed our clothes in. I'd seen weapons in it as well. "Let's go." He turned and marched toward the cabin's driveway.

Chapter 20

Gage had instructed me not to speak while he paddled across the inky black ocean. Said voices carried for miles across water. He'd used night-vision goggles to find his way, while I'd been as usual, left in the dark. Just as well. He'd barely said three words to me that weren't direct instructions. Locating a kayak to *borrow,* and waiting for nightfall before taking off, had been painful with his refusal to make conversation.

When the hull scraped bottom, he reached back and grabbed my hand. Helped me out of the craft and into foot deep water. I stumbled a couple of times because my legs were short on circulation and rubbery after being stuffed in the narrow two person boat for heaven knows how many hours.

His grip tightened and he tugged me along at a relentless pace until we were away from the water's edge. He sat me down on a log and disappeared into the dark. I heard the boat scraping on rocks, then his footsteps before he dropped the waterproof bag down beside me. He stripped down and pulled on his dry clothes with speed and efficiency. What a shame it was too dark to enjoy the show.

Once he was all set, he stripped me out of my wetsuit. Cursed, under his breath when he discovered that I was naked. Not that my underwear—had I worn some—would have covered all that much. He helped me get dressed and tied up my bootlaces as though I was a helpless child. Okay, so I was acting like one.

I suppose it was easier this way, no accounting for my emotions or my behavior. But deep down, I was still smarting from the mini-lecture Angie had given me. Thinking about it though, I wasn't completely responsible for Delia's involvement. They'd set me up to run away, so hadn't they sort of forced me to contact her? Surely they deserved a little bit of the blame?

Nice try Cass. The blame game was as useless an exercise as the regret game. I refuse to have regrets for things I've done, or not, in my life. Because really, if one little thing had been done differently, every other little thing would be altered. I heaved a sigh.

"Now what?" Gage was turning the kayak on it's side, slipping the paddle things inside.

"That's my question. What happens now?"

"We're going to hike across this island, then, settle in and wait for Angie to make contact, maybe pick us up before dawn."

"How long will it take?"

He lifted the kayak up over his head saying, "A while." Then he turned and hiked into the darkness.

What the heck? "Hey." I scurried after him. "What are you doing?"

He stopped, turned and his voice was emotionless. "I'm leading the way. Getting us to a safe place to rest for a while."

"And why exactly are you pissed at me?"

"I'm not. Now can we just get on with this?" He turned away, marched on.

"Can I help you carry that?"

He ignored me.

Okay so now *I* was pissed off. Been that way a lot lately. I suppose that's something I needed to think about. I trudged along behind him, stumbling now and again, cursing under my breath when I did.

By the time he stopped and laid the kayak on the ground, I was bone weary. I watched in silence while he magically produced two very thin black blankets and a bag of what looked like protein bars from the waterproof bag. He pulled me around and sat me down with my back to a tree trunk, handed me one of the bars, a small plastic bottle of water and draped a blanket over my legs.

He sat beside me and we munched together. I didn't know what to say so I stayed silent. It was pretty darned obvious that he didn't want to talk so what the heck, silence would be fine by me for a while. I finished my snack, folded the wrapper and stuck it in my pocket. Setting the empty water bottle alongside the bag, I leaned my head back against the tree and closed my eyes.

I must have fallen asleep, as the next thing I knew, Gage's lips were against my forehead and his low gravely tone vibrated through me when he said, "Easy baby."

"Tell me we're in my nice warm bed at home."

"You asking me to lie?" His warm breath brushed my ear.

I sighed and he wrapped me even tighter in his arms. I

could smell the trees and the ocean over the warm male scent I was snuggled into.

My eye-lids shot up as I pulled away and cold air slipped between us. Awake now, and in the faint light of dawn I noticed the blanket draped over my head.

"Come back here, it's cold and too soon to move."

I'd been sleeping on top of him and he'd covered me, us, with the blanket. He was half propped against the upside-down kayak.

"Don't we have to be ready for Angie? No, wait. She's supposed to pick us up before dawn. While it's dark. But-"

He looked away.

"Why isn't she coming?"

"I don't know."

"Is that a good I don't know? Or a bad one?"

"Neither. Just means we go to plan B."

"Will I like plan B?"

He had a little smirk on his face. "Depends."

Okay, so I got a quick mental flash of old people and protective undergarments. I shook it off and said, "Just tell me what's going on."

"I got a message from Quinn two hours ago that translates into, we're going to Plan B. "

Something twisted inside me, made me feel queasy. *Ohmygod. Had the helicopter crashed? Or did the Minnows capture them? Or? Whoa. Hold it.* Why exactly was I panicking? I sucked in a long hard breath and exhaled slowly.

Gage was watching me. "Feel better now?"

"Marginally. I still need facts. What happened?"

"I have no clue. Could be anything, including a need for the Steed or Angie elsewhere. On another assignment."

"Okay, I can work with that. What's Plan B and when do we get started?"

By ten in the morning we were back in the kayak, tucked into a tiny cove behind some huge boulders. I could hear the voices. Gage started to paddle, easing us out toward a group of passing kayakers. I dipped my paddle ends into the water and tried to emulate his moves. It was hard not to laugh when he gave me a dirty look over his shoulder. Guess I still wasn't doing it right.

Amid a quiet chorus of hellos and welcomes we settled in at the back of the pack. A man in the middle of the group of around a dozen kayaks gave a nature talk while he paddled.

I whispered to Gage's back. "How did you know about this?"

"It's well advertised at the local store and the ferry terminal."

Sometimes getting information out of him was like trying to pull teeth. "So what, these people all meet somewhere, pay a fee, rent a kayak?"

"It's a local thing. That guy lives on one of the islands. He leaves his own dock at six am and follows a set route. People join in as they please.

What a cool idea. "How long will we be with them?"

"About an hour. Until Gandolf Island."

We paddled along, in the brisk cold air with the winter sun doing little to warm us so early in the day. We should have been wearing our wetsuits as the others were. But I suppose they wouldn't be good for whatever the next step in our journey would be.

I contemplated Gage's shoulders as he moved the paddle with a lovely rocking rhythm. Made me wish I could just reach out and touch him, feel the heat. Reminded me of how his body felt naked. Okay, well, that warmed me up. I dipped my paddle hard and felt the kayak wiggle in the water. Shit. Don't want to dump us in the drink.

I laid the paddle across my lap and listened to the nature talk, enjoyed the man's voice, distant as it was, while he shared facts about killer whales and sea lions, and told amusing stories of pirates, smugglers and secret caves. Made me think of bedtime stories my dad used to tell Dean and I once Syd fell asleep. She'd been too young for scary stories.

My mind wandered to Sydney and Wes. They certainly seemed happy together. It was nice to see my sister that way again. I guess that's why I couldn't stand to be the reason she was separated from him. Of course in the back of my mind I still didn't trust him completely so I figured she must be a bit uncertain. Maybe she feared she's lose him again if he stayed with Gage.

And maybe I didn't want to let Gage out of my sight either.

I thought about his sudden attitude change. From hot to cold in the blink of a lie. Aside from the one microscopic moment when I'd woken up this morning, he'd not so much as looked at me with anything more than tolerance.

Great. I admit to myself that I might have real feelings for the guy about ten minutes before he turns into a walking talking popsicle.

Just as well. He'd only break my heart if I let myself

fall for him. Better this way. We'll go our own separate ways soon, likely in the next couple of hours. Won't ever have to see him again. My new life will be a fresh slate, not taking any sad memories with me.

No friends, no family. No worries. No problems. I could take up painting. Or photography, less messy. Maybe I could write a book about this adventure. It would certainly sound like fiction. Too much work. I could take up journaling though, so one day I could look back on all the amazing experiences I'd had in such a short time.

"Hey, where are you?"

I blinked a couple of times. Gage was turned around staring at me, and the others were way ahead of us. "What?"

"Change of plans." He dipped the paddle in on the left side and held it still so the kayak turned left and I spotted an opening between the rocks. He steered us into the small bay and right up to a wharf where a float plane was tied. *Oh boy.*

"Tell me we're not going to *borrow* an airplane." Geez, thievery just wasn't something I was comfortable with. Sure he'd left a note, a promise to pay, when we'd taken the kayak, but it still felt wrong. But now an airplane? Man that had to be grand theft.

"Oh shit." The words slipped out as a man walked down the dock toward us. He held the front of the kayak and Gage grabbed one of the rubber tire bumpers to steady us.

"Go ahead, climb out," he said over his shoulder.

I scrambled up onto the wooden float and held the craft still so he could get out too.

Once on the dock, he grabbed the other guy in a back slapping one armed man hug. Good thing I was holding onto the kayak or it would have floated away. Thankfully, Gage reached down and dragged it up out of the water.

The stranger held his hand out to me. I shook it and nearly did a double take when I looked up at his face. "Another one," I muttered.

He grinned. "Trent, nice to meet you Maddy."

I turned to Gage. "How many more brothers do you have?"

"A few," was his non-committal answer.

"He's the old wise one. I'm way more fun." Trent winked. "You ready to go?"

"Will it be a long flight? Should I pit stop first?"

Gage took my arm and pointed me away from the house tucked into the gorgeous windswept Arbutus trees. "No. There's no time."

I stared at him and the words popped out. "What the hell crawled up your ass last night?"

"Hey, Gage, I like her." Trent was grinning as he stepped onto the pontoon and opened the passenger door. He held out his hand for mine, pulled me over and helped me up into the seat behind the pilot's. Before long we were all on board and airborne.

Trent and Gage both wore big pale green earphones with a microphone attached and they appeared to be talking to each other. Just as well. I watched the world from about a thousand feet. I could still see little boats and barges piled high with sawdust as we winged across the water.

I could tell we were headed toward the mainland—as opposed to Vancouver Island—because the sun was on the right of the craft—to the south. The drone of the engine was a comfortable noise and I was content, until Trent reached a hand back and waved to get my attention.

He pulled his mike up out of the way and shouted, "Pass me that bag on the seat."

It was a cooler type bag. I handed it to him. He took out a couple of water bottles, handed one to Gage and passed the bag back to me. "Help yourself."

They were those cute little water bottles, the half-size ones that didn't make you concerned about where the next bathroom stop was. Not that I needed to worry. I was drier than a popcorn fart.

I opened one and swallowed down half the contents in one go, then wiped my mouth while I took a breath. I finished the bottle, twisted the lid back on and dropped it into the cooler bag. Now I could use a big fat hamburger.

In an effort to keep my mind off my empty stomach I watched the men in front of me, thought about what it would be like to grow up with so many siblings. So far, I'd met two brothers and two sisters, and if I'd interpreted Gage's comment correctly, there were more. I sighed. All I had was Syd. Maybe.

The drone of the engine was making me sleepy. I bundled Gage's jacket up and put it against the window so I could lean my head there. I tried to watch the ocean going by while inhaling the scent of the man I was in lust with. Pissed me off that he hadn't spared me a glance since we'd boarded the plane. I tried staring at the back of his head to make him look my way, but my eyes refused to stay open. An odd, yet now familiar feeling washed over me.

Chapter 21

I woke up smiling. Felt warm and safe and... my eyelids shot up like window blinds. Black. Nothing. I could smell a hint of ocean, earth and trees over the warm scent of Gage. My eye-lids lifted higher, as I tried to move, got tangled, and struggled in earnest. I sat up and the jacket wrapped around me—over my head—fell away. I was sitting on a bed, still fully dressed. I tried to focus, remember where I'd been before I fell asleep. I let out a furious yell.

"*Arrggh.* This is getting really OLD."

I flopped onto my back and stared up at the familiar stars sparkling on the ceiling. My fingers played with the seams and lines of the quilt I lay on. "I'm awake now. Any of you chicken-hearts want to come in and torture me a little more?"

Soft fur tickled my knuckles. "Merlin." My fingers automatically rubbed around his ears.

'*pprrrlt.*'

Glad he was talking cat instead of human this time, I lifted my head to smile at him. *Holy shit.* "Harris?"

'*pprrrlt.*'

265

I bolted off the bed, wrapped my cat in my arms, and tried to ignore the brain cells clanging like cymbals. Had they brought Harris here? He purred happily against my chest as I walked around the room, opening drawers, the closet. My clothes were all here. Is this home? Did I dare to lift the window blind?

Not sure if I was ready for the truth, I decided to take a shower first. Peal off a layer of grime. I set the cat on the dresser, dug out clean jeans and a t-shirt. Smiled at a drawer full of my own underwear, the sweet mix of Victoria's Secret and cotton grannies somehow helped me feel grounded. Perhaps I'd just been ill, having nightmares. Right. And this was Kansas.

I shook my head. "Harris, is this home or are they messing with my mind??"

As if in answer to my question, the dogs began to bark and the door flew open, then closed after Connie strode through. She stopped short. "You're awake."

I nodded.

"Get back in bed. I have to get you ready."

Huh?

She pushed and shoved until I was stretched out on the bed.

From the night table she pulled something made of clear plastic, unfolded and slid it over my left leg before passing me a long attached tube. "This inflates it. Blow it up. Now."

Of course I did, and soon the plastic morphed into an inflated brace that covered me thigh to ankle, the kind used to stabilize fractures. There was red coloring of some kind on the inside, making it look like there were streaks of blood on my jeans.

While I'd blown up the brace, Connie had worked on my face with brushes and fingertips, messed up my hair and wrapped a hard plastic cervical collar around my neck.

I was amazed by my lack of question, the way I went along with what she was doing while cataloguing each move in some corner of my mind. This was Connie and I trusted her, didn't I?

Nothing more than mild surprise flitted through me at the sound of a helicopter approaching. The dogs became much more agitated, their barking escalated into full throated baying.

Connie helped me to my feet, pulled my arm across her shoulders and we shuffled out into the hallway. My hallway. We'd just turned into the kitchen when the back door opened and Jared came in. I could see Sheriff Porter close behind him, craning his neck to stare at me.

Jared reached my side and took over for Connie by swinging me up into his arms. "Sheriff, she's going for x-rays right now and I'm paying that pilot by the minute so you'll have to ask your questions later."

I stayed mute. Was pretty sure that was what they expected of me. I sighed, also pretty certain that my weird adventures weren't over yet.

One thing about Porter, he didn't back down easy. Although I couldn't see him from where I was, I heard him clomping after us and then the questions began rapid fire. "Where was she found? Who found her? Where'd that jacket come from? Where's the horse?"

I tuned him out while I thought about the big jacket I'd woken up wrapped in and Connie had pulled around me before we'd left my room. It was light brown camo, like it came from Desert Storm. I'd never seen it before but it smelled like Gage. I know we didn't have it with us when we left the island.

"What day is this?" I whispered.

Jared's eyes met mine. "What honey?"

Silence settled around me. I went with my instincts and raised the whisper a notch or two. "What day is this? How long have I been gone?" Then I groaned for effect.

Jared kept walking at a steady pace as Connie answered from somewhere behind us. "You've been gone eight days. The mares and Blue came home without you a week ago and we've been searching ever since. They found you yesterday, nearly fifty miles south of here."

Nice story. Could it be true? Had this whole adventure filled with invisible helicopters, mysterious houses hidden from satellite cameras, and talking cats been a dream? Did I hallucinate Gage? Have I lost my mind? Aren't delirium and hallucination by-products of dehydration and concussion? I felt tears well when the helicopter came into view. It was a blue and white Bell. The pilot swung around to smile at me and I saw the face of a total stranger.

Connie popped into the co-pilot's spot while Jared settled me into a seat in the back and belted into the one beside me after he slid the door closed. The helo lifted up off the ground, then slid forward across the deer meadow, before we zipped up over the trees.

I wanted to ask where the hell we were going but figured there was little point. I was getting used to not having a clue what would happen next in my life. I lifted the jacket to my face, sucked in a deep gulp of Gage-scented air and clung to the hope that he was real.

I blinked to clear my senses when I thought I saw Connie's tote-bag move. She'd set it on the floor before she'd crawled forward into her seat. I recognized the old carpet bag as the one she took everywhere with her. I stretched my right leg out until I could poke the bag with my toe and nearly squealed like a girl when something inside it moved.

Jared picked up the bag and plunked it in my lap. He opened it just a little and Harris popped his head up. I lifted him, bag and all, against my chest so I could rub my face against him. I could hear his purring, feel it, and was nearly settled by it. Until I realized that if they'd brought Harris along, I was likely never going back.

I looked up at Jared. "This is really happening. None of it was a dream."

He nodded.

My life as Cassandra Mallory was over. I no longer had a home. No longer existed. I suppose the good news was that Gage wasn't a figment of my imagination. As if that meant anything now.

We landed alongside a hospital and Jared lifted me out, onto a rock hard gurney. Then people with big red parkas over their pale green scrubs, took over with straps and sand bags and blankets before they wheeled me inside.

I kept my eyes moving, taking in my surroundings as best I could while strapped to a backboard. Ceilings were white. Light fixtures clean. And bright. Very bright.

After rolling along for what seemed like miles, I was parked in a room with what looked like an x-ray machine. There were very few lights on, and they left me there.

Alone.

Just about ready to panic, I nearly screamed when a voice close to my ear asked, "You ready to get out of here?"

Shit. I knew that voice. "Any chance I can stay awake for the trip? I'm getting real tired of what feels like time travel."

Eve laughed and started undoing the straps holding me in place. "Yup, just you and me this time and no way I'm carrying you."

Once my hands were free I ripped the Velcro off the c-collar, sat up, pulled the plug on the inflated leg brace and began squeezing the air out. Eve chuckled at my efforts, produced a tiny foil packet, ripped it open to expose a scalpel blade and dissected the plastic in two quick moves.

"Scary."

"Efficient," she countered. "Jump down and use this." She handed me a jar of Vaseline and a cloth then pointed at the mirror by the door.

While I wiped off the makeup Connie had used on my face to make me look beat up, Eve wrapped the collar and cast remains in the bed-sheet and stuffed it into a laundry cart.

"But won't the laundry people report it?"

"Nope, they get this kind of stuff out of the ER all the time. And chances are, anybody doing a search here would check the garbage, not the laundry, besides, laundry pickup is every hour, trash is twice a day."

Good thing she knows her stuff. I didn't bother to ask her if my being missing would be an issue, because I'd already figured out that I wasn't wearing a hospital bracelet so that should mean I wasn't in the system.

I ran my fingers through my hair, then wove it into a tidy braid. Eve tossed me a lab coat from behind the door. I held it for a minute. I really didn't want to take off Gage's jacket.

"Let's go."

I stared at her and somehow, she understood. "We have to take the jacket too. Put the lab coat on, and toss the jacket in this. She handed me a cloth laundry bag.

Of all moments to have a completely off topic thought. But there it was, my applause for the hospital using reusable cloth bags instead of plastic. I gave my head a shake and did as I'd been told.

Eve clipped an ID badge to my collar. "You're a new candy striper, we're having trouble locating uniforms." She opened the door and led the way down the hall. People were busy everywhere. Nobody so much as looked at us until we went through the security door to the parking lot.

"Hey doc."

"Hey back Charlie, what's new?"

"Nothin' much. Where you headed? Shift's not over. Got an emerg somewhere? You should have coats on, you'll catch your death."

Eve had continued to march on, I followed. She looked back at the guy with a smile. "House call. Coat's in the car, too big for my locker."

We rounded a corner and Eve clicked the button that made a car chirp. When the trunk of a dark green Buick popped open I dropped in the bag with the jacket.

"You too," said Eve.

Oh well, whatever, I climbed in.

We must have passed through an exit gate because we stopped and I heard a man's voice, "off early doc? Lucky you."

We drove a while then, fast and slow, making sharp turns that had me convinced she was trying to either kill me or loose a tail. My teeth were chattering and my lips probably blue by the time she stopped and opened the trunk.

She reached in to help me out. "You okay?"

"Sure, fine, but if we're gonna do this again, go ahead and drug me."

She was already walking away so I grabbed out the bag with the jacket and followed, looking around at the inside of a huge warehouse. "Don't suppose you'll tell me where we are?"

"En route."

Well, gee, thanks for all the information. Grr.

Eve took me through the door at the end which led to a giant garage with two big trailer loads of square baled hay, hooked to a truck. An eighteen wheeler type rig with a second trailer they call a pup. We stopped at the cab and I watched her climb up the ladder-like steps to settle into the seat. A few minutes later the big diesel rumbled to life, sounding less than happy. I watched the double plumes of exhaust swirl upward toward a big fan that sent it out through a hole in the ceiling.

When Eve climbed back down, she explained that there was a hidden compartment within the load of hay. I crouched to follow her under the pup-trailer to a trapdoor. She twisted the handle and the heavy door flopped down silently. Eve stood with her head through the opening and reached above her. Soft light appeared. She backed away and said, "Take a look."

Able to stand straight up and look around, I was impressed. It was a camper, the kind like off the back of a pickup truck. There was a bench seat with a table, a kitchen counter with a hotplate, a tiny fridge, sink, cupboards and yes, even a closet sized room right in front of me with a toilet in it.

I crouched back down. "How long will we be in there?"

She smiled. "I'm driving. You'll be inside for about two days."

"Why don't I just hide in the cab-sleeper?"

Her smile turned into a grimace. "Because I'll be dropping the pup off in a few hours and going an entirely different direction."

Not a surprising answer, I was getting the hang of the games they played.

She touched my arm. "If it's any consolation, this might be your last big move. If we can pull off the transfer without any major glitches, you'll have a chance at getting settled into your new persona, maybe even enjoy normal life for a change."

Still, no mention of Gage. "Can you tell me where I'm going?"

"Sorry."

"What about my sister, my brother, will I have contact with either?"

"Sydney's a possibility. But your brother's been in hiding for so long even we've lost him." She checked her watch, shuffled out from under the trailer and I followed her.

She went to the big doors at the end of the building and hand-cranked them open. It was full daylight but the area from the warehouse out, about a city block or two, was shadowed by camouflage netting, like the safe house we'd been in.

"So," I said, "I'm on the road again."

"Did Gage explain to you about misinformation and false trails and stuff?"

"No."

"Dolt." She shook her head. "We're laying false trails so that the Minnows think they're following you and concentrate all their efforts in one area while we get you set up somewhere else."

"Gage went pretty silent on me after the others left on the Steed." She didn't say anything else but I thought I was getting the picture. "Syd, Wes and Dee have to be hidden as well, right?"

"Mm hmm."

"So your family's company is handling all of this."

"Pretty much. There's food in the cupboards and little fridge—with a milk jug of frozen water to keep it cool because there's no electricity or propane in there. There's a Kindle, a DVD player, lots of movies, games, and three power packs. Pencil and paper and cards in the drawers. Battery operated clock and lights to last you a couple of days. Tubes run from the ceiling vent up through the hay for fresh air."

She checked her watch again, moved around the rig, pulling out chocks, stowing them in compartments, checking the load and the hook-up stuff between the trailers before pointing at the underside of the pup.

"You want me to get in there now?" Duh. Of course she did. I sighed, bent and headed underneath. Tossed in the bag with the jacket, put my hands on the sides of the opening and hefted myself up so my butt landed on the camper's beige linoleum floor. As I swung my legs in, Eve poked her head through the hole.

"When I close the hatch, pull the handle up towards you, that'll sink the outside of it into the depression and make it blend in." She pointed to a little hook. "It will set over this so it's locked from the inside." She held her hand out to me. I looked at it for a moment then reached and held on.

"Is this goodbye?" I asked.

"Nope, good luck."

"So we'll see each other again?"

"Hard to say." She ducked down and closed the hatch door before I could reply. I pulled up the handle, hung it over the hook and leaned back against the cardboard thin door to the tiny room where the biffy was. I felt the rig start to move and said out loud, "Onward ho." But somehow, it just didn't sound the way it was supposed to.

I sat there for a very long time, tears, of all stupid things running down my face while I clenched my jaw and fought back the lump in my throat. I'm hopeless. I have no home, no people, no animals even that love me. I thought about Blue. He was a working dog. He'd hate life off the ranch.

And Harris. Oh man, now that was hard. I'd been packing that cat around for years. He'd heard all of my problems. Listened attentively while I poured my heart out then dutifully purred and rubbed against me as though he knew what I needed. He did of course. I needed comfort, the comforting that came from touch, from warmth and caring.

Oh there'd been a few men that passed through my life, but none were as solid and loving as Harris. I'd dubbed him Sir Harris Tweed because he was just like the fabric—a warm mix of browns in his plain striped coat, yet nothing plain about the resulting color. I suppose I should be thankful to know that Connie had him safe somewhere.

Like the cat, I was squirreled away in a traveling case, my current destiny completely out of my own control. At least he got to pop his head out now and again. I looked around at the curtains. Were there real windows behind them? Shouldn't I check just in case I decided to be TSTL again and not go along with their plans?

I stood, and left my pity party behind. I pulled all the drapes aside and studied the windows. They were small, of course, and gave a lovely green view of hay bales. And these weren't the old fashioned back yard bales that weigh about fifty pounds. Nope, these were the big boys. One of these would fill the box of a pickup truck and at upwards of five hundred pounds, there was no way I'd be able to push one aside, or pop the strings and pull the hay into the camper while I made a tunnel.

But there should be some natural space between the bales as they'd never stack exactly flush. I spent the next several hours opening windows and measuring spaces until I'd come up with a plan.

I broke out the long skinny window up by the bunk, the part of the camper that would be over the truck windshield in normal circumstances. That would put me near the top of the load so that I'd only have the upper bales to deal with. I used cupboard doors from inside and braced them against the bales, so that the steady vibration and movement of the rig would eventually create a bigger space.

*

Two full days of road. I wrote the words on the page and underlined them. I tried to think of all the places I could be. Fifty miles an hour, equaled twelve hundred miles a day which equaled twenty-four hundred miles so far. Holy Christmas I might be in New York State! Or they could have been driving back and forth any old place. Only thing I knew for sure? This bus couldn't be in Florida, yet.

The rig had stopped rolling dozens of times but never for much longer than an hour. Sometimes I'd feel the jerking motions that I'd figured out as my trailer being transferred to another rig. There'd been seven changes so far. In the beginning I'd tried to track everything from stops at scales to train crossings.

My tunnel was coming along nicely, and it gave me comfort to know that I had a way out, even if the rig was moving. Not that I'd likely use it but I liked having a backup plan. Even if it meant there were bits of hay blowing in through the upper window.

I was tempted to just slip out the trap door and disappear on my own each time the rig stopped but I kept reminding myself that I didn't want to screw up my chances for a safe relocation.

I watched movies, played solitaire and occasionally wrote journal type notes. I'd eaten two of the sandwiches in the fridge, four chocolate fudge pudding cups, an apple and three bananas.

And I hadn't slept for more than two hours at a time.

Forty-eight hours had passed without a word from anyone. I'd grown to hate the clock with its red bars that formed numbers. I thought about who might be driving my rig and laughed as it occurred to me that I could have been kidnapped again and not even know it. I promised myself that if they didn't let me out in the next twenty-four hours, I was opening that hatch myself.

But for now, the lack of sleep was catching up with me. I crawled up into the drafty bunk and let the gentle sway of the rig, lull me to sleep.

I woke up to a weird smell, blinked for a second or two, orienting myself in the dimness of the weakening battery lights. Camper ceiling about a foot and a half from my face, warm air moving through the punched out window beside me and pot? Definitely smelled like someone was smoking marijuana. I nearly sat up but caught myself before mashing my forehead on the ceiling.

The rig wasn't moving, which is probably why I woke up. I glanced at the clock and frowned. Two o'clock in the morning? Not possible. I couldn't have slept for ten hours.

There was no sound of a diesel engine. The driver must be taking a sleep break. Geez, I hope he's not using pot as a sleep aid. My heart started to thump hard and fast against my ribs as my brain finally cleared of sleep and recognized the smell.

Fire.

Chapter 22

The hay was on fire!

Mentally slapping myself upside the head for stupidity, I dove from the bunk to the hatch door. I grabbed the handle, twisted and nothing happened. I lifted, twisted, pushed, turned, shoved but the latch wouldn't give. I sat, dragged on my boots, then pounded them on the stubborn door with all the strength that went with fear. Nothing happened.

The smell of burning hay was getting stronger. I looked up at the bunk knowing I'd have to go out through my tunnel, fire or not, I wasn't staying in here to die of smoke inhalation. Nor was I going to be a crispy critter. Chances were, I'd lose a layer or two of skin on my way out but it would be a small price to pay. I tied the boot laces as fast as my fingers could move, shoved my arms in Gage's army coat and I did up all the snaps. I grabbed the fabric grocery bag my food had been in, and headed up onto the bunk.

Pulling the sleeping bag to the window, I laid it over the edge where broken bits of glass were still stuck in the rubber edge, and crawled out into pitch black.

Smoke burned the insides of my nostrils and I coughed when it reached the back of my throat. Having dragged the sleeping bag out, I shoved it in front of me as I crawled through the scratchy hay tunnel. I was nearly at the end when I saw the light of flames. The good news? This meant there was lots of oxygen which confirmed I must be almost out.

Time for the grocery bag I'd stuffed into the front of my jeans, I pulled it over my head and scrambled forward as fast as I possibly could. The instant stink of burning fabric scared me spit-less. I could only hope it was the sleeping bag and not my clothes or the bag over my head on fire. So far, I didn't smell burning hair.

Bursting out of the bales and into the open air I was momentarily stunned to see that I was surrounded by flames. About then it occurred to me that one, I was over twenty feet from the ground, and two, my pup-load of hay was an island in the middle of nowhere.

I ran to the back of the load where there seemed to be less fire, grabbed hold of one of the straps and went over the side, hoping that the strap hadn't burnt through anywhere. My feet found the end of a bale for just a second, then it gave way and my knee hit the edge of the trailer with a nasty wallop. I landed on the ground in a heap of snarling pain with the air knocked clean out of me.

Gasping for a new breath, I lay on my back, terrified, synapses firing hard and fast. I was a sitting duck this way, but first I needed air. An old hand at getting the wind knocked out of me—learning to ride ranch horses hadn't come easy—I pulled my knees up and felt a familiar line of fire, as air burned its way to my lungs.

I rolled, shoved myself up, and ran. I knew on some level that my knee was screaming with pain and trying to buckle under me but I drove forward, stumbling to get clear of the burning trailer.

When I lurched into a clump of bush I recognized the scent of sagebrush. Scenes of acres and acres of the stuff as far as I could see flitted through my mind. I shuddered, there would be no trees for cover or shade.

Rattlesnakes and sagebrush went together. Crap. I'd rather die a crispy critter than meet up with a diamondback. Hell, a peaceful, backyard garter snake could send me running for my life. I shut down the foolish thought.

Taking slow deep breaths, I stared at the burning load of hay while I took in what had happened.

The trailer had been unhooked and abandoned in the middle of an open desert-like area, and lit on fire. Chances were, my trap door had been locked from the outside and that was supposed to take care of me. On the upside, whoever had lit the match to whatever they'd used to get it started would have bolted in a hurry so they wouldn't be caught.

Counting on not being spotted wasn't exactly smart but it gave my nerves a bit of a break—lowered the terror level. So now what? Get gone I supposed. Or should I hang around in case a sheriff or fire department showed up. Wouldn't that be a sure way to get rescued? But by whom? Did I know who I could trust? Maybe the fire was exactly here because the Minnow's had connections to the local authorities? Hell, they could own the friggen property I was standing on.

Would I always have this underlying edge of doubt in

my life? I sighed, then nearly laughed out loud as a single word formed in my mind. Inconvenient.

I'd listened to a self-help tape years ago about how life's twists and turns were easier to deal with if you changed the labels from devastating or earth shattering, to simply inconvenient. Granted, this was a *damned* inconvenient situation, but not something I couldn't overcome.

I looked up into the sky wondering how one navigated by the stars. As I did a slow circle, it was at least encouraging to see light on the edge of the horizon that hopefully indicated the presence of a city or town.

With one last glance at the burning hay I turned and wound my way through the sagebrush as fast as I dared. No telling how long it would be before someone took me out of the deceased column and painted a fresh target on my back.

I had no concept of time, but felt like I'd been walking for hours when the yipping and howling of coyotes on the trail of a meal had me feeling sorry for some poor creature about to be breakfast for the pack. They'd tear it to pieces before it was dead. I hated that about coyotes. But had to respect an animal so able to adapt. Survive.

Getting coyote-like myself, I thought. Adapting. Next thing you know, I'll be scavenging in trash bins. That thought made me feel almost faint. Likely because I was breathing too hard.

Slowing down to catch my breath, I wondered about how I'd ended up here. Had the rig been stolen or hijacked? Had someone been hurt or killed?

Worry about Gage and his family distracted me as I trudged on. They were people I'd come to both like and respect in spite of the kidnapping, lying, and manipulation. I understood their position, though I wished they hadn't kept me in the dark like a mushroom.

I frowned, bothered by my breathing. Must've sucked in too much smoke. I stopped, hoping to ease the pressure on my chest. I was getting light-headed. Snicker. Not the first time I'd been called a feather-brain.

Maybe if I just sat down for a minute, I'd get some strength back. But the light of civilization was still an awful long ways away. Best to keep walking. No time to sit. Daylight would probably bring heat and all kinds of other trouble like snakes... and fish. Minnows.

I plodded on. And on. Felt like hours had passed. Put miles between me and the burning hay. Lost track of my thoughts. They wandered as I did.

Someone was singing, badly, then laughed when I tripped and landed on my hands and knees with a nasty jolt. I sat back on my heels to get my bearings and almost tipped sideways. Sat instead. Wrapped my arms around my legs for support, rested my forehead on my knees. Smelled blood and lifted my head, blinking hard, trying to focus on my pant leg.

I stuck a finger through the tear in the knee of my jeans and found a wet hole. Ick. All of a sudden I felt the pain in my leg. That's really stupid, I thought.

It was when I worked my jeans up to check it out that I noticed my boot and sock were soaked in blood. I tugged until the pant leg was up over my knee and saw the slice, about two inches across and deep enough that blood still oozed out and over the edge to follow the dark pathway downwards. Shit.

No wonder I'm light headed, I held my hand over the wound—probably driving all kinds of dirt into it—and sat back to think about what to do. Tried to wrap my head around a plan.

It took a while, searching the same pockets of Gage's jacket over and over again but in the end, I did find the pocket knife thing with a gazillion little tools in it that had been in a drawer in the camper. I amused myself, opening out each one, seeing what I had to work with, until it dawned on me that I was stupidly wasting time. I tried to focus on what I was doing and conveniently noticed the metallic smell of blood.

Attention drawn back to my leg, I stared at the thin wet stream edging its way toward my boot and wondered why I'd taken my hand away. I needed to put pressure on the wound. Make it stop bleeding. Must make pressure.

Shrugging out of the jacket, I pulled my shirt over my head and stuffed my arms back into the jacket. I wrapped the shirt around my leg and leaned back against a nearby bush, exhausted, and cold. All of a sudden I was really, really cold.

Must move.

Don't want to.

Must move.

A coyote yipped—short, staccato pieces of a howl cut into the air. Close. Too close.

Must move.

I turned toward the bush, used it for balance as I struggled to my knees, pulled one foot forward, put my palms on the ground and pushed my ass into the air. I reached for the bush again and worked myself upright. Felt like it took an hour.

Wasting time. MUST get going.

My head stopped spinning. However, I'd somehow lost touch with my senses. I didn't smell the sage anymore, and the sound of coyotes was muted as though I'd donned ear muffs. My vision was sort of blurry and sparkly like when a fine mist rises from the damp ground in spring sunshine. But the sun wasn't out and everything was dry. Except me. I knew that there was a dampness like sweat on my skin, yet I think I was still cold.

Even the vibration of my feet hitting the ground seemed to be coming to me second hand.

With single minded determination, and a chant of *never quit,* in my head, I slogged toward the light as it grew brighter on the horizon.

Even when I felt the earth against my mouth, tasted it, the words went on, *never quit, never quit.*

*

Gage paced beside the helo, cursing himself for never learning to fly the damned thing. At least Angie taught him how to prep it for takeoff.

He wouldn't allow himself to look at his watch again. She'd be here as soon as she could.

They'd have to think about housing one of the birds at her house, make it easier, faster ... his head came up at the sound of her SUV barreling down the drive.

She parked, bailed and sprinted toward the machine. Gage tossed her the black helmet and she hopped through the pilot's door as he dove in the other side. Within minutes they'd lifted off the deck and shot forward, gaining altitude. He filled her in with details as they flew.

"Bottom line according to my contact, the local authorities had yet to access the melted camper shell."

"I've got a good feeling about this Gage."

While he never discounted Angie's 'feelings' because they'd proven over the years to be pretty accurate, he couldn't stop worrying, mentally beating himself over the head for his stupidity.

"Not your fault bro."

He turned his head to meet her look. "You know, you're spooky sometimes."

She grinned. "We all have our little perks." The smile faded. "You know I'm right. It's not your fault."

"Sure it is. I made a stupid decision based on assumptions. I'd been watching her on screen for months and somehow felt like I knew her, thought I understood her. Figured I'd be able to get her to come with me if I could engage her emotionally."

Angie snorted and he felt it double through the earphones. "Hey."

"Your stupid decision was based on your heart you idiot. You fell for her. Assumed you could make her fall for you right back. Might've worked out if she hadn't been called home from Vegas."

"Lust."

She snorted again and he winced. "Wrong L-word brother dear. It may have started by watching her get naked for weeks but –"

"We only had cameras in the kitchen and office. I'm no voyeur."

She gave him a sideways look. "I believe you. Doesn't change anything though."

They were silent for a long time. Angie's attention was on her flying, avoiding contact with area towers and restricted airspace. Staying unnoticed was routine.

Gage was lost in memories of Cass, his Maddy. He wished now that he hadn't pushed her away but it seemed like the best thing to do at the time. He'd needed to break the connection so he could make good decisions that would keep her safe. He hated that his mistakes had put her in danger. Galled him that she didn't trust him.

What seemed like a simple order, 'bring in Cassandra Mallory for protection' had morphed into a total fuck-up.

His mind kept trying to get him to look at the mental image of Cass trapped in the camper screaming for him to help her. And he kept shutting it down. His gut clenched and his heart ached. He rubbed his fist over his chest to ease the pressure, but it didn't help.

Angie reached over, squeezed his knee and met the resulting look. "Believe Gage. You need to believe."

With his words trapped behind the lump in his throat, he shook his head, looked out the front of the bird and sucked in a breath when the charred carcass of the trailer came into view.

Angie put them down in a clear patch of scrub a little ways away so they didn't spew dirt and sand all over the people gathered near the burn. She shut down the engine and looked at Gage.

"You ready for this?"

No. Never would be. "One thing." He swallowed hard. "If she's in there. Give me some space. Don't come after me."

"I'm telling you she's not in there."

They stepped out into air that stunk like water soaked fire. Gage kept his eyes on the rig, where a melted blob of grey was being lifted off the blackened bed of the trailer by chains hooked to a crane. As it was lowered onto the flatbed tow truck with a Rangers' star on the door, he could see the hole that had been cut in the bottom for access through the trailer's trap door.

Angie stepped close to the camper as though looking at it but Gage could see her nostrils flaring as she searched for scent. His sister the hound. He was shocked that he could have such a thought right at this moment. He realized then, that the weight on his chest had lifted just enough for breathing to become easier. The weight of death, loss, was gone.

He wandered to the trailer, crouched to get underneath, check out the trap door. A heavy piece of metal rebar wedged in made the handle useless. He carried on through to the other side, walked a wide lap around the rig, paying close attention to the ground, stopping now and again, kicking the dirt with his foot. Covering the evidence while they were all poking at the camper.

He joined the others, hands in pockets, shoulders slouched. "Yup, looks like our rig by the numbers on the underside, don't know what's up with the addition though." He looked over at the Ranger. "Looks like an elaborate method to smuggle illegal's to me."

The Ranger nodded. "We'll open it up and have a good look inside, see if we can get anything from it. We'll take the trailer too."

"So you don't want us to arrange for pickup?"

"Not until we're done with it. Probably take a week or two with the backlog in the garage."

"We'll be off then if you don't need us." There was handshaking and nodding all round while Gage's mind screamed for him to get going and find her.

Once they were in the bird, he updated Angie. "She's bleeding some, no blood close to the rig but it shows where she stopped about twenty feet away. Looks like she headed east."

"Nearest town's northeast."

"That's our route then. Low and slow. Engage the infra-red search alert."

She pushed buttons, twisted dials. "It's on, but remember, it'll pick up everything from a human on down to a field mouse."

"Fine, good, it'll catch what I miss." He was leaning forward moving his gaze back and forth across the land about a hundred feet below them. They covered close to ten miles before a quiet beeping became much louder.

"What the hell?"

Angie pointed to the right. "I've got visual at two o'clock." She hesitated. "With four coyotes."

As the helo descended, he opened his door, searching, and spotted Cass as a coyote darted toward her, grabbed her by a boot and started tugging.

*

"Maddy."

I heard him but just didn't want to wake up. The

pillow was soft, the covers warm, and drugs still muddled my brain. I was beginning to like it that way—an absence of confusing and scary. I sighed and snuggled in.

"Maddy, wake up love."

"No," I whispered into my pillow. *This is a dream, he's saying that name like he did in Vegas and I want to keep it that way. I want to... sleep.*

The next time I came to, a stranger stood over me, pointing a little flashlight in my eyes. I turned away. "Stop."

A large hand gripped my head, fingers pried my eye open and the bright light flashed.

"Go. Away."

"Told ya, she's a feisty one." Eve or Angie, I couldn't see past the silent doctor's white coat to know which one.

"Bug off."

She snorted. Angie. "She ready to transport soon?"

The man at my bedside smiled and said. "She's fine. There shouldn't be any problems. We've loaded her up with antibiotics so she won't need anything orally until tomorrow morning. Meds are in the bag, 2 pills, four times a day, directions are on the bottle. We dug an awful lot of debris out of that wound so the drugs are important, and keep her hydrated."

I thought about protesting at the way they were talking over and around me but couldn't be bothered as bits of memory flashed. Crawling through the smoky tunnel, hiking across a desert , the hole in my leg and coyotes. A vague recollection of the helicopter ride, Gage holding me close and saying he loved me. That part must have been a dream. I wanted to close my eyes and go back to dreamland. Avoid being buzzed away to a new location by Angie. I was sick to death of being manipulated. And what was I getting out of it? Did I feel comfortable or safe in this game? No. I felt like a pawn. I'd probably be just as well off on my own, but what got in my way were my feelings for Gage. And wasn't that a waste of emotion? Wouldn't I be better off cutting the threads that stretched between us?

The click of the door closing behind the doctor drew my attention.

Angie passed me a little pile of clothing from a large tote bag. "Get dressed and we'll blow this pop-stand. We need to talk."

Sitting up and swinging my legs over the side of the bed, my head spun just a bit. I took a deep breath and looked down at the bandage on my leg. "Geez, it wasn't that big a cut, they've wrapped half my leg."

Angie poked at the bright pink wrapping. "Looks like over-kill to me. Guess they didn't trust you to keep it clean."

I held up the skinny-leg jeans she'd brought me. "I can't bend my leg. No way I'll get these over the bandage anyhow."

"Hmm." She went out, came right back with a pair of scissors and grabbed the jeans.

"Hey, give me those." I reached out, palm up.

She frowned and handed me the jeans.

"No. The scissors." She passed them over. I slipped the blunted end under the bandage and began cutting a few layers at a time, didn't stop until the whole works fell to the floor. I swung my leg up onto the bed and we both studied the medical handiwork.

"No stitches, only butterfly bandages," I muttered.

"Guess that's why they didn't want you to bend your leg. Nothing much here to hold things together."

Shit.

"Don't move." Angie bolted from the room. Came back with a roll of adhesive tape and a wad of gauze pads. She secured the pads over the wound with enough tape to keep it there until next year. We slid the jeans onto that leg first, then I finished dressing. She handed me the tape before we left the room. "Stick this in your pocket, we might need it."

Hot dry air burned my throat when we stepped outside and once we settled into a black SUV, her questions started. I wasn't much help, didn't have any idea when the rig had last stopped or if there'd been any warnings that things had changed etc. I explained that I'd been asleep.

When it was finally my turn, I asked, "Where are we?"

"Arizona."

"How did you find me?"

"You mean after the fire? We spotted you from the air."

I smiled. "So you see me sprawled on the desert, land, pick me up and poof, I'm all better now."

"The infra-red picked up the body heat from you and the coyotes about to share you for breakfast. If I hadn't grabbed him by the belt Gage would have jumped out of the helo at a hundred feet to get to you."

"I heard them yipping far away and then closer. Then I couldn't hear. Everything went really weird for a while and then nothing."

"Shock. You were bleeding to death. Lucky for you, we have Eve. She keeps us well trained and supplied for emergencies. Gage had a bitch of a time finding a vein, but managed to pump a bag of fluid into you before we landed at the medical center. They loaded you up with blood and all sorts of fancy stuff."

"Blood transfusion." That gave me a shiver. Some stranger's blood swishing around in my body. Somebody who just walks into a clinic and offers up their blood, not knowing or caring if it will be an innocent child or an axe murderer they help.

"Lucky for you, we're all boring old O negative. We each gave you a pint of fresh stuff, to top off your tank."

I had to smile at that. Well, at least I knew who to thank. That and I hadn't been hallucinating Gage.

"Where did he go?"

"Gage?"

"No, Santa Claus."

"Testy. That's a good sign." She grinned. "You want a time line? Easy. We picked you up, I left you both at the clinic and flew off as a diversion. Trent met me, we switched seats, he took the helo, I flew the Citation to Flagstaff, rented a car and drove back to the clinic to relieve Gage who then left in the ME's wagon, with a dummy in the body bag. They drove to the local Ranger's office, picked up a Ranger who then flew out with them."

I shook my head. All so freaking complicated. I sighed and asked the next logical question. "Where are we going now?"

"Home."

Way too simple. "In this? A rented car?"

She smiled. "This car, my dear, belongs to the doctor at the clinic. We'll be leaving it at the airport in Vegas.

Of course we will. I closed my eyes and thought about the last time I'd been in Vegas and the pressure in my chest became almost unbearable. I let my mind wander over the events that consumed me since then and dozed off, exhausted.

Three hours later, we'd left the car in the long term parking lot at the Vegas airport, stole into, then out of the terminal, stepped into a limo and ridden the few miles to the hotel. Same one I'd stayed in about two weeks ago. Angie shook hands with the doorman? Whatever. We went straight to the bank of elevators. No surprise when we stopped outside the door of 1708, the room I'd been in before.

Angie magically produced the key card, swiped it and at the green light, turned the handle, and pushed the door open for me to go in first. I didn't move. Couldn't.

The room was dark but for the light of the hallway. I searched the interior for Gage. Found him standing in the deepest shadows near the drawn curtains. My heart rolled over in my chest. This would be my last chance to tell him that I'd fallen, madly, stupidly, in love with him. I had to do it now before he could distract me. I stepped forward.

But the moment he moved I knew it wasn't Gage.

Chapter 23

At a click behind me I spun around and saw that the door was closed and Angie was gone. My heart thumped hard. I turned back. To face the man I hadn't laid eyes on in over twenty-five years. A man I'd tracked relentlessly and then believing I'd found him murdered, had mourned for months.

He stepped further out of the shadows, turned on a lamp, stood silent, unmoving, waiting for me to make the next move, say words that would open the invisible door between us.

He was taller than I'd expected. And thin. His hair was dark grey, cut short. He wore a solid outdoorsman tan that looked all wrong with the elegant charcoal suit. The lamp's reflection glowed on the toes of his well-polished black shoes.

I huffed out a sigh and looked away, at the bed where Gage and I had made love and I felt an embarrassing heat work its way up to my cheeks. I blinked at my own ridiculous reaction, I strode toward the bathroom but stopped with my hand on the door. I could hide for a minute, until I got a grip on the confusion of so many emotions clattering together. But what were the chances he'd still be here when I came out? Slim and none. Time to cowboy-up.

I turned, looked him in the eye for the first time, and shock radiated through me. Like looking in a mirror. His eyes were identical to mine. Or mine to his if a person was getting technical. He smiled then and I saw my teeth.

Freaking spooky.

He chuckled, making me ask, "Did I say that out loud?"

He nodded. "You look like me."

"I think we can skip the DNA tests. Why are you here?" Okay so that was a stupid question but my conversation skills had deserted me.

"To see you, meet you and thank you."

"For what?"

"For being tough enough to overcome your mother. I hope you can understand the reasons and forgive me for leaving you and Sydney with her."

"Did you ever love her?"

"I thought I did." He shrugged. "And to be fair, I think she was as much a victim of circumstances as the rest of us."

I lifted an eyebrow.

He closed some of the space between us. "She'd had dreams of being an actress but ended up pregnant, married, tied to a family she'd never planned on having."

As he got closer, I frowned. "I know you."

The smile lines around his eyes deepened and he said, "rumor has it that the caves on this side of the island were once used for smuggling."

Holy shit. "The kayak guy. You're the kayak guy."

"Guilty as charged."

"Did you know about our cabin on Mayne?"

"Not until a couple of days ago. Odd isn't it how you two found a special place so close to my hideaway?"

"Where?"

"Gandolf Island. I bought it twenty years ago as a backup plan. Was handy when the Minnows found the ranch."

"Did you know I was searching for you?"

He shook his head. "Not until I picked up a message from the security company last month. Said they were pulling both you and Sydney in for protection. I can't tell you how sorry I am that you two got caught up in this mess."

"I thought you were dead." I stared at him. "I found you. Dead. With the horse." I shook myself like a wet dog, changed the subject. "I don't know what happened to Buck after I left him on the lookout mountain."

"He's safe."

"God how I hate that word."

He frowned. "He's been taken to a refuge. A lady I know rescues misfits. She's given him a permanent home." And that was apparently the end of it.

We talked for a while longer, eventually settling in a pair of leather chairs. My gut twisted each time he glanced at the clock on the nightstand. I watched the lines deepen on his forehead and his shoulders start to rise up long before he told me he had to go.

"Will I ever see you again?" The words seemed so flat in the midst of my internal turmoil.

He swallowed hard. "You were my first little girl, I adored you. It broke my heart to walk away from you and your sister but there was nothing else I could do. I gave you up to keep you out of danger."

"You kept Dean." I know it was awful of me to say that, but the words came from the center of who I was. From the little girl that still thought he'd chosen one child over the others. "Would you have kept me if I'd been a boy?"

He reached for my hands, held them and looked right into my eyes when he said, "I don't know. I honestly don't know."

"Why?"

"My first responsibility was to protect Dean from the people who wanted to find him, and most likely kill him after they discovered what he'd seen. Why put the rest of you in that kind of danger? And I thought it was best to keep you and Syd together. I actually envisioned taking both of you and cutting your mother loose but I just wasn't equipped to deal with little girls. So when the FBI agent working with us said that it was best to spit the family, well, I just went along. I'm sorry, for everything you went through, for not being there when you needed me."

He stood and pulled gently until I was wrapped up in his arms. His hands ran up and down my back, soothing in a way that was gut-deep familiar. And I held on to this man who was a stranger, yet not.

When his fingers squeezed my shoulders, I stepped back and my arms fell away. I stared into his eyes and tried to put my thoughts into words. "I know you have to go and I may never see you again. What about Syd and Dean. Will you visit them too?"

"I spent some time with Sydney when you were here a while back. I see Dean occasionally."

"Will I ever find him?"

"Maybe someday, if it's sa– okay, he'll find you."

I felt his discomfort along with my own. Now what? Would he just walk out the door and disappear again? "If Dean gave up the information, would it end?"

His smile was sad. "We'll never know." He held out his arms and I walked back into them. "I have to go." The gruffness in his voice gave away more than the words did.

"Thank you for risking your life and coming here to meet me."

"If it wasn't risking *yours*, I'd stay forever." He planted a kiss next to my ear and memory stirred as he walked away.

"I love you Daddy."

He half turned. "I love you too baby." Then he was gone.

I shook my head. "No Daddy, Sydney's the baby now." My hand clamped over my mouth. The words were a memory of what we used to say at bedtime. I could still feel the rough cheek under my hand when I kissed him goodnight.

My legs folded and I sat. Right where I was. With arms wrapped around my middle, silent tears ran down my face, dripped onto my jeans as I rocked.

Boots appeared on the carpet in front of me. Dust covered brown girl-boots. I hadn't heard the door. My Dad had been wearing shiny black shoes I'd never see again. I sighed at my weepy self, swiped across my cheek with the back of my hand.

The boots left and returned. A damp washcloth dangled in front of my face and I just stared at it. Man I'm pathetic. The cloth dropped into my lap and the boots left again. I heard the door snick closed.

The deep breath I sucked in burned. Time to move on. I took the cloth with me to the bathroom, used it to cool my stinging eyes, washed up, noticed the ache in my leg. Probably opened it up again. I dropped my jeans and checked, no blood seeping through the bandage.

Having no clue what they had in store for me next, and being plumb wrung out, I pulled aside the spread, stretched out on the bed with a cool damp cloth over my swollen eyes thinking that now would be a good time for someone to come along and drug me again. I'd welcome the oblivion.

I stayed very still when the door opened and someone walked toward the bed. When a hand landed on each side of my head, I sat bolt upright expecting a pillow to be held over my face but instead clunked my forehead into something hard, yet soft.

Hands grabbed my shoulders and pressed them to the mattress. My eyes were wide open but the damned cloth still covered my eyes. Warm lips grazed mine. Gage.

I stayed very still while he ran his mouth over mine and down my throat, back up to my ear and nibbled. His tongue moved around the edge and a moan escaped me.

He chuckled, lay down on the bed and wrapped me in his arms. Somewhere along the way the cloth had disappeared and I was staring into those dark blue eyes. "You okay?" he asked.

"Depends."

"On what?" His mouth started a journey toward my ear.

"How much time do we have before the next move?"

"Which move?" His voice was low and rough and then he did something with his tongue in my ear that made me forget to breathe. I was brainless jelly on a plate. My body vibrated and two words rolled to the front of my mind. Who knew?

"Maddy."

"Hmm?"

"Look at me."

I thought I was. I opened my eyes and his beautiful blues were staring into mine.

"We have to make a plan."

"You're doing just fine without one." My head lolled back and his mouth moved to my oh so sensitive throat. I was floating somewhere pleasant when I thought I heard the door open.

I definitely heard the snort, followed by, "well gee, I was just going to ask if you're ready to go but I guess that's a no."

"Give us a minute," Gage replied.

"Make that ten." I added, which still wouldn't be long enough but neither would forever so I was learning to make do with what I had. I rolled away from him as the door closed and sat on the edge of the bed staring at the curtains. "I'm really not good at this good-bye shit but I'm trying to get the hang of it."

"Maddy."

"I don't want to keep that name. It reminds me too

much of you. I'll need something else, something new and fresh that has no ties to the life I'm leaving behind."

"What are you talking about?"

I got up and went to the window, stopped myself before I peeked out because I'd learned not to do that. I was beginning to think the way they wanted me to. I sighed and paced back and forth between there and the door, with my arms wrapped around my aching stomach. On about the third pass he stepped in front of me, stopped me in my tracks. Glancing up, I saw the crease between his eye brows that meant I was confusing him as usual. This was so not fair.

I laid a palm against his chest. "Saying goodbye to my father pretty much depleted my resources." Drawing a deep breath I forced myself to continue because I knew there were no guarantees I'd get another chance. I pressed on, trying to ignore the sensation of security as his hands moved up and down my arms.

"Goodbye is hard for me Gage. I understand that the night we spent together here was all about you getting me to a safe place, willingly. And I'm pretty sure that we have an amazing amount of chemistry and you'd like to make love again, and of course, I would too, but …"

I gave myself a mental head slap and got back on topic. Blurted out my truth. "Look. I'm sorry if it makes you uncomfortable, but I have to say this, just once out loud. I know it's stupid, but I've fallen in love with you. It's probably that syndrome where the captive falls for the captor so I'll get over it okay, but I don't think it would be a good idea to get naked together. I mean, I want you, your body, bad. Too much. Kind of like lusting after a big slice of chocolate cake. I know the short lived pleasure will be followed by long-term pain like I'd have to run ten miles to burn off the memory or something." Had I made any sense at all? I felt like banging my head against a wall.

He placed a hand on either side of my face, stared into my eyes for a long time, then kissed me. A long, deep, soul searching kiss that made my heart climb up my throat, had me longing to crawl inside his skin. My hands sunk into his hair and his migrated to my ass. Begging sounds rose from my throat as he lifted me up and my legs wrapped around his waist. I wallowed in sensation, vaguely noticing that we were on the bed again. His mouth left mine and he wrapped me tight, his face in the crook of my neck while his breathing slowed. He rolled us over until he had me pinned to the mattress. Surprised me by propping on his elbows above me.

Passion darkened the eyes staring into mine. "If Angie hadn't grabbed me by the belt I would've jumped from the helo at a hundred feet to get that coyote off of you."

Yet after delivering me to the clinic, he'd disappeared, until now. "You have a deeply ingrained sense of responsibility."

"Not the same thing." He touched his lips to my forehead in a move so tender I felt tears well. He was killing me.

"I can't do this. You're walking away from here today with a big enough piece of me." My voice became a pathetic pleading whisper. "Leave me something."

"How 'bout this." His mouth dropped over mine, taking, giving with each stroke of his tongue.

I reached for the strength to fight, found none, had no

defense, and my heart opened to store one last memory. Answering the sound from deep in his throat my body arched, asking for everything. I reached for his belt buckle, but he collared my hands, drew them over my head and held them there while he, nipped at my throat and teased the sensitive tips of my breasts through the fabric of my shirt before he stripped it away.

He worked his way lower, baring my skin as he went and I stored memories of his touch, his hungry gaze. Mental snapshots to be savored in the coming months when loneliness was sure to gnaw holes in my gut. Those eyes watching me as he kissed a trail down my stomach. As he went lower.

Sensation swamped me and conscious thought evaporated when his mouth settled on my center and mind numbing sensation drove me up and over the edge of a brilliant internal explosion, I silently screamed his name. Wave after wave of aftershock pleasure seemed endless until I became aware of someone pounding on the door.

I opened my eyes as Gage shifted off the bed. A little shiver ran through me when he pulled a cover over me and walked to the door, still fully dressed. He cracked it open using his body to shield me and I heard a murmur of voices but not the words.

I grabbed my clothes and sprinted to the bathroom. Stood with my face in the spray of the shower for long minutes, focusing on nothing but the tingle of water from several nozzles.

My body knew when he stepped in behind me.

He turned me around. "Look at me Maddy."

I opened my eyes. "Why are you still here? I thought

our ten minutes was up."

"I'm not leaving without you."

"Oh?" My heart raced as I began to actually believe that maybe...

"I talked to your father before you got here."

And what did that have to do with the price of coffee? I frowned.

"I asked if it was a problem that I wanted to spend the rest of my life with his daughter."

Ohmygod. Can hearts gallop? Mine seemed to be doing a double thump in my chest. "What did he say?" Like it mattered?

"Said he's good with whatever makes her happy."

I tilted my head like a curious puppy. "So when are you and Syd riding off into the sunset?"

"You're work, you know that?" And then he kissed me until I couldn't feel my feet.

Sometime later we emerged, fully dressed, to find Angie waiting for us. She grinned. "All better now?"

I smiled. "He wants to keep me."

She snorted. "Before or after shower sex."

I frowned. "Before. I suppose that was just to get me naked then?"

"Chances are."

"You were already naked."

Angie was grinning. "So, you gonna marry him?"

I shrugged. "Dunno. He hasn't asked yet."

"Oh for crying out loud, Maddy." He shook his head and with an exaggerated sigh for lead in said, "will you marry me?"

I took one step toward him and he reached out,

grabbed me by the arm, pulling me into his chest with a thump.

"Hey."

"I said, will you marry me?"

"You haven't said you love me."

He glanced over my shoulder at his sister. "She's work." He cradled my face between his hands in a way that made me weak at the knees and with that dark blue gaze locked on mine he said slowly, "I love you Maddy, more than breath. Will you please marry me?"

I swallowed hard and asked one last important question, "What about Harris, my cat?"

"Packed and ready to go. Merlin too, as he's apparently decided you belong to him as well."

I smiled and nodded. He leaned down to kiss me and I whispered against his mouth, "Yes."

Angie's voice interrupted. "We have to get a move on folks."

Gage lifted his head. "Right."

I leaned my forehead on his chest. "Where to this time?"

"Home."

Dear reader,

I sincerely hope you enjoyed this story as much as I loved writing it!

As an author, I spend most of my time alone with my computer in a room I call my writing cave, and have little interaction with my readers.

Because of this, when someone loves one of my stories and takes a minute to leave a review on Amazon or one of the other sites, spontaneous happy dancing happens in the writing cave!

And not to worry, Wolfe and Bear, my obnoxious tuxedo cats are no longer offended by this silliness.

So if you'd like to make me happy, happy, happy, and imagine me jumping around the room like an idiot, just click on my book on Amazon and leave me a review. And honestly? You don't need think of it as one of those dreaded book reviews we had to do in school. A simple, "great story" or "good read" or "interesting characters" will thrill me to no end.

And if you didn't like the book? Well, kudos for reading to the end anyways, and I hope your next reading experience is happier.

Cheers!

Kathryn.

Acknowledgements

I'm told it takes a village to raise a child. As my books are my children, I have a village to thank, so here goes.

Many thanks to: author L. j. Charles for your wonderful critiquing skills and advice; Barb and Donna for the sharp-eyed reading; Judi Fennell of www.formatting4U.com for the awesome copy edits, formatting, and uploading services; Kim Killion for the fabulous cover; Scarlet E. for the picture in my head when I wrote about Fred; Lincoln City, Oregon for the hospitality; Cherry Adair for her no-nonsense encouragement (virtual butt kicking); Brenè Brown for Daring Greatly—an inspiration to me and my characters; Sandy James for encouraging me to rock the words; Al for keeping me and the pets loved, fed, and cared for while I was immersed in this story; Wolfe and Bear for the purring company while I was holed up in the writing cave, and for not minding how loud I cranked the music; Barb and Judy—how do I put it into words? You have loved and supported me my entire life. You are the constants in my journey. You've egged me on and believed in me, always. I love you both.

About the Author

Award winning author Kathryn Jane writes about the kind of women she'd like to hang out with—smart, self-reliant, think on their feet ladies who are just as happy eating a loaded hot dog at a ballgame as they are sipping champagne in the back of a limo. Women who laugh as hard as they cry, appreciate good sweaty sex, and know how to keep a secret.

Kathryn lives in a cottage on the west coast of Canada with her very own prince charming. Among her favorite things are the smell of the ocean, crisp sunny days, the warm breath of a horse, cats with a sense of humor, dogs that love to please, music, and kind people. She collects beach glass and rocks, has a single string of tiny Christmas lights that she turns on all year round, and loves to walk on the beach with her sisters.

For more information about Kathryn and her other books, check out her website, or join her on facebook and twitter.

http://kathrynjane.com/
www.facebook.com/kathryn.jane.921
https://twitter.com/@Author_Kat_Jane

Other books by Kathryn Jane

Intrepid Women Book 1 - **DO NOT TELL ME NO**
    Kindle http://amzn.to/1d1hFLR
    Print http://amzn.to/1cdTycs

Intrepid Women Book 2 - **TOUCH ME**
    Kindle http://amzn.to/1fhFFhQ
    Print http://bit.ly/NpagQ1

Intrepid Women Book 3 – **DARING TO LOVE**
    Kindle http://www.amazon.com/dp/B00I13NB9U
    Print http://bit.ly/1d8Wq0w

Intrepid Women Book 4 – **VOICES**
    Kindle ....
    Print ....

www.ingramcontent.com/pod-product-compliance
Lightning Source LLC
Chambersburg PA
CBHW051408170626
46809CB00006B/2072